# GLAMOURIE

Alice Starmore's

# GLAMOURIE

Knitted Costumes & Designs by

## Alice Starmore

Stories & Photographs by

## Jade Starmore

CALLA EDITIONS
Mineola, New York

*Glamourie* is a new work, first published by Calla Editions, Mineola, New York, in 2018.

*International Standard Book Number*
ISBN-13: 978-1-60660-083-2
ISBN-10: 1-60660-083-4

CALLA EDITIONS
An imprint of Dover Publications, Inc.
www.doverpublications.com/calla

Printed in China by RR Donnelley

*To Thomas*

for all possible futures

# Contents

# INTRODUCING GLAMOURIE

**Glamourie** (noun) – a Scots word meaning a charmed condition in which everything is invested with magical properties and possibilities

**Glamour** (verb) – in Scots means to bewitch, bedazzle or enchant

The story of *Glamourie* begins with a breakfast in Chicago. Jade and I were shattered and jet-lagged after a particularly difficult journey, and were stoking-up on bagels to get us through a day of "show and tell" about the new edition of *Tudor Roses* at a major textile event. We began the discussion by having a good moan about how "enough was enough" and we would never do another book ever again; the time, commitment, effort and sacrifice was just too much. Our wish at that moment was to be able to shape-shift and make the journey home on our own wings, thus avoiding the rigours of trans-Atlantic air travel. It is a testament to our effect on each other that by the time the last crumb of bagel was consumed, we had mapped out *Glamourie* and were fired up with the possibility of having the perfect vehicle to show knitters a stage of the imaginative process which – for very practical reasons – I had never revealed before. What if, we thought, I actually knitted the ideas that came into my mind before I applied the usual constraints to them? My original concepts are often quite fanciful, but at the end of the day I have to provide designs that can be knitted in several sizes and have instructions that can be fitted into a reasonable page length.

On occasions – *Eala Bhan* and *Anne Boleyn* spring to mind – I have pushed the boundaries in terms of complexity and length of instructions, but usually the constraints rule the day. I have never regarded these working constraints to be anything other than an interesting challenge. It is a further step in the imaginative process: the challenge is to stylise and hone down my ideas so that practical issues can be solved and yet the final design will be original and imaginative in itself. But in *Glamourie* I would break free of this. Jade would write seven new tales rooted in

9

our Gaelic culture, which has a powerful tradition of storytelling centred around the theme of shape-shifting, where wild creatures have the ability to alter their bodies and even appear in human form. I would then "illustrate" her tales by creating *Designs Minus Zero* – no limits!

When creating costumes for Jade's other-worldly creatures, I would cast off all constraints and give free rein to my needles, yarn and imagination. I would show how fanciful, elaborate and extraordinary ideas can be portrayed through the medium of hand-knitting. The glamourie of knitting is that one single thread can be shifted into clear space to create any shape – no frame or canvas is required. My aim would be simple – to play the enchantress and put a spell on you.

Our breakfast in America was three years and several hundred thousand stitches ago. During that time I found that working on one *Glamourie* costume led to ideas for the next. For example, one of the types of feather I made for the Raven became – with a very small change and some felting – the tentacles of the Sea Anemone. One thing definitely leads to another and one of the most enjoyable aspects of the project was to explore an idea and technique and let it run. Looking back on the finished project now, I realise that not only did the stories and the wild things inspire, but the sequence in which I made them also had an effect. Had I not worked on the Raven first, I may well have come up with a different Sea Anemone. I surprised myself by using, for the most part, just a few simple techniques – increasing, decreasing and short rows were the backbone of the work. I have made a career of teaching knitters in detail not only about techniques, but also about pattern and colour design, so they will be inspired to create their own works. My book of Fair Isle knitting,

*Aran Knitting* and *Charts for Colour Knitting* are prominent examples of my endeavours in this field, and have been used extensively by knitters the world over. But *Glamourie* has enabled me to teach an unexpected but wonderful lesson – that endless possibilities abound even if your capabilities run to no more than the basics. Such is the glamourie of knitting.

These *Glamourie* costumes are not the stuff of everyday wear and are well beyond the practicality of written instruction, but they serve to show what can be done with a single thread and a pair of needles. While the first half of this book is an unrestrained flight of fancy, the second half is where duty calls and I gently return to earth, for here you will find full instructions for knitting designs based on the costumes. As ever, it is of paramount importance to me that my instructions are clear and accurate so that the design can not only be made exactly as illustrated, but can also be modified to suit the knitter's personal requirements. But not as ever – in fact for the very first time – I have demonstrated how my mind works and how my imagination led me from the first inspiration through to the finished design. The costume is the initial concept in my head; the practical pattern is what came out when I put it through the constraints mill and turned the handle. The hardest part of this exercise was creating only one design from each costume, for the various possibilities kept spiralling off in fractal fashion ... but every book has to end somewhere.

Making these costumes was creatively rejuvenating and I have no doubt that the exercise has added a few pages to my personal *Book of Future Possibilities*. I sincerely hope that you will be similarly inspired to add a few pages to your own.

Alice Starmore

# About
# the stories

I was brought up in a quirky little village in the centre of an island that lies out on the wild edge of the Atlantic Ocean. In the past, Achmore was a stopping-off point for people making the journey from the west side of the island into the town of Stornoway. At some point roughly a hundred years before I was born, some of those people decided to stay (or, as was sometimes joked, were left behind) and create a village in the middle of the moor.

Being moorland, the ground was not very suitable for crofting, and the rush-filled strips of land that run down from the houses to the shore of Loch an Ach are a continuing testimony as to why Achmore was not settled in earlier years. The moor does not accept human habitation in the way that the dry and sandy potato-friendly land around the shoreline does. From an agricultural point of view the only upside to the village's moorland position is proximity to deep peat that can be cut conveniently close to the houses. This was something that our family and all the others in the village took advantage of every summer, and the resulting peatstack heated the house and water and cooked our meals for the entire year. So the moorland gave, as did the myriad lochs scattered throughout it. My grandfather was an expert salmon fisher and he frequently dropped by late in the evening to share his catch.

In addition to the acidic and difficult land, the weather could also be a trial. The village faced directly into the teeth of the wind with no shelter for miles, and when there were storms our living room windows were put under so much pressure that we all had to retreat to the kitchen in case they blew in. And when the wind did not blow, a stillness could settle which would trap you indoors as much as any storm as dark clouds of midges would gather at the corners of the house and lie in wait.

You may wonder from this what the benefits of living in such a place were, and that question is simple to answer – it was (and still is) incredibly beautiful. The view from our house was out over an expanse of moor filled with lochs and streams, and beyond that were layers of hills in varying shades of browns and blues, stretching all the way from Pairc in the east, across Harris in the south, and over to Uig in the west. The constantly changing weather meant that a drama from light to dark, storm to colour and brilliance, was played out every day, and you could sit at the window and look out over it for a lifetime and not become tired of it. This ever-shifting panorama was the backdrop to my childhood years.

In addition to this wild, wide landscape, if you walked up behind our house for a few minutes you came to a mostly buried ancient stone circle, put there thousands of years ago, presumably as a satellite to the larger and better-known circle at Callanish. That it has not been excavated and was left at the disposal of any child who happened upon it, has given it an air of secrecy and adventure – an imprint of ancestors who lived so far in the past that the island they looked upon would not have been recognisable to my eyes.

School was a stone building in the centre of the village. At the height of its occupation it catered to 14 children of differing ages, who were ruled over by the at turns benevolent, at turns formidable, Mrs Maclean. After school, on days when the wind sat comfortably at a speed between midges and storm, I would sometimes ride my bike up the single track road (known as the High Road) behind the village. This road was dotted with *àirighs* – little huts painted in bright colours where people used to spend their summers to extend the grazing of their animals. There was a magical charm to these places which were nestled into dips and hollows, and I felt that they were more than just the dwellings of people and were in fact inhabited by things stranger and more mysterious. Amongst them were even older stone àirighs, some no more than a collection of tumbled stones in a circle of green grass.

Growing up amid this landscape with its beauty and danger, and the evidence of mysterious constructions stretching back like a pathway to the past, meant that as a child I was fascinated by fairy tales more than any other genre of book. The tales I liked best were the most dangerous ones, which were invariably Scottish. There are few princesses in Scottish myth and legend, and instead there is constant danger. These tales are not for the faint-hearted and serve as warnings: for example, the tale of the Kelpie tells you to be wary of freshwater lochs, which I know from experience is very sound advice. Any fairies encountered are certainly not of the benign English garden variety: they represent the land and must be respected and appeased, and if you forget that then you will pay a price in blood. Endings tended to be ambiguous at best in those tales, which seemed to fit well with the moody landscape that I lived in.

My *Glamourie* stories specifically reflect the Isle of Lewis and Harris – the beauty and the wildness, and the potential dangers that lurk within. In some cases I have subverted a familiar tale, like that of the Selkie, and turned it into something which seemed to me to be more possible and believable (albeit in a world where seals can transform into women). In others I have taken an old superstition and created a story around it, so the notion that it is bad luck for a sister to brush her hair while her brother is at sea had a touch of *Macbeth* added to it and became the Sea Anemone story. Similarly, the myth that the last person buried in a cemetery becomes the graveyard watcher until they are relieved of their duty by the next death, turned into the story of the Mountain Hare, who becomes a guiding hand in the final darkness. Other stories, like the Otter and the Raven, simply came into being by themselves from ideas sparked while sitting eating gingerbread on a rock in the moor, and when seeing the pattern left by a feather entwined with seaweed in the sand.

All the stories in this book originate from a child's view out over the moorland from that quirky little village in the middle of the island, and I wanted to write them because that view is inevitably changing. In the same way as my mother's experience of the island is different to mine (she actually spent her summers living in an àirigh rather than just cycling past one), my son's experience is even further removed from my own. Achmore School shut the year after I left due to lack of children. The fishing boats in Stornoway harbour, which were moored three deep on a Sunday in my childhood, have dwindled to a few remnants. The àirighs about which I made stories in my head have almost all (for reasons that I cannot understand) been pulled down. My grandfather no longer stops at the house late at night with freshly-caught salmon for next day's dinner.

Of all the changes, the biggest is that we no longer cut peat. Every summer I sat and played by Loch an Ach while my parents cut the peat. Being there was not an entertainment or a choice: it was a requirement. The peat were cut by hand, providing enough to keep us warm until the next year. The turf was put back carefully so the peat banks would be ready again the following summer. The skill was handed down from beyond memory. We took carefully from the land and created a connection with the moor, and also with the rest of the village, as taking the peats home was a communal activity and we all relied on each other for help. Then, when I was in my teens, people started building new houses which didn't have ranges and were powered by oil, and suddenly – almost overnight – the peat banks became overgrown. My generation is the first in centuries not to go out into the moor as adults, to work and benefit from the land and pass the knowledge on to our children. This perhaps explains why I picked the Otter costume to design when there were more flamboyant choices available. The Otter is the one character that is entirely and solely of the moor and lochside of my childhood.

These *Glamourie* stories and the Otter costume shown opposite are my way of saying that, even though my grandfather's peat iron lies stored beneath the floorboards and I do not use it, the memory of watching the process is still with me. As is the feeling of how magical it felt as a child to sit on a rock beside Loch an Ach with the moor spreading out on every side, making up stories in my head while listening to the water lap against the stone and watching the cotton grass blowing in the heather.

Jade Starmore

14

# Glamourie

# Costumes & Stories

# The Mountain Hare

*There was once a shining tranquil sea that stretched unbroken from horizon to horizon – until one day the serene silence was riven by a falling star that burnt hot through the air and was violently quenched in the cold clear water. The star was made of an ancient, magical stone so potent that when quickened by salt it gave rise to life itself. One by one, ornate fish began to populate the newly-disturbed waters and an island rose up from the ocean bed; it reached for the sun and clothed itself in a myriad of plants and flowers. Then animals awoke and chose their forms, and the air was filled with birds and sounds. For many ages that was how it remained, with the land in harmony and endless sunshine, and the sea stretching not quite unbroken from horizon to horizon. But after a time the days began to turn and in the first twilight one last creature was born from the very heart of the fallen star – the Mountain Hare. She was swift and fleet of foot, and danced in the magic hour – that space between day and night when the doors between worlds lie open.*

*At first she ran for the joy of running. Then she began to pause and look about her. She watched hidden amongst stones as the deer grazed the heather on the hillsides and the eagles swooped high above. She saw the Sundew coil and uncoil, merging the lives of others within itself, and she saw the distant tranquil sea and the pure sands calmly reflecting the moonlight. She was shy and gentle, curious and playful, and she longed for a companion to run with through the twilight, but the other creatures were bound to the night or to the day and she remained solitary in the strange half-light.*

*As time passed, the Mountain Hare became sorrowful and lonely, and lost pleasure in running; instead she would watch the daylight world – always just out of reach – from her mountain fastness. One day she saw a sleek Solan Goose flash like a white arrow from sky to sea in a single blink of her eye. But instead of a fat fish, the Solan Goose surfaced with a stone which it dropped in disgust upon the sand. With her magical eyes the Mountain Hare could see it was no ordinary stone and her thoughts teemed with possibilities.*

*When the twilight hour finally fell she stole down to the sand and gathered up the stone – which was the very last piece of the fallen star – and raced away to the hilltops. Recognising the life at the heart of the stone she went to the highest hill and as night fell she caught the first beam of moonlight. She waited hidden throughout the long cold night, which was not her domain, and in the morning she caught the first ray of sunshine; with these forces at her command she called forth from the star a creature that was bound to neither day nor night.*

*This creature had no allegiance to light or darkness and was different from all the other living things upon the island; she walked upright on two legs, had deft use of her hands and had a voice all of her own. She ran with the  Mountain Hare in the twilight and they both delighted in each other's company, For many weeks they were happy together, but the seasons inexorably turned and winter came. The Mountain Hare shivered so her companion climbed to the highest hill top and spun yarn from the starlight to make her a coat that would keep her either warm or cool all the year around. So once again they were happy and ran together — but it is a hard truth that nothing alive remains unchanged.*

*The Mountain Hare's companion became entranced by the starlight, and went again and again to spin with it, faster and faster, until one day she became entangled and the magic wound itself all around her. Her body began to swell and her steps became slow until she gave birth to a multitude of children. Nimble and clever with their hands, they were not bound to night or day, and neither were they bound to the hills. They sought the undulating fertile lands near the machair, and the companion of the Mountain Hare, with a sorrowful backward glance, followed her children downwards and went no more to dance in the twilight.*

*The Mountain Hare watched from the hilltop as the creatures born from her companion multiplied until the race that is now known as the Children of Men came into being. They fashioned metals with their industrious hands and they broke the skin of the earth and dug down, forcing the soil to do their bidding. They went to sea in boats made of Rowan wood and brought back fish and salt. They forayed to the hills and killed the deer, and the Mountain Hare hid in fear behind the stones. The land itself shivered and shook with their enterprises and the first tides began to turn; the days and nights spun faster and the seasons grew harsher, but still the Children of Men multiplied.*

*The Mountain Hare viewed this with great sorrow. She climbed to the top of the highest hill and in the magic hour she ran, pulling the twilight around her and opening the door to another world – a distant place where time does not exist and light cannot penetrate. As she ran, she wove strands of starlight and caught a creature of the darkness which she released into the night – and thus she brought Death to the Children of Men.*

*From that day on, men, women and all other creatures no more lived lives as long as the ages of the hills, but instead they grew old and died.*

*The ageless Mountain Hare watched as the animals and birds were born, glimmered briefly in the sunlight and then fell to the earth. But her sorrow was mitigated by the ease with which their bodies returned to the soil, and their spirits flew to the worlds beyond the starlight and the hilltop. The Children of Men however were bound to neither day nor night, and though their bodies were easily claimed by peat or water, their spirits lingered and wept on the shoreline. When the magic hour fell the Mountain Hare called to them in the language of her old companion, and she led them to the hilltops and opened doors with starlight so they could pass through and be at peace.*

*From that day to this, the Mountain Hare has been known by my kinfolk as the **Faire Chlaidh** – the graveyard watcher. She runs in the twilight: a swift-moving figure at the edge of sight, neither in this world nor the next. She is fleeting and transient, but at the very last breath she offers a comforting hand in the darkness and opens the door to a new and different world.*

# Notes on the Mountain Hare costume

I firmly believe that the supernatural properties endowed upon the Mountain Hare (called in Gaelic, *maigheach-gorm*; literally "blue hare") are a product of its extraordinary ability to appear and disappear before your very eyes. Though they do occasionally travel to the lower regions of the hills, they spend most of their time up above the heather-line where the terrain changes and becomes rarified. Plants and lichens grow on, and around, numerous blue-grey rocks and boulders in a landscape where no human could permanently sustain life. To be in this landscape is to feel a powerful sense of leaving the everyday world behind and stepping closer to the stars – the perfect theatre for a cosmic legend.

As our photographs show, there is austere beauty all around – in form, colour and texture – and into this the Mountain Hare fits perfectly. The mountain boulders, worn and shaped over aeons, are their cities; the montane lichens and mosses are their gardens, and so they change the colours of their mantles to match the changing seasons. So it is that a hill-walker will see a rock or a clump of moss or a snowdrift suddenly leap into life and vanish in a flash. The traces they leave can be as magical and evanescent as the sight of them. Once, near the summit of a hill called *Liuthaid*, I came upon a winding trail of unmistakable hare's foot and tailprints in the snow, alongside which ran the tiniest four-legged prints of a shrew. It was impossible not to imagine the glamourie inherent in the hare and the shrew's adventure around the mountain.

The hare's costume evolved in my head and in my hands as an inextricably linked blend of sightings of these creatures, the colours and textures of their montane landscape, and the legends I grew up with. I chose colours evoking the "blue hare" and the boulders, lichens and mosses of the rarified landscape. The soft pelt and shapely curves of the hare led to the idea of felting the pieces after I had knitted them.

I wanted to create some surface design that would echo the hare's legendary power to slip between worlds. At the time I was rising at 3am to check on my cattle who were imminently calving.

Experiencing a diamond-sharp Hebridean winter sky in the silent dead of night is something worth losing sleep over, and the icy stars and Jupiter with its attendant moons conspired to focus my imagination on the hare on the mountain top, drenched in starlight, with innumerable parallel worlds at its disposal. This led me to think of the ways in which humans have expressed their relationship with the universe. I am fortunate to live in a place where people built monuments to the cosmos which we can still marvel at five thousand years on; the Callanish Stones cosmic clock marks the movement of heavenly bodies to this day. Ancient humans also carved abstract imagery of circles, spirals, stars and lines into rocks in remote places; these images evoke the profound mysteries of the universe and can be interpreted as a powerful visual expression of the possibility of travel from one dimension to another.

I didn't want to draw up a plan for the embroidery in advance so I just worked a quick swatch to try out ideas in stitches and shapes. I decided to work the embroidery on the centre back and front pieces and my first step was to arrange very small drifts of carded wool in Driftwood, Sundew and Sea Ivory which I needle-felted in place so that they became barely visible. Then I threaded the needle at will and proceeded to create the cosmic shapes with a variety of embroidery stitches. For the spirals, circles, arcs and lines I laid out shapes of strands of yarn and closely overcast them. I worked stars and French knots in abundance and also made star shapes by working Bullion Stitch radiating from overcast circles. Since heavenly bodies were a powerful part of the theme, I decided to create knitted and felted spheres to decorate and fasten the jacket. This proved to be a fast and fun exercise and so I upscaled the idea and created an orb to serve as the magical stone that the Mountain Hare finds in Jade's story. I finished the hat "tail" with a wave of blackface sheep's wool found on the hillside. Jade digitally created a subtle fabric design from a photograph of montane lichen and then designed and made the skirt to complete the costume.

My embroidery test swatch in the domain of the Mountain Hare

# The Raven

*After the land and sea had settled into a form that the eye could recognize, the first of the birds began to appear. The Robin grew out of berries and twigs; the Gannet came from sleek, sea-honed pebbles, and the piratical Great Skua materialised from a particularly vicious gust of the north wind. All came forth from that which represented their nature, and they chose their colour and form as was appropriate to their wants and needs.*

*The mother of all ravens was the very last bird to appear on the far north-western islands, and she grew out of the blood and tears of the fallen and became the colour of bleached bone. Her nature was to take what life had already left – the unwanted and the forgotten. She was a shy and lonely bird, and when she tentatively approached the warmly-coloured berry eaters they scurried away in fear because she had grown larger than they were. She made her way to the cliffs and watched the gannets dive beneath the waves, but she could not follow them as the sea was not her domain. She followed the skuas over the moorland, but they were brigands of the air with great disdain for those who did not live constantly for the chase. So she remained alone, a scavenger seeking temporary refuge on the cliffs and moors, still unsure of her purpose and form.*

*As the months of spring and summer passed, the land was plentiful and the birds multiplied, and the Raven too saw her kind grow in her likeness. But although the seasons passed more slowly in those early days, they still had to turn. When winter came it was dark and harsh and cold, and the children of the Raven began to starve.*

*As the birds and animals had appeared, so had men and women, and although the Raven had been wary of these creatures who were so*

*different from herself, she began to venture nearer in search of food. She tried many times to approach them but found herself driven back with stones, and so she returned to the cliffs with nothing.*

*One day she noticed that a dwelling had been built near the foot of the cliffs; it was a small house made of stone, but neatly kept. It was lived in by a woman and her children, and although the Raven had become wary of men, desperation made her venture closer. Upon seeing the starving white bird the woman brought out some berries, but the Raven could take no nourishment from them. The woman then brought out some scraps of meat, and the Raven feasted. As the long nights of winter passed the Raven grew comfortable in the woman's presence, and even after the days began to warm again and food was once more plentiful, the Raven still visited her and they often sat side by side in the evening, sharing stories and watching the night chase the sun over the horizon.*

*As the years passed the woman grew older and her children grew up and had children of their own. One evening when the days were at their shortest, the Raven and the woman sat on the shore beneath the cliffs and watched the weak winter sun as it melted into a hundred colours and disappeared into the sea. The woman turned to the Raven and said, "Goodbye my good friend, I have seen the sun set and rise many times, but this is the last." The Raven was filled with pain and horror as she realised that her friend was dying, and said, "But this must not be the end; there must be a way that we can stop it; there are herbs I have heard the blackbird speak of that prolong life in mortals; let me find some for you."*

"No," the woman replied. "My life has been long, and I have seen my children and my children's children grow. It is time for me to go, just as the sun is eclipsed by the night."

"But you cannot want to end," the Raven replied. "For when you are gone it will be as if you have never been."

"That is not true," said the woman, "Yes, I am mortal, and my body will turn to dust as all mortal things do, but I will live on through my children, and through the stories I have told you. Though I will be long-gone when the world reaches its end, you will still remember me and my life will not be forgotten." And as the night claimed the sky the woman contentedly breathed her last, and the Raven was left alone on the shoreline.

Through the night the Raven shed tears which turned into black stones and covered the body of her friend until nothing more of her could be seen. By the time the pale morning sun had crept into the sky, the Raven had shed her last stoney tear, and her feathers – and those of all her descendants – had taken on the colours of midnight.

And from that day to this she has lived on the edges of the lands of men, watchfully keeping her distance while diligently collecting their stories and lore. My kinfolk talk of fios a fitheach – the wisdom of the Raven – and there is truth in this, for she keeps the knowledge of men alive in her boundless memory long after their spirits have taken the dark and mysterious pathways beyond the realm of day.

# Notes on the Raven Costume

Sinister and menacing are words often used to describe the raven. However, I have the great privilege of sharing my croft cliffs with a resident pair, so I find neither of these words to be a fair description. Intelligent, resourceful, hardworking and fun-loving are words that fit my daily observations of them. They are the first birds to start preparations for nesting: as soon as the winter solstice passes they involve themselves in long and rapturous amorous displays and very shortly thereafter they can be seen flying purposefully to and fro over the house bearing twigs they have scavenged or snapped from shrubs and heather to mend their nest in the cliff. I know that they have completed the mending stage when they move to the machair to pull up marram – a tough yet pliable grass that is laid inside the nest. Then finally, they scour the crofts for scraps of wool fleece which they diligently gather and cram into their massive beaks. Not only is wool the perfect lining for incubation, I have observed on more than one occasion that when both birds have been compelled to leave the eggs and the newly hatched chicks, they use wool as a blanket to cover them in their absence, thus keeping them both warm and hidden from predators.

Their aerobatics are astonishing to watch and most exuberant when the young have just fledged and they join up with other families for an aerial jamboree. This often involves passing a twig from a great height and allowing it to drop before flying upside-down to catch it. But I love them best of all when I have the opportunity to be very close to them. They habitually sit on fence posts or on the ground and if I am there a while and careful not to move around in any way that could be construed as threatening, they will enter into a long and rambling oration full of varied vocabulary which makes their distinctive throat feathers bristle. I have no idea whether they are being profound or profane, or perhaps both at once, but there is undoubtedly a wide and subtle range of raven information being conveyed. It is as though they are reciting *The Voynich Manuscript* – the world's most mysterious book whose language has eluded decipherment for centuries. The Gaelic expression *tha fios fithich aige* (he has the knowledge of the raven) said of a wise man, was surely born from those who worked the land and observed their intriguing lives.

It seemed right to begin *Glamourie* with the wild creatures I share my croft with, and so I found myself devising methods to convey the blue-black bristling throat feathers in knitting. Perhaps, subconsciously, I wanted to begin with something that was connected to some form of communication. From there I went on to build the upper body, beginning from the centre back vertical panel and working shapes to form the back. Once I had made the core I set to thinking of how I would convey the plumage.

Watching ravens diligently preening is a lesson in identifying all the different components of their plumage: the primary and secondary wing feathers; the outer and central tail feathers; the upper-tail coverts; the median wing coverts; the chest feathers; all engineered with absolute precision. I created shapes that would convey the complexity of their plumage and along with this I wanted the construction to allow a sense of motion so that both the air and the movement of the wearer would echo the shapes cast by the bird when flying and in repose. So it became all about knitting individual feather shapes and then knitting them together into the silhouette. This was a major task and after I completed the costume I calculated that I had cast on a total of 17,963 stitches. I felt satisfied that I had honoured the ravens by working as hard and diligently as they always do themselves.

# The Otter & the Damselfly

*Damselflies were born long ago in the sparkle of sunlight on the gentle waves of a peaceful loch. They were made to flit and dart along the stony water's edge, and, as creatures of the meeting place of earth, water and air, they had a magic all of their own. They danced above the lapping waves and used the sun-warmed stones to spin magical doorways that opened onto other lochsides far away across the moor, to which they could pass instantly no matter how many miles in between. These 'passing places' were full of potential and change, and the damselflies delighted in their speed as they darted from one water's edge to another.*

*The Otter was born much later, when the world was a harder and less forgiving place. He was a curious mixture of the playful light on the softly undulating moorland hills, the transient charm of the briefly-flowering heather, and a desperate hunger for fat fish. He was at his most solitary in the winter: a season for survival, with no time for pursuits of a more convivial nature. In the spring he was entirely given over to industry, repairing the damage of the harsh winter while hunting and eating prodigiously. By the summertime he was sleek and comfortable. He spent his nights poaching or stealing any opportunistic delicacies that came his way, but at the height of the noonday sun he would frolic and laze on the banks of the peaceful loch. It was in this way, at the beginning of a long warm summer, that he first met the Damselfly.*

*Despite her long life the Damselfly was of an innocent nature and she was much charmed by the Otter who dallied on the riverbank and seduced her with tales of his daring* exploits. The Otter for his part was quite enchanted by her beauty, and for many days they were most content in each other's company. But where the Damselfly was eternal and constant, it was in the Otter's very nature to be capricious and changeable. As time passed, his interest in the beauty of the Damselfly waned and was replaced by an overpowering curiosity about her ability to travel without distance from one water's edge to another. As he lay by the loch he contemplated the Damselfly as she disappeared from one place to materialise in another in the blink of an eye, leaving only an echo of her magical doorway behind her. As more days followed he decided that he must have this magic for himself.

When the summer was at its height, the Otter quite suddenly and with no warning broke the delicate and insubstantial heart of the Damselfly and walked away from the loch and into the moor. The bereft Damselfly left her peaceful loch and familiar happy stones and followed him for many miles, but the Otter was a master of concealment and kept himself always just out of reach. Exhausted, the Damselfly lay down in the heather and the moor claimed her body for its own, while the deceitful Otter stole her magic and fashioned it into a walking stick that would open doorways across the moor.

As the summer started to fade the bold Otter used the stolen magic to leap from place to place without effort. One day he took his ease by a loch, quite unaware that he was being observed – by another young Damselfly who had secretly watched from afar the doomed romance of the Otter and her older sister.

*The young Damselfly had found the cruelly-broken heart and watched while the moor claimed the body of her sister for its own. The wings of this young Damselfly flashed sunlight as she wove her magic around the Otter, who was oblivious to its thistledown touch and went on his way unencumbered by doubt or worry.*

Soon the Otter tired of the loch, as he tired of most things after a time. He picked up his magic stick and went on his way, and when the time felt right he opened a doorway and passed through to another place. This time the passage did not feel as light and easy as it had in the past, and the Otter felt a shiver of apprehension. He was not at a lochside, or on the hills of the moorland, but instead was at the mouth of a river that was unfamiliar to him. A feeling of strangeness settled over him, and he found himself altered in ways he could barely comprehend.

And as the magical walking stick turned to ash in his hand he realised he was no longer he, but instead was **she**. From that day on he was cursed to bear the cares and worries of all female creatures, and could no longer wander the moor as a happy roving bachelor, ever free and content. Instead the Otter was bound to the river, never again to trouble the hearts of damselflies as they shimmered around their peaceful lochs.

# Notes on the Otter & Damselfly Costumes

The moorland of Lewis exists in its own mysterious world of gentle sounds – of wind in the heather and water lapping in streams and lochs. When I was a child I thought of it as a magical place, filled with colour, warmth and beauty, but also full of deception. There were still and deadly peat bogs, hidden holes under sturdy-looking ground and a strange bending of distance. On the many walks that we took through the moor, a landmark was fixed upon which looked achievable, but after what felt (to a small child) like miles had been covered it would remain a tantalising distance away, and at times disappear altogether. It was a place with its own rules, which were difficult to define.

Despite all the time I have spent on the moor, I have seen an otter on only a few occasions. Those elusive creatures make paths from loch to loch but rarely show themselves. Once we came across one beside a stream: unusually it hadn't seen us and so remained quite at ease until it looked up and made eye contact before slipping away.

The story I have fashioned for the otter paints him as a heartbreaker, an expert in concealment and a thief, but I am not without sympathy for the character. I imagine that those industrious creatures making paths through the heather would be entitled to look up at the damselflies glinting easily overhead and wonder why they could not have the freedom to move so fast and so far.

For the otter costume I wanted to make a garment that represented both beauty, industry and protective concealment on the moor. The result is almost armour-like: it is close fitting and because of its thickness it practically stands up by itself. The ridges that cover it are studded with knots representing the beauty of the moor in summer, sprinkled with cotton grass and flowers. The element of industry came in the making. The ridges are fashioned by picking up and knitting together a previously defined row, thus making a ridge with a centre of knots that stands out proud from the garment, so essentially I knitted the design three times over. Finishing it was like trying to achieve a moorland landmark on those childhood walks – far longer and much more exhausting than first realised. JS

Damselflies and their larger dragonfly cousins have been a source of facination to me from my earliest days of living on the Lewis moor. The sight of those gorgeously colourful creatures whirring around on shimmering wings over loch and bog still remind me of the long summer days of my childhood. Their beauty captivated me and opened the door into their world of *glamourie* for they truly are shape-shifters. It was easy to believe a yarn spun around any creature that could transform itself into another, when I could watch it actually happening right before my eyes. I spent many happy hours crawling as close as possible to the quaking edges of bogs in order to catch a sight of the real *glamourie*. Warm, windless early mornings were the perfect time to look out for a damsel or dragon larva clambering out of the water and up a bogbean or moorgrass stem. There it would begin the mesmerising metamorphosis in which it burst out of its skin, all pale and fragile. I was spellbound as it slowly pumped fluid into its intricate wings and colour into its pale body, to become one of the most spectacular creatures on earth.

I designed the damselfly costume for a child in remembrance of those far-off summer days. I sketched and planned this costume in detail before I began knitting as there were diverse aspects that I wanted to convey, such as how the creature changes from underwater swimmer to winged beauty and from a pale form to its final bright colours. Each species comes with its own defining colours and I chose my favourite, the Emerald Damselfly. The sides of the body and the sleeves reflect the pale form, and I worked these side-to-side with thin, vertical bands of colour.

I then created an abstract pattern based on the wing veins and worked this in the colours of the Emerald for the wing-shaped front panels. Using these same colours, I worked a central vertical panel on the back which echoes the long narrow shape of the segmented tail. I then created a lacy design for the detachable wings. Hidden hooks hold them on the shoulders and also under a patterned border along the centre of the sleeves. Finally, I made a larger matching wing to serve as a wrap for the heartbroken sister damsel, so that she could rest on the moor in comfort. AS

# The Selkie

*At the turning of the very first days, the islands of the far west and
north were potent with a new and wild magic; it danced across the
moorland, through the machair and far out to sea until everything it
touched was filled with vibrant colour and texture. During this time
of possibility and chance, the Selkie took their shape. Carefree and
wild, they grew wings and sleek silver feathers and they swooped and
wheeled above the water. They dared each other to soar ever-higher,
questing up towards the sun for doorways to other worlds. However,
there are very few creatures upon the earth or in the sky who can follow
the ever-shifting path between the worlds, and the Selkie were not
among their number. They reached too far, too fast, and the blistering
magic of the rising sun tore their wings from their bodies and they fell
for many heartbeats until they were embraced by the cold sea.*

*In their new watery domain they lost none of their carefree nature.
They chased the wandering salmon far out to sea before the swift
and cunning fish distracted them with trails of beautiful pebbles.
Then they dived deeper below the waves and teased the crabs until
pain made them seek a new entertainment. They looked towards the
land and used the moonlight magic that glittered across the waves
to make a pathway to the shore, where they danced across the sand.
They returned to the water only with the return of the rising sun, whose
magic burned their delicate silver skins.*

*And so it remained for many years; the Selkie slept beneath the waves in the day and at night they leapt and danced without thought or care. They paid no heed to the coming of the Children of Men and they barely listened to the shoals of herring, who whispered fearfully of the dangers of wood and metal.*

*On one night much like any other, the Selkie danced recklessly before the coming of the dawn. They did not notice the coming of men and were brought down in the blink of an eye by knife and spear until the sand was dyed with blood. Only one Selkie survived; she unconsciously turned* deiseil *(sunwise) and the knife meant for her heart pierced her arm instead. She ran from the sand and hid herself amongst great, sea-smoothed boulders while the men cooked the bodies of her sisters in a vast metal dye pot. They dissolved the magic from them and worked it into the tormentil-coloured sails of their boats to give them speed and luck upon the water.*

*The last Selkie hid beneath the stones until the men sailed away and the sun had disappeared below the horizon. She pulled the knife from her shoulder, cut off her silvery hair, dipped it in salt and bound her wound, healing it instantly. Then she reached toward the shingle and used the moonlight to fashion the rounded stones into a strong, thick coat to protect herself. The coat was dark and tinged with the colours of sea and storm, and it protected her from blade and sunlight. The knife she kept in her hand as she dived into the sea and called mournfully to the shoals of herring, understanding at last the danger of wood and metal.*

*From that day to this the Selkie holds her domain within the sea, but she has not lost her curious nature. Sometimes, when the sky is cloudless and the magic of the moon is strong, she ventures onto the shore and into the domain of men, but she never dances without the protection of her stone-armoured coat.*

# Notes on the Selkie Costume

*Sgeir Leathann* (A Gaelic name meaning *Broad Tidal Rock*) lies just out to sea from the foot of my croft, and appears and disappears according to the tides. Any visitor taking a walk along the shoreline may pass by without realising that many of the rounded, smooth boulders scattered among the sharp crags are in fact grey and common seals. A large colony of each species share the crags and appear to live side-by-side in a state of harmony, although on a relatively windless day or on a moonlit night you may be forgiven for thinking that murder is taking place as the seals howl their banshee songs into the still air. I am lucky enough to be able to fall asleep to these eerie, other-worldly sounds.

I have never lost the compulsion to call to them when they come close-by, because they will invariably disappear only to pop up even closer for a good look at me. A little song will keep them watching and though I have never heard them make a sound in reply they will keep pace with me as I move along the shore. There is always a feeling of some elemental connection when you can see yourself reflected in their huge watery eyes and so it is not surprising that so many stories have been woven around them over the generations.

Jade's story of the seal's coat of stone was at the forefront of my mind when I began to think about the Selkie costume: it had to be strong and powerful and reflect the colour of both seal and its habitat. So I doubled up my 3 Ply Selkie-coloured Hebridean yarn and set to make a coat of stone, both sleek and powerful. I saw the outline as a fitted double-breasted coat with a collar in which one could hide and then suddenly re-appear. The cuffs play a similar role so that the hands can disappear and make the arms seem like flippers. I created dense knotwork patterns for the collar and the cuffs and I lined both with felted, stranded knitting, worked in doubled 2 Ply Hebridean in Mara and Shearwater. The body and centre sleeves feature simple waving cables and I embroidered the body panels in waving lines echoing the weed forests through which the seals weave their splendid sea dances. The buttons are knitted, embroidered and felted and are placed strategically within the waving cables.

# The
# Sea
# Anemone

It is said in Gaelic-speaking lands that witches with green
eyes are able to catch the wind and trap it in a knot on
a thread. It is also said that it is unlucky for a sister to
brush her hair while her brother is away at sea.

*Far out to the North and West lay the Long Island: a place either
scoured by storms or blessed with a beautiful crystal light that
illuminated more colours than existed anywhere else upon the earth. Of
the Children of Men who made their home there, some saw the beauty
while others saw only the hard and jagged rocks, and their characters
developed accordingly.*

*On this island, near the base of a high-rising cliff, lived three sisters,
full of youth and vigour, and each possessing her own particular mark
of beauty. The first sister had eyes as green as the bogbean that grew
within the treacherous places of the moorland; the second had long-
fingered hands that were full of grace, and the third had thick, lustrous
hair that shone and glimmered with all the colours of the moorland
in the heart of autumn. They also possessed the knowledge and ways
of herbs and incantations and were frequently sought out to help, or
hinder, depending on the nature of the request.*

*One day the third sister was sitting on a stone brushing out her
hair nine-times-nine, when a young man came by with a request for
a favourable wind to take to sea with him. The third sister smiled at
him (for he was comely in all respects) and with the last stroke of her
hairbrush she caught a happy and swift westerly breeze and passed it*

to her sister, who wrapped it in an intricate knot of yarn and sent him on his way. However, the young man was so captivated by the sight of the third sister that he came back day after day, and as she smiled at him day after day it was not long before they were married. They settled in a blackhouse at the top of the rising cliff where the breeze was strong, for she liked to tame the wind with her brush and make it do her bidding.

At first, when the marriage was young, all was well, but as time went on the sister found less and less peace. She was used to being always in the company of her sisters, and as her husband was often at sea she felt the lack of company, and the chores of the house and land multiplied around her as the seasons turned. It befell that the only pleasure she had in her lonely day was when she sat near the door of the house and brushed out her hair and chased the North wind.

On one particular morning, as she sat and brushed her hair nine-times-nine, her counting was interrupted by the stew pot boiling over. No sooner had she seen to that and settled back again to her counting when the cow lowed for milking. Once that was seen to and she was settled again, her ducks charged the front door and created a cacophony within the little stone house. Once she had restored order with a hard broom she was quite overwrought, and when she returned to her counting she made a terrible mistake – she brushed her hair nine-times-ten, summoning the sharp and bitter East wind. Different from the West, North and South, the East wind had rules all of its own and no witch could tame it.

The East wind – full of fury at being called from its favourite pursuit of jabbing sharp, cold knives into the hearts of ill-clad travellers – whipped at the sea until the waves towered and the swell heaved. And the third sister could only watch as her husband's fishing boat was shattered against the rocks at the foot of the cliff. Satisfied, the East *wind veered away to the horizon, leaving the third sister to climb down and pull the body of her husband from the waves and bury him beneath the beautiful but treacherous shingle.*

*The third sister climbed down to the shingle day after day and shed many tears over the grave of her husband. At first these were tears of guilt and sorrow, and her hair became dull and straggled. Then, as time passed, she shed tears of loss and pain and her body became thin and bony. Then she began to begrudge the happiness of others when she had no comfort of her own, and she shed tears of malice and rage. These fell from her eyes as blood and rained down upon the shingle until there was nothing left of her body but her red tears. The sea washed them back and forth until they coalesced into a single smooth red pebble, and as night fell the half-waxed moonlight danced upon it and the Sea Anemone was born.*

*For a time she dwelt half-formed in a cave, looking out upon the colourful pebbles and the world beyond, her smooth stone heart brim-full with the malice of the third sister's tears. Slowly she began to explore the sea and shoreline beyond the cave; she observed the fragility of all warm-blooded beings and learned the value of beauty and of salt. She then took her shape and walked out amongst the shingle; her skin was as pale as sea foam and her eyes as blue as the sea itself. Her hair she coloured from a memory of the third sister, and her face and form were as smooth and perfectly curved as the many-hued pebbles that lay upon the shore. She fashioned garments from the seaweeds upon the beach and climbed the cliff in search of young and tender flesh. For a time she seduced and feasted on the unwary, until the shoreline villages were depleted and the Long Island was ruled by loss and fear. The villagers tried to fight her but her stone-hard flesh repelled all weapons, and still her beauty ensnared those she encountered in solitude.*

*In desperation the villagers turned to the first and second sisters, who had just returned to their blackhouse at the foot of the rising cliff after a twelvemonth spent deep in the moorland colouring cloth with rare plants. They were distressed to hear the plight of the villagers, and they grieved beyond measure for the life of their sister. But they recognised the warped and twisted form of her magic within the Sea Anemone and they stopped their own tears lest they call into being yet more malign forces. They asked the villagers to bring them the very finest fleece from the very purest sheep. The first sister – whose green eyes could determine the nature of plants – dyed the fleece into the warm and rich colours of the moorland. Into her dye pot she also mixed love and the strength of her ancestors. The second sister used her elegant hands to spin yards and yards of a soft strong yarn, full of her most cherished memories. Thus armed, they went forth to the shoreline under a waning moon, and spun and wove until they had created a net so fine that it was invisible in the darkness.*

*The Sea Anemone, complacent and sated, walked unsuspecting into a net so strong that she could not break a single strand. As her skin was hard as stone, the sisters could not harm her, but as the night passed they sang and danced spells and incantations which bound the Sea Anemone to the very rock. Though they could not destroy her, they called out to their sister's blood; they entreated until her clothing changed colour to a rich red that would warn the unsuspecting of her deadly nature.*

*Though the sisters have passed long out of time and memory, the Sea Anemone still lives on. Anchored to the rocks, she cannot pass onto the land, but she waits by the shore in lonely places, ever vigilant for the tender and the unwary; the careless and the easily seduced.*

# Notes on the Sea Anemone Costume

Blood-red beadlet sea anemones stand out like sirens among the myriad forms of life stranded in rock pools at low tide. They survive periods out of water by withdrawing their tentacles and enclosing water within so that they look like innocuous blobs of jelly, but they are hungry creatures and once immersed it does not take long to see them open up to expose their waving tentacles. Their beautiful flower-like appearance belies their predatory nature as each of their tentacles is armed with many tiny cells containing poison barbs. The instant a fish touches a tentacle, triggers in the cells fire and barbs shoot into the prey. Held by the tentacles and poisoned, it has no chance of escape and is very quickly consumed.

Although they appear to be static, attached to rocks by a strong basal disc, they actually do move very slowly from one place to another and these are times when they can display some interesting behaviour. If one happens to touch another, then the larger of the two will withdraw its touching tentacles and then slowly it begins to "grow" taller until it towers over the smaller one and at the same time the body at the base of the tentacles grows into a pronounced collar. It then quickly bends over and strikes the smaller anemone with its collar, releasing spots of stinging cells onto the smaller one which then retreats to nurse its injuries.

This astonishing behaviour no doubt serves the practical purpose of ensuring that territorial boundaries are adhered to but it served to inspire me to design the costume and Jade to write her story.

Deadly, alluring glamour were my bywords as I lived and breathed Sea Anemone red for a good many weeks while constructing the costume. I began with the tentacles which I knitted in a similar manner to the collar feathers I designed for the Raven. I felted them until they stood by themselves and then knitted the collar in the round in one piece. I then rolled it in on itself so that it formed a trench into which I stitched the tentacles.

I based the silhouette on the columnar curvy shape of the anemone and extended the length in a nod to its attachment to rocks. I designed a textured pattern for the upper body and embroidered little "beadlets" in a brighter red and centred these within the textured waving pattern lines. I then made the lower body with a curving extended hemline in panels worked from side-to-side and shaped it to fit from hips to ankles using short rows.

By way of her "catch" I knitted and felted a mermaid's purse encrusted with free-form embroidery. I then created various smaller felted forms – a felted starfish caught in a net and various knitted forms of seaweed.

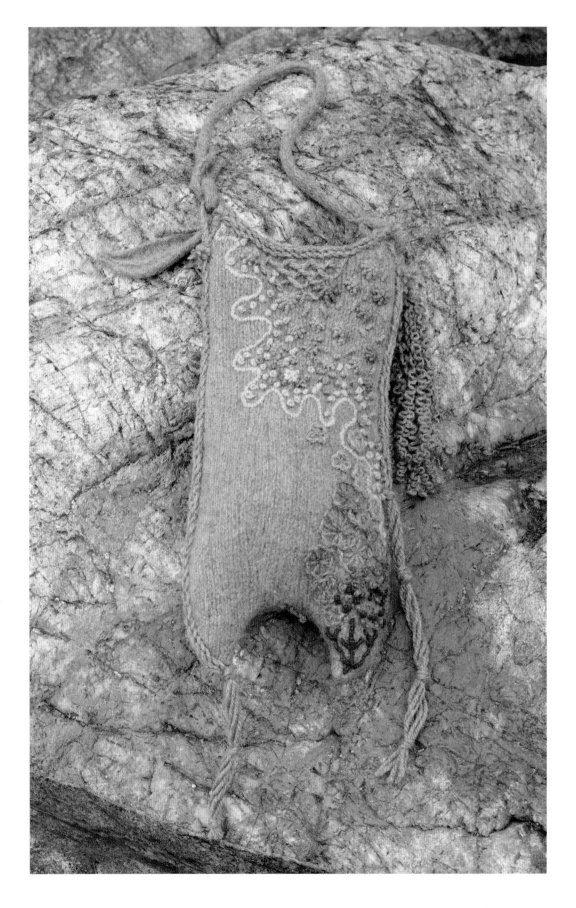

The Eagle & the Lapwing

*Back in the early years upon the Earth, the Island awoke with a great burst of starlight upon sand, sea and heather; it was then that the pulse of the seasons began to quicken and the days lengthened and shortened accordingly. The years spun past but in the gaps between the seasons there was a static time, like a held intake of breath – a pause when neither summer nor autumn held sway, and the flowers on the machair and the moor were both vibrantly alive and dying away in the same instant. The moon above the sea was neither fully waxed nor fully waned but equally split down the middle – half a disc of shining light and half of deepest midnight. In this pause, in this brief moment of respite upon the great spinning wheel, a strange girl-child was born into the world of men.*

*As soon as she became able she ran ceaselessly between shore and moor, feeling most at home during the twilight hours and sensitive to the life beneath her feet. As she grew she became separate from the villagers, shuddering when they drove iron too deep and far into the soft peat or trampled the machair flowers.*

*One day she turned her face away and walked until she could no longer see or hear the bustle of the village, and she rested in a quiet dell situated exactly between moor and machair. Here she built a house out of stones and lived a life apart,*

93

*but she was not solitary as long as she had the beat of the earth beneath her feet. Soon she was feared as a powerful witch and she chased away all those who came near, protecting both the heather and the clover from the blade of the* **tarrasgeir** *(as the peat iron is called in Gaelic) and the careless trampling of many feet.*

*As the years went by she brewed and dyed the richest of colours and spun the softest of yarn, which she wound into the very fabric of the surrounding land until it was filled with colour. No stretch of moor or breadth of machair was as vibrant as that which stretched out from her dell to the edges of the horizon. Yet, even though it was so beautiful, none dared set foot upon it for fear of her power. The children were told stories of the witch who sat spinning upon the shore and could catch an errant child with a flick of her thread, but no child ever dared test the tale to see if it was true. For her part she simply smiled and continued to spin her yarn in many colours.*

*After the turning of many seasons, and despite the pauses in between them, she who was once a girl grew old and could no longer run between moor and machair. Her footsteps became slow and her movements painful, and in the pause between summer and autumn, when the moon had neither waxed nor waned, she spun her very last two hanks of yarn.*

94

One she mixed with heather and soft, black peat; she added a touch of her blood and fed the whole concoction to a giant hungry sundew. The other she blended with machair and sea, and added a shard of polished flint which she had kept next to her heart. This she fed to the clover and the orchid. Once all was done she scattered her possessions until nothing was left to mark her but the tumbled stones of her dwelling set within a circle of green grass. As the moon set she sighed her last and sank back into the earth, exactly between moor and machair.

As days passed, rumours spread their wings and flew, and all through winter the Children of Men whispered of the passing of the witch. By the time spring had brought colour back to the earth and warmed the snow-bleached sky, they had gained enough courage to pick up their peat irons and walk toward the witching place. But as the land awoke so too did the flowers, and as the giant sundew unfurled, a golden Eagle burst out from it in a whirl of feathers. She was as gold and layered as the moss, rich as the peat, many-hued as the sundew and as sharp as a blade. Her talons yearned for blood and as the Children of Men brought their irons to the moor she swept forward and drove them away in a fury of talon, blood and bone.

*What was left of the Children of Men ran toward the shore and the safety of the machair. As they sheltered together at the coming of the night, the clover and the wild orchid unraveled and faded and the Lapwing grew from their tender petals. She was sleek and her colour spoke of rich grasses and the mystery of the sea, but her eyes were like polished flint and all those who looked into them forgot themselves and wandered uselessly upon the shore.*

*In the village, wives and children wept for the loss of their men, and down the years the stories of witchcraft strengthened. None dared venture to the secret place where the moor and the machair meet, for high on the rocky horizon the Eagle could still be seen, a perched silhouette ever-ready to fly – swift and sharp, with blood in her mind.*

*And on the machair the Lapwing sat, her polished flint eyes reflecting the colours of the flowers. Sometimes, in the pause between summer and autumn, when the moon shines brightly and eclipses darkly all at the same time, the Eagle and the Lapwing take on human form. When the land holds its breath in that magic hour, they walk hand-in-hand where the moorland meets the machair.*

# Notes on the Eagle Costume

The Isle of Lewis and Harris is home to a quarter of Britain's population of Golden Eagles and so there is always a good chance of spotting at least one at any time of the year, soaring on raised wings, high above the hills. I have watched them since childhood and yet familiarity does not diminish the excitement and reverence I feel every time I see this iconic monarch of the birds. I admit to feeling some envy for their command of their wild territory and I try and imagine how it must feel to be able to soar and glide effortlessly from coast to coast and view the island from innumerable vantage points.

They spend around five years growing up and once they have passed the tough tests of survival, including persistent persecution by man, they find a partner and set up a territory. One of the most thrilling sights to see is a courting pair in the air when they grab each other by the talons and whirl around in an elemental dance of wings. A close encounter is quite rare but always truly memorable, for this is when the overall dark appearance at long range proves to be a deceit and the beautiful bronze and golden markings on its plumage are revealed. The pointed golden nape feathers, which are raised up when the bird is angry, are the defining feature of its name.

I have always associated the Golden Eagle with strength and power: a warrior at one with the unforgiving climate and landscape. It was from this basis that I began to work on the Eagle costume. I started by doubling up my 3 Ply Hebridean yarn for warmth and strength. The moorland shade of Tormentil would be a perfect shade for cover in the wild. I planned touches of gold around the neck and on shoulder feathers which would rise when worn. The doubled yarn gives textured stitches a strong, bold appearance so for the front I worked a textured trellis pattern as a stylised form of the chest feathers, and bounded this with a curved cable design in recognition of the bird's broad rounded chest.

To convey an idea of the eagle's speed, I worked a pattern of diagonal lines on the back and sleeves which spread out from strong cabled centres. For the tail, which I worked in the lighter single 3 Ply, I made short-row shaped pieces and attached them to the V-shaped lower back. I designed the studded collar so that the 3 Ply gold cords could be threaded through and would stream behind in the wind. In this case, I wanted the knitting design to work with the costume and so I designed the Eagle Wrap by way of wings.

Jade designed and made the skirt, panelled in two shades of fine suede. The crowning glory is the exquistely hand-crafted leather headpiece and mask designed and made by Pete Williamson.

# Notes on the Lapwing Costume

The lapwing's distinctive peewit call and exuberant tumbling aerial display was always a signal note of the arrival of spring in the Hebrides. Suddenly the sky above the pasture lands would be filled with the sound and sight of these beautiful birds as they arrived to breed from southern Britain and continental Europe. In past days they were generally regarded as being quite ordinary creatures – undoubtedly because of that strange human propensity to take all things numerous for granted. It is only when people have the opportunity to view them at close quarters that they realise how exquisitely exotic the bird really is. Now, because of industrial farming practices further south, lapwings are a rare sight, and for the last decade I can count the yearly number on my croft with one hand.

The sight of a lapwing running around catching insects on the flower-filled machair – with its crazy "fascinator" crest and its purple-green iridescent plumage, sharply contrasting with its pale chest and its honey-coloured bottom – is one of the most joyously colourful sights of summer. My intention was to convey all of this in a costume that would be a fitting homage to these extraordinary birds.

I started with the crest, which I thought would be an interesting experiment in just how well my Hebridean yarn would felt, as the crest had to be tall, curved and vertical on top of the head. I thought I would worry later about how well anything so tall would stand up in a place like Lewis, where hats regularly blow right off heads. I made a simple sleeveless top with a lightly curved hemline for the chest and a feathered neckpiece to evoke the lapwing's underside colours. The jacket was constructed to echo the shape when its wings are closed, with a tail worked side-to-side which I felted very lightly then folded to form loose pleats while it was still wet. I then decorated the jacket with knitted and felted flowers, stems and leaves and touches of purple embroidery.

Jade and I greatly admire the intricate and ingenious costume designs of our lovely model Rachael Forbes, and so I sent her a picture of the finished costume – whereupon she designed and made the wonderful and suitably exotic skirt to complement my efforts. The photography day proved fair and the crest stood up well in a very light breeze. *Rara avis* indeed.

---

# The Cailleach

*The wheel of history turns and times change, though not necessarily for the better. The peace must ever be fought for, and if the good cease this struggle then the door is left open for evil. Thus it was that the Island on the Edge fell into discord and vice.*

*The Otter brewed a potent liquor from the flowering heather and watched with glee as the Children of Men drank until they forgot to tend their land and fought amongst themselves instead.*

*The Damselflies grew bold and careless and flew up and down the crofts, leaving portals to other lands lying open behind them. The flash and dazzle of their wings enchanted small children, half-dreaming in the sun, and they stumbled into other worlds never to return.*

*The Sea Anemone picked up discarded driftwood and using the last sharp rays of sunlight on the water set it alight. It burned through the midnight hours and lured boats onto the rocks where she drank her fill of sailors' blood.*

*The Raven grew melancholy and reclusive as her stories were ignored or mocked and forgotten.*

*The Lapwing stole into the houses of those who slumbered late, and, taking whatever bright and beautiful things she could find, she adorned herself and strutted up and down the shoreline.*

*The Selkie grew vicious and warlike, came up into the harbour and slashed the sails of boats while the men were incoherent and heavy with liquor.*

*The Golden Eagle strayed from the bounds of the moorland and hunted untended livestock which she devoured; she flung their bones down chimneys where they rattled into iron pots.*

*The Mountain Hare hid from all the clamour, too afraid to venture forth, and the souls of the dead once more walked upon the land and wailed in the moonlight.*

*The tides turned erratically, shoals of fish avoided the coastline, livestock grew thin and wary, the birds flew aloft in fright and would not nest. The island grew dark and stormy and the sky turned red in warning. In the midst of this turmoil, when the sea heaved and dashed against the rocks and the wind tore the thatch from the blackhouses, a single shaft of moonlight pierced through the clouds and lit down upon the moor. This silver light fell upon the fading heather and into the ageless peat, and that is how the Cailleach was born between the moor and sky.*

*She was a woman who could not be placed in years, with steel strength in her body and the wisdom of the land in her heart. From the left side of her belt hung a pair of sheathed needles, and from the right, a pattern book from which the very future itself could be knitted. She saw the moral chaos about her and as the year turned she knew the time was ripe for action. In the spring, when the Children of Men cut their peats, she walked close by and blew favourable drying winds across them. She called to the Golden Eagle and helped her build nests in high, stony places far away from houses. She walked the boundaries of the moor and showed that rapacious bird the limit of her territory.*

*When summer came, she watched over the crofts and chided the Damselflies; she then sent them back to their lochs and closed their portals behind them. And as autumn approached and the heather bloomed, she ran swiftly across the moor, and gathered up the flowers in her arms. The wind of her passing spun them into yarn as she leapt over mossy bogs and through the hills. In the evenings she paused by the lochsides and knitted, fashioning a jacket that spoke of her past and looked to her future. By the time the vindictive Otter came to harvest the heather, the flowers were all gone and the Cailleach chased her away back to the river.*

*Without the distraction of the Otter's heady, dangerous brew, the Children of Men turned once more to peace and industry. The Cailleach spoke words over their dye pots that strengthened their garments and sails, so they had no more need to spill Selkie blood. The Selkie in turn went back to her rocks, sheathed her knife and rent men's sails no more. The Cailleach sang as she plaited heather stalks and seaweed into ropes that bound the Sea Anemone to the rocks. Then she walked across the machair, pricked her thumb with a needle and bright flowers bloomed wherever the blood fell. The inquisitive Lapwing was entranced by their beauty and lost the urge to steal from the houses of men.*

*As the days dwindled towards the Solstice, the Cailleach's knitted jacket grew dusky and softened into winter shades; it glowed around her as she sat by the shoreline and listened attentively to the tales of the Raven. With those stories lodged firmly in her mind she gathered the souls of the dead about her and led them back to the foot of the Ben, where the Mountain Hare came out from hiding and guided them onwards to the world that lay beyond sight and sound.*

123

*And so the world still spins, the seasons still turn and the island still lies out upon the edge, amidst the passing storms. It is filled with many lives and many deaths, but the Cailleach is ever-present, making sure that whatever fades or falls silent in winter is renewed every spring. She walks the boundaries between moor and shore, between loch and hill. She turns the animals away from bogs and lights a beacon to guide the boats back to harbour. And if you, Traveller, should ever be beguiled by Glamourie and stray upon hill or heather, shore or machair, she will guide your steps – a distant figure upon the horizon, marking the way from the mysterious world of the Shapeshifters back to the safety of your own familiar fireside.*

# Notes on the Cailleach Costume

(In Gaelic, *cailleach* means an old lady)

I grew up in a time and place where people were intimately connected to the land. My maternal grandparents were both born in 1875 and both were still alive when I reached adulthood. My grandmother lived for 100 years, which was not too unusual, and so I grew up knowing many of her generation. Their lives were so very far removed from our lives today, that thinking back is to look into a different world. It is a world that I am powerfully connected to and one to which I owe much that I hold dear.

It is easy to romanticise lives spent at one with the natural world, far removed from the innumerable complexities of the twenty-first century. But that would fail to acknowledge how difficult and precarious life actually was back then. Nature is not always merciful and to survive, both men and women had to have a high level of stamina and endurance. Knowledge of the natural world was essential and resourcefulness often made the difference between life and death. Women in particular, had extremely tough lives: they had to look after the home at all times and the land in the busiest seasons, while the men went on fishing voyages. They clothed and fed their families, tended their animals, raised crops and brought home winter fuel on their backs. They milked the cow, sheared the sheep, gathered plants, dyed and spun wool, wove cloth, knitted socks, shawls, petticoats and ganseys.

These were all tasks of absolute necessity and for the most part were regarded as chores to be got through before the failing light. When it came to making, as always, some did it better and with more enthusiasm than others. This was ever the case with the women of my family: my grandmother, aunts and especially my mother, loved to make things and they were very resourceful. My father's aunt Seònaid spent her summers at a sheiling very close to where our Cailleach is standing in these photographs. Before she went out to the moor she gathered up every scrap of yarn she could lay her hands on and returned home for the winter with a huge basket of beautiful, colourful gloves which she handed out to everyone she knew. Nothing was ever wasted.

*The Cailleach* is my homage to all those I knew who were creative and resourceful and who understood the ways and rhythms of the natural world. I wanted to make her a jacket that would symbolise her essence. To this end I plundered the chest of drawers that holds all the swatches I have knitted over all the years of my career as a designer. I chose a selection of Hebridean 2 Ply swatches, felted them and then inlaid them in a panel made with fine cabled strips. I also utilised the diagonal pattern I had made for the eagle costume as a nod to the Cailleach's tireless endeavours. Then I created gradually expanding, eternal knotwork patterns for the sleeves and front panels. At the lower back and sides I made little flourishes and finished them with tiny felted flowers, and at the front hemline I attached little knitted tabs so that she could transport her small important accoutrements, such as the magical pattern book from which she knits the future. For her knitting needles, I made her a felted and flower-appliquéd needle case. Finally, I felted buttons to ensure that every last scrap of yarn was used up.

Jade designed and made her luxurious purple wool dress, and we made sure that our Cailleach had plenty of yarn on hand for the future.

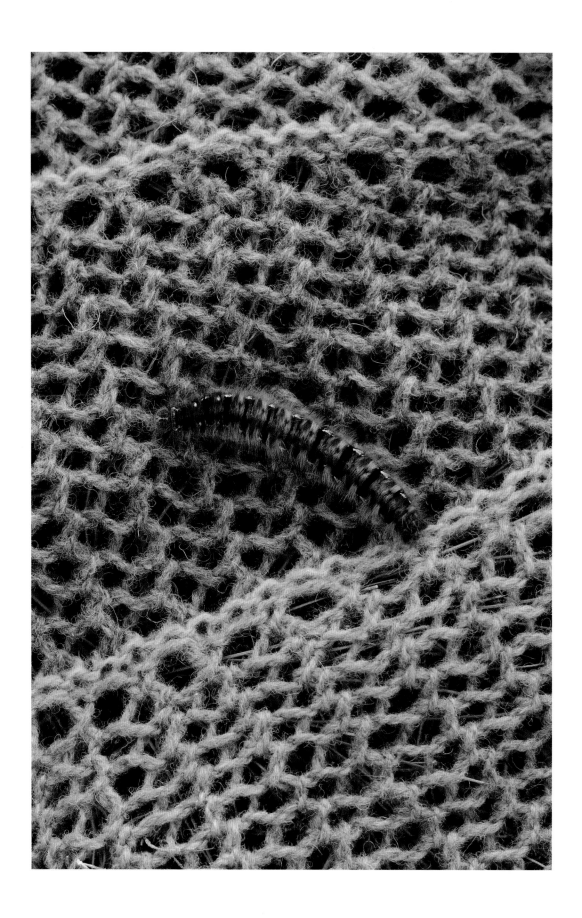

# The Mountain Hare

## Design Notes ——————————————

I wanted these designs to echo the salient features of the costume, and to this end I used a simple finely-textured pattern for the sides and sleeves, and panels of textured zig-zag lines that climb upward, with a single ladder pattern at the centre back. The zig-zag panels are lightly embroidered with stars and French knots, both self-coloured and also in contrast colours.

The collar of the jacket and the brim of the hat are worked in a textured stranded colour pattern, and both jacket and hat feature buttons that are embroidered then felted into little orbs.

The jacket is lightly shaped to the waist with all the shaping taking place within the side panels (charts A & E). It is worth spending a few moments studying these simple charts so that

when you work the shaping, and decrease or increase stitches, you will effortlessly maintain the continuity of the pattern. There is a lot of scope for variation in the embroidery as it is entirely optional, being worked after the pieces are knitted. I have detailed within the instructions how I embroidered both jacket and hat. If you are new to embroidering on hand-knitted fabric then I highly recommend that you make a swatch of either chart B or D and try it out before working on the garment. On these charts I have indicated the position of the French knots (row 1) and the stars (centred on row 14). See pages 266 and 267 for the embroidery stitches I used and also page 268 for felting, should you wish to make the buttons.

## Sizes

To fit small [medium, large, X large].
Directions for larger sizes are given in square brackets. Where there is only one set of figures, it applies to all sizes.

## Knitted Measurements

Underarm (buttoned) 91[97,103,109]cm.
Waist 79[85,91,97]cm.
Length 57[59,61,63]cm.
Sleeve length 43[44,44,45]cm.

## Materials

Of **Alice Starmore® Hebridean 2 Ply** –
350[400,450,500]g in Pebble Beach.
20g each in Corncrake and Mountain Hare.
10g each in Sundew and Driftwood.
1 pair 3mm needles. Stitch holders.
Stitch markers. Tapestry needle.

## Tension

27 Sts and 43 rows to 10cm measured over chart A patt using 3mm needles. To make an accurate tension swatch, cast on 36 sts and rep the 6 patt sts of chart A 6 times. Rep the 8 patt rows and work 48 rows. Pin the swatch on a flat surface and measure tension using a ruler.

## Left Front

■ With 3mm needles and Pebble Beach cast on 55[59,63,67] sts. Work lower border as follows –
**Row 1 (RS):** Purl. **Rows 2 & 3:** Knit.
**Row 4:** Purl.
**Row 5 (RS):** * K3; Make Knot (MK) thus: (k1; k1b) twice into the next st then pass the first 3 sts made over the last st made; rep from * to the last 3 sts; k3.
**Row 6:** Purl. **Rows 7 & 8:** Knit.
**Rows 9 & 10:** Purl.
**Next Row (RS) – Inc:** (K 9[10,11,12]; m1) 3 times; k 10[11,12,13]; m1; k17; m1; k1. 60[64,68,72] Sts.
**Next Row (WS):** P1; k1; p17; k1; p 40[44,48,52].
**Set Chart Patts**
**Row 1 (RS):** Reading from right to left, work chart A over the first 40[44,48,52] sts working the first 3[1,5,3] sts as indicated; then rep the 6 patt sts 6[7,7,8] times; patt the last st as indicated; work chart B over the next 19 sts; k1.
**Row 2 (WS):** P1; reading from left to right, work chart B over the next 19 sts; work chart A over the last 40[44,48,52] sts working the first st as indicated; then rep the 6 patt sts 6[7,7,8] times;

patt the last 3[1,5,3] sts as indicated.
Continue as set and work 12[14,16,18] chart patt rows in total.

▲ **Next Row (RS) – Work Side Dec:** K1; k2tog; keeping continuity, patt to end of row. Continue in patt as set for 7 rows. ▲▲
**Next Row (RS) – Work Inner Dec:** Patt as set to the last 2 sts of chart A; k2tog; patt as set to end of row. Continue in patt as set for 7 rows. ■ ■
Rep from ▲ to ■ ■ 2 more times, thus working 3 side and 3 inner dec rows in total with 34[38,42,46] chart A sts rem.
Work from ▲ to ▲▲ once more, then work another side dec row, thus having 32[36,40,44] chart A sts rem. 52[56,60,64] Sts in total and 69[71,73,75] chart patt rows worked from beg, thus ending on row 17[19,21,23] of chart B and row 5[7,1,3] of chart A inclusive.
Continue in patt as set for 17 rows.
* **Next Row (RS) – Work Side Inc:** K1; m1; keeping continuity, patt to end of row.
Continue in patt as set for 7 rows. +
**Next Row (RS) – Work Inner Inc:** Patt as set to the last st of chart A; m1; k1; patt to end of row.
Continue in patt as set for 7 rows. ++
Rep from * to ++ 2 more times, thus working 3 side and 3 inner inc rows in total, thus having 38[42,46,50] chart A sts.
Work from * to + once more, then work another side inc row, thus having 40[44,48,52] chart A sts and 60[64,68,72] sts in total.
Continue in patt without further shaping until piece measures 39[40,41,42] cm from cast on edge with RS facing for next row.

### Shape Armhole
** Keeping continuity of chart A patt throughout, cast off 5[6,6,7] sts at beg of next row. Patt 1 WS row. Cast off 3[3,4,4] sts at beg of next row. Patt 1 WS row. Dec 1st at armhole edge of next 3 rows. 49[52,55,58] Sts rem. Patt 1 WS row. Dec 1st at armhole edge of next and every foll alt row until 41[44,47,50] sts rem. Continue straight without further shaping until armhole measures 12.5[13.5,14,15] cm from first armhole cast off row with RS facing for next row.
### Shape Front Neck
Patt as set to the last 6[7,7,8] sts and place these sts on a holder for front neck. Turn and keeping continuity of patt throughout, dec

**CHART A**

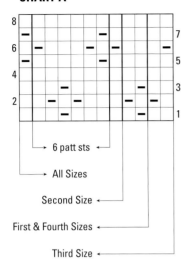

→ 6 patt sts ←

→ All Sizes ←

Second Size ←

First & Fourth Sizes ←

Third Size ←

**CHART B**

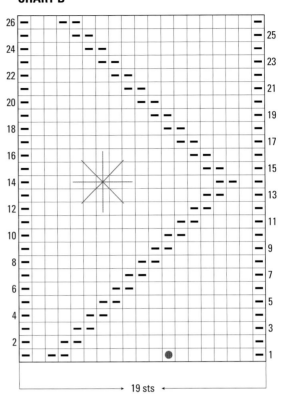

→ 19 sts ←

**CHART C**

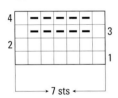

→ 7 sts ←

**CHART D**

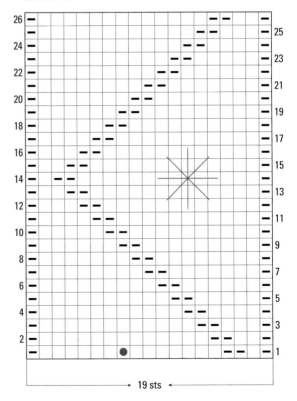

→ 19 sts ←

**CHART E**

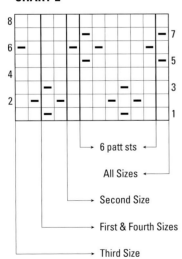

→ 6 patt sts ←

All Sizes ←

→ Second Size

→ First & Fourth Sizes

→ Third Size

138

## CHART F

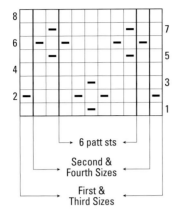

## KEY FOR MOUNTAIN HARE JACKET

☐ k in Pebble Beach on RS rows: p in Pebble Beach on WS rows.

▬ p in Pebble Beach on RS rows: k in Pebble Beach on WS rows.

❙ k in Corncrake on RS rows: p in Corncrake on WS rows.

▬ p in Corncrake on RS rows: k in Corncrake on WS rows.

❙ k in Mountain Hare on RS rows: p in Mountain Hare on WS rows.

▬ p in Mountain Hare on RS rows: k in Mountain Hare on WS rows.

## CHART G

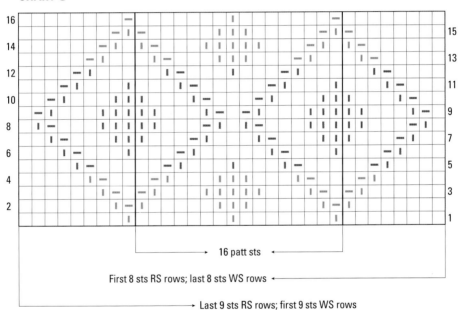

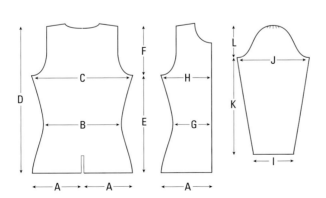

A = 22[23.5, 25, 26.5]cm
B = 39[42, 45, 48]cm
C = 45[48, 51, 54]cm
D = 57[59, 61, 63]cm
E = 39[40, 41, 42]cm
F = 18[19, 20, 21]cm
G = 19[20.5, 22, 23.5]cm
H = 22[23.5, 25, 26.5]cm
I = 19.5[21, 21.75, 23.25]cm
J = 30.75[33, 35, 37.5]cm
K = 43[44, 44, 45]cm
L = 15[15.75, 16.5, 17.25]cm

1st at neck edge of next 4 rows. Patt 1 row without shaping then dec 1st at neck edge of next and every foll alt row 4[4,5,5] times in all. 27[29,31,33] Sts rem. Work 2 rows without shaping then dec 1st at neck edge of next and every foll 3rd row 3 times in all. 24[26,28,30] Sts rem. Armhole measures 18[19,20,21] cm from first cast off row with RS facing for next row.

## Shape Shoulder

Cast off 8[8,9,10] sts at beg of next row. Patt 1 WS row. Cast off 8[9,9,10] sts at beg of next row. Patt 1 WS row. Cast off the rem 8[9,10,10] sts.***

*Right Front*

■ Cast on 55[59,63,67] sts and work the first 10 border rows as left front.

**Next Row (RS) – Inc:** K1; m1; k17; m1; k 10[11,12,13]; (m1; k 9[10,11,12]) 3 times. 60[64,68,72] sts.

**Next Row (WS):** P 40[44,48,52]; k1; p17; k1; p1 .

## Set Chart Patts

**Row 1 (RS):** K1; reading from right to left, work chart D over the next 19 sts; work chart E over the next 40[44,48,52] sts working the first st as indicated; then rep the 6 patt sts 6[7,7,8] times; patt the last 3[1,5,3] sts as indicated.

**Row 2 (WS):** Reading from left to right, work chart E over the first 40[44,48,52] sts working the first 3[1,5,3] sts as indicated; then rep the 6 patt sts 6[7,7,8] times; patt the last st as indicated; work chart D over the next 19 sts; p1. Continue as set and work 12[14,16,18] chart patt rows in total.

▲ **Next Row (RS) – Work Side Dec:** Patt to the last 3 sts; ssk; k1.

Continue in patt as set for 7 rows. ▲▲

**Next Row (RS) – Work Inner Dec:** Patt as set to the first 2 sts of chart E; ssk; patt to end of row.

Continue in patt as set for 7 rows. ■ ■

Rep from ▲ to ■ ■ 2 more times, thus working 3 side and 3 inner dec rows in total with 34[38,42,46] chart E sts rem.

Work from ▲ to ▲▲ once more, then work another side dec row, thus having 32[36,40,44] chart E sts rem. 52[56,60,64] Sts in total and 69[71,73,75] chart patt rows worked from beg, thus ending on row 17[19,21,23] of chart D and row 5[7,1,3] of chart E inclusive.

Continue in patt as set for 17 rows.

**\* Next Row (RS) – Work Side Inc:** Patt to the last st; m1; k1. Continue in patt as set for 7 rows. **+**

**Next Row (RS) – Work Inner Inc:** Patt as set to the first st of chart E; k1; m1; keeping continuity; patt to end of row. Continue in patt as set for 7 rows. **++**

Rep from **\*** to **++** 2 more times, thus working 3 side and 3 inner inc rows in total with a total of 38[42,46,50] chart E sts.

Work from **\*** to **+** once more, then work a final side inc row, thus having 40[44,48,52] chart E sts and 60[64,68,72] sts in total.

Continue in patt without further shaping until piece matches left front in length but with WS facing for next row.

Shape armhole, neck and shoulder as given for left front working from **\*\*** to **\*\*\*** but beg all shapings with WS facing for next row.

*Back*

## Lower Left Back

Work as Right Front from ■ to ■ ■. Then work from ▲ to ■ ■ once more. Then work from ▲ to ▲▲ once more. Then work another inner dec row. 54[58,62,66] Sts rem with 53[55,57,59] chart patt rows worked in total, thus ending on row 1[3,5,7] of Chart D inclusive. Keeping continuity, patt the next WS row. Break off yarn and place the sts on a spare needle.

## Lower Right Back

Work as Left Front from ■ to ■ ■. Then work from ▲ to ■ ■ once more. Then work from ▲ to ▲▲ once more. Then work another inner dec row. 54[58,62,66] Sts rem with 53[55,57,59] chart patt rows worked in total, thus ending on row 1[3,5,7] of Chart B inclusive. Keeping continuity, patt the next WS row.

## Join Right & Left Pieces

With RS facing and keeping continuity of patts, work across the 54[58,62,66] sts of lower right back as set; cast on 5 sts; with RS facing work across the 54[58,62,66] sts of lower left back. 113[121,129,137] Sts.

**Next Row (WS):** Keeping continuity, patt as set over the 54[58,62,66] sts of left back; k5; patt as set over the 54[58, 62,66] sts of right back.

**Next Row (RS):** Keeping continuity, work the next row of chart A as set over the first 34[38,42,46] sts; work row 5[7,9,11] of chart B over the next 19 sts; work row 1 of chart C over the next 7 sts; work row 5[7,9,11] of chart D over

the next 19 sts; work the next row of chart E as set over the last 34[38,42,46] sts.
Continue as set for a further 3 rows.
**Next Row (RS) – Work Side Decs:** K1; k2tog; continue in patt as set to the last 3 sts; ssk; k1.
Continue in patt as set for 7 rows, then work another side dec row as before. 109[117,125,133] Sts rem and 69[71,73,75] chart patt rows worked from beg, thus ending on row 17[19,21,23] of charts B & D.
Continue in patt as set for 17 rows.
**\* Next Row (RS) Work Side Incs:** K1; m1; patt to the last st; m1; k1.
Continue in patt as set for 7 rows. **+**
**Next Row (RS) – Work Inner Incs**
Patt as set to the last st of chart A; m1; k1; patt as set to the first st of chart E; k1; m1; keeping continuity; patt to end of row. Continue in patt as set for 7 rows. **++**
Rep from **\*** to **++** 2 more times, thus working 3 side and 3 inner inc rows in total thus having 38[42,46,50] chart A and chart E sts.
Work from **\*** to **+** once more, then work another side inc row, thus having 40[44,48,52] chart A and chart E sts and 125[133,141,149] sts in total. Continue in patt without further shaping until back matches fronts in length at beg of armhole shaping with RS facing for next row.
**Shape Armholes**
Keeping continuity of patt throughout, cast off 5[6,6,7] sts at beg of next 2 rows. Cast off 3[3,4,4] sts at beg of next 2 rows. Dec 1st at each end of next 3 rows. Patt 1 WS row, then dec 1st at each end of next and every foll alt row until 87[93,99,105] sts rem. Continue straight without further shaping until armholes measure 17.5[18.5,19.5,20.5] cm (2 rows below first shoulder cast-off of fronts) with RS facing for next row.
**Shape Back Neck and Shoulders**
Patt 26[28,30,32] sts; place the next 35[37,39,41] sts on a holder for back neck; place the rem 26[28,30,32] sts on a spare needle. Turn and work the right neck/shoulder as follows –
**Row 1 (WS):** P2tog; patt as set to end of row.
**Row 2 (RS):** Cast off 8[8,9,10]; patt as set to end of row.
**Row 3:** As row 1.
Cast off 8[9,9,10] sts at beg of next row. Patt 1 WS row.
Turn and cast off the rem 8[9,10,10] sts.
With RS facing rejoin yarn to the 26[28,30,32] sts of left shoulder and patt as set to end of

row. Shape left neck/shoulder as follows –
**Row 1 (WS):** Patt as set to the last 2 sts; p2tog.
**Row 2 (RS):** Patt as set to end of row.
**Row 3:** Cast off 8[8,9,10]; patt as set to the last 2 sts; p2tog.
**Row 4:** As row 2.
Cast off 8[9,9,10] sts at beg of next row. Patt 1 RS row. Turn and cast off the rem 8[9,10,10] sts.

*Sleeves*

With 3mm needles cast on 47[51,51,55] sts. Work the first 10 rows of border as Left Front.
**Next Row (RS) – Inc**
K 1[3,1,3]; \* m1; k 9[9,7,7]; rep from \* to the last 1[3,1,3] sts; m1; k 1[3,1,3]. 53[57,59,63] Sts. P1 WS row.
**Set Chart F Patt**
**Row 1 (RS):** Reading from right to left, patt the first 2[1,2,1] sts as indicated; rep the 6 patt sts 8[9,9,10] times; patt the last 3[2,3,2] sts as indicated.
**Row 2 (WS):** Reading from left to right, patt the first 3[2,3,2] sts as indicated; rep the 6 patt sts 8[9,9,10] times; patt the last 2[1,2,1] sts as indicated.
Continue in patt as set and working all inc sts into patt throughout, shape sleeve by inc 1st at each end of 7th and every foll 8th row until there are 69[75,87,95] sts; then inc 1 st at each end of every foll 12th row until there are 77[85,95,101] sts.
**First & Second Sizes Only:** Continue as set and inc 1st at each end of every foll 16th row until there are 83[89] sts.
**All Sizes:** Continue in patt without further shaping until sleeve measures 43[44,44,45]cm from cast-on edge with RS facing for next row.
**Shape Cap**
Keeping continuity of patt throughout, cast off 5[6,6,7] sts at beg of next 2 rows. Cast off 3[3,4,4] sts at beg of next 2 rows. Dec 1st at each end of next row. 65[69,73,77] Sts rem. Patt 2 rows without shaping, then dec 1st at each end of next and every foll 3rd row until 25[27,29,31] sts rem. Patt 1 WS row and on 2nd & 4th sizes only, dec 1st at each end of this row. 25[25,29,29] Sts.
Thread a darner with a spare length of yarn and transfer sts to the yarn. Block sleeves as given in *Finishing* and once blocked, transfer the sts back to the needle and work the final row to gather the sleeve top as follows –

**Next Row (RS) – Dec:** K2tog 6[6,7,7] times; k1; ssk 6[6,7,7] times. 13[13,15,15] Sts rem. Cast off purlwise on WS.

*Finishing*

Block out all pieces RS up to measurements shown on schematic. Cover with damp towels and leave to dry away from direct heat.

**Back Vent Edgings – Right Side**

With RS facing and 3mm needles beg at top of vent and knit up 42[43,44,45] sts evenly to cast-on edge, working into the inside loop of the edge st.

**Row 1 (WS):** P1; k to the last st; p1.
**Row 2 (RS):** K1; p to the last st; k1.
**Row 3:** Purl. **Row 4:** Knit. **Row 5:** As row 3. With RS facing, cast off purlwise.

Work left side of vent as right, but knit up the sts from the cast-on edge to the top of the vent. Darn in loose ends and sew the top ends of the edgings to the centre cast-on sts of back so that the edgings meet at the centre. Press the seams and edgings very lightly on the WS using a warm iron and damp cloth.

Embroider the back and fronts with French knots and stars at will. The garment can be embroidered to a greater or lesser degree, as preferred. I have used both the ground colour, Pebble Beach, and some contrasting colours. Here is what I did —

On the back I worked all of the embroidery in Pebble Beach, placing a star (centred on row 14) and a French knot (centred on row 1) of charts B & D as I have shown on the charts.

I placed three French knots across the top vent edging seam. On the fronts I worked the same arrangement of stars and French knots but worked pairs from the neckline in the colours, Sundew, Mountain Hare, Corncrake and Driftwood then completed the rest in Pebble Beach.

Sew fronts to back at shoulder seams and press seams lightly as before.

**Collar**

With RS facing and 3mm needles, pick up and k the 6[7,7,8] sts from right neck holder; knit up 26[26,27,27] sts evenly to back neck holder; pick up and k the 35[37,39,41] sts from back neck holder; knit up 26[26,27,27] sts evenly to left front holder and pick up and k the 6[7,7,8] sts. 99[103,107,111] Sts in total.

**Rows 1 & 3 (WS):** P1; k to the last st; p1.
**Row 2 (RS):** K1; p to the last st; k1.

**Row 4 (RS):** Knit.
**Row 5 (WS):** Purl. **Row 6 (RS):** * K3; MK; rep from * to the last 3 sts; k3. **Row 7 (WS):** Purl.
**Row 8 (RS):** Knit. **Row 9 (WS):** As row 1.
**Row 10 (RS):** As row 2. Place a marker at each end of this row. **Row 11 (WS):** Purl.

**Next Row – Inc**

**First, Second & Third Sizes:** K4[2,1]; * m1; k 7[11,21] rep from * to the last 4[2,1] sts; m1; k 4[2,1]. 113 Sts.

**Fourth Size:** K1; m1; k to the last st; m1; k1. 113 Sts.

**All Sizes:** P1 WS row. Joining in colours as required, and stranding the yarns on the WS throughout, work the patt from chart G as follows –

**Row 1:** Reading fom right to left, patt the first 8 sts as indicated; rep the 16 patt sts 6 times; patt the last 9 sts as indicated.

**Row 2:** Reading from left to right, patt the first 9 sts as indicated; rep the 16 patt sts 6 times; patt the last 8 sts as indicated

Work the 16 rows of chart as set.

Break off contrast colours and with Pebble Beach k1 row; p1 row. Work outer edging as follows –

**Row 1 (RS):** K1; p to the last st: k1.
**Row 2 (WS):** P1; k to the last st; p1.
**Row 3 (RS):** Knit.
**Row 4 (WS):** P38; m1; p37; m1; p38. 115 Sts.
**Row 5 (RS):** K1; * MK; k3; rep from * to the last 2 sts; MK; k1.
**Row 6:** Purl. **Row 7:** Knit. **Row 8:** As row 2.
**Row 9:** As row 1.

With WS facing, cast off knitwise.

Darn in ends. Block out collar and cover with damp towel or press **very** lightly on the WS using a warm iron and damp cloth.

**Left front Band**

With RS facing, 3mm needles and Pebble Beach beg at marked st of collar and knit up 158[162,166,170] sts evenly to cast-on edge.
**Row 1 (WS):** P1; k to the last st; p1.
**Row 2 (RS):** K1; p to the last st; k1.
**Rows 3 & 5 (WS):** Purl.
**Rows 4 & 6 (RS):** Knit. **Row 7 (WS):** As row 1.
**Row 8 (RS):** As row 2.
Cast off knitwise on the WS.

**Right Front Band**

As left, but beg at cast-on edge and knit up sts to marked st of collar and work 9 buttonholes on row 4 (RS) as follows –
K17[21,25,29]; * cast off 2; k15; rep from * to

the last 5 sts; cast off 2; k3. On next row, cast on 2 sts over those cast off on the previous row.

### Front Collar Edgings

With RS facing beg at cast-off edge of right collar end and knit up 21 sts evenly to top of right front band, working into the inside loop of the edge st. K1 WS row. P1 RS row. Cast off knitwise on WS. Work left end of collar as right, but beg at top of left front band and knit up sts evenly to cast-off edge.

Darn in loose ends and sew end of collar edgings to top of front bands on WS. Press very lightly on WS using a warm iron and damp cloth. Sew up side and sleeve seams and press seams very lightly as before. Pin centre top of sleeves to shoulder seams and underarm seams together and then pin and sew sleeves into armholes. Press seams as before.

### Felted Buttons

With 3mm needles and using colours at will, cast on 3 sts.
**Rows 1 & 3 (WS):** Purl.
**Row 2 (RS):** (K1; m1) twice; k1. 5 Sts.
**Row 4 (RS):** (K1; m1) 4 times; k1. 9 Sts.
**Rows 5, 7 & 9 (WS):** Purl.
**Row 6 (RS):** Knit.
**Row 8 (RS):** (K2tog; k1) 3 times. 6 Sts.
**Row 10 (RS):** (K2tog) 3 times. 3 Sts.
Turn and cast off purlwise, breaking off yarn with enough to sew up the sides tog. Finish and embroider the cast off end (top of button) in contrasting colour and felt as given for hat button on page 147. For further information on felting see page 268. Sew buttons on to left front band.

# Mountain Hare Hat

## Design Notes

The hat can be embroidered at will. See pages 266 and 267 for illustrations of French knots and stars. I chose to encrust the hat with embroidery in contrasting colours to emphasise all the knitted elements, but there is plenty room for variation. For example, you can embroider just a few of the elements and/or use self colours for a more subdued result. You can also make the stars of varying sizes, sometimes working a long vertical on the upright cross with shorter horizontal and diagonal stitches.

Here is how I embroidered the hat –

I began by placing a French knot in Sundew at the centre of each of the 9 small Corncrake diamond shapes (shown split at each end of rnds 1-5 of chart); a Pebble Beach star within each of the 9 Mountain Hare centre shapes (rows 6-11 of chart); a Driftwood French knot on the Pebble Beach ground within each of the 4 points of the enclosed coloured diamond shapes. This completed the embroidery on the stranded section of the knitting.

Starting at the top of the hat and working towards the brim, I worked a Mountain Hare French knot at the centre of each of the 4 purl-framed diamond shapes shown at the centre of the chart (rows 62-34); then a Mountain Hare star at the centre of the largest purl-framed diamond shape (rows 34-22); a French knot in Corncrake at each double decrease point, working from the top decrease down each line of decs to the first dec on row 35. Finally, I worked a larger star in Sundew in the St.St. space below each of the first double decreases.

## Knitted Measurements

Circumference 51.4 cm. Brim to Crown 20.5cm.

## Materials

Of **Alice Starmore® Hebridean 2 Ply** –
45g of Pebble Beach.
15g each of Mountain Hare and Corncrake.
5g each of Driftwood and Sundew.
1 Set of double-pointed or circular 2.5mm and 3mm needles. If using a circular 3mm needle, then a set of double-pointed sock needles will be required to complete the crown as it decreases. 1 Stitch marker. 1 tapestry needle.

## Tension

28 Sts and 39 rows to 10cm measured over chart patt on 3mm needles.

## Hat

With set of double-pointed or circular 2.5mm needles and Pebble Beach cast on 132 sts. Place a marker at beg of rnd and making sure cast on edge is not twisted, work border as follows –

**Rnds 1 & 2:** Purl. **Rnd 3:** Knit.
**Rnd 4:** * With Driftwood, k1 then sl the st back to the LHN and make knot (MK) thus: (k1,k1b) twice into the st to make 4 sts; then slip the first 3 sts made over the last st made; k3 Pebble Beach; rep from * to end of rnd, stranding the Driftwood yarn across the WS.
Break off Driftwood. With Pebble Beach continue as follows –
**Rnd 5:** Knit. **Rnds 6 & 7:** Purl. **Rnd 8:** Knit.
**Next Rnd – Inc:** * K11; m1; rep from * to end of rnd. 144 Sts.
Change to 3mm needles. Joining in and breaking off colours as required and stranding the yarns across the WS on the first 16 rnds, read all rnds from right to left and rep the 16 patt sts of chart 9 times in the rnd. Break off Corncrake. With Pebble Beach continue in patt as shown and work through rnd 34 of chart.

**Next Rnd (Rnd 35) – Begin Crown Shaping**
* Patt as set to the last 2 sts of rep; sl the next 2 sts tog knitwise as indicated on chart; k the next st (first st of next rep), then pass the 2 sl sts over the k st; rep from * to the last 2 sts of rnd; sl these sts as indicated; remove the beg of rnd marker and k the first st of next rnd and pass the 2 sl sts over this st; replace the beg of rnd marker. 126 Sts rem.
Continue and work through the rem chart rnds as set, having 18 fewer sts after every dec rnd until 18 sts rem after working rnd 70.
**Next Rnd:** (K2tog) 9 times. 9 Sts rem. Break off yarn leaving enough to fasten off the rem sts. To fasten off, thread the yarn end into a tapestry needle and pass it through all rem sts, then bring the needle through the centre of the sts to the WS and pull gently to close the hole. Secure and darn in the yarn end on the WS. Darn in all loose ends.

## Finishing

Dampen the hat by spraying with water inside and out and then roll lightly in a towel to allow the water to be absorbed. Then fit the cap over a head form or suitably shaped item such as a bowl or balloon and leave to dry.

## Felted Button

With 3mm needles and Corncrake or chosen colour, cast on 3 sts.

**Rows 1, 3 & 5 (WS):** Purl. **Row 2:** (K1; m1) 3 times. 6 Sts. **Row 4:** (K1; m1) 5 times; k1. 11 Sts. **Row 6:** (K2; m1) 5 times; k1. 16 Sts. Work St.St. for 5 rows. **Row 12 (RS):** (K1; k2tog) 5 times; k1. 11 Sts. **Rows 13 & 15:** Purl. **Row 14:** (K2tog) 5 times; k1. 6 sts. **Row 16:** (K2tog) 3 times.

Break off yarn, leaving enough to fasten off the rem sts and sew up the seam. Thread the needle and pass it through the rem 3 sts and sew up the seam about half way to the cast-on edge. Cut up spare yarn ends into very short pieces (1-2mm) and stuff into the piece to make a firm round shape, then sew up the rem seam to the cast-on. With Pebble Beach or preferred colour, embroider a star on the top end of the button. Felt by plunging the ball into very hot soapy water (see page 268 for felting) and wearing a pair of household gloves roll the ball vigorously between the palms of your hands using a circular motion. Once the button shrinks and feels solid, plunge into cold water for a few moments then rinse thoroughly in warm water and leave to dry for at least 24 hours, away from direct heat. Sew through the cast-on end of the button and then sew to the centre top of the hat.

## KEY FOR MOUNTAIN HARE HAT

☐ k in Pebble Beach.

❙ k in Corncrake.

▬ p in Corncrake.

❙ k in Mountain Hare.

▬ p in Mountain Hare.

▬ p in Pebble Beach.

SL2 slip 2 sts tog knitwise.

☐ pass the 2 slipped sts over this k st.

147

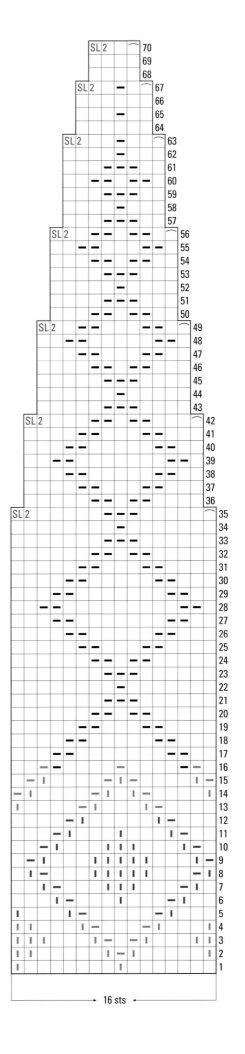

16 sts

# The Otter

## Design Notes

The otter design is sleeker and lighter than the costume. The studded ridges are a striking feature at the neck, cuffs and hem, while the body is lightly shaped in Stocking Stitch. The Heath colourway shown in the cropped design is taken from heather and cotton grass; the Moss colourway, shown in the classic version, is based on the rich green grasses and golden mosses that grow beside the waters of the bogs and lochs. The directions for the all the colours used in the Heath colourway are stated first and the Moss colours are stated second and <u>underlined</u>.

The ridges are formed by knitting 6 rows, then knitting the next row together with the loops from a row worked before beginning the 6 ridge rows. In order to make this easier and more accurate I have highlighted the row by having it worked in a contrast colour. You will not see this row on the finished piece but it serves as an excellent guide while you are working.

## Sizes

To fit small [medium, large, X large].
Directions for larger sizes are given in square brackets. Where there is only one set of figures, it applies to all sizes.

## Knitted Measurements

Underarm 89.5[97,102.5,108.5]cm.
Waist 79[86.5,92.5,98.5]cm.
Length Cropped Version: 40.5[42,43.5,45]cm.
Length Classic Version: 57[59,61,63]cm.
Sleeve length 44[44,45,45]cm.

## Materials

**Alice Starmore® Hebridean 2 Ply** in –

**Cropped Version Heath:**
275[300,325,350]g in Fulmar.
50[60,70,80]g in Spindrift.
25[30,35,40]g in Driftwood.
20[25,30,35]g in Solan Goose.
15[18,21,25]g in Golden Plover.
12g in Mountain Hare.

**Cropped Version Moss:**
250[275,300,325]g in Bogbean.
50[60,70,75]g each in Corncrake and Machair.
40[50,60,70]g in Mara.

**Classic Version Heath:**
340[370,390,425]g in Fulmar.
40[50,60,70]g in Spindrift.
25[30,35,40]g in Driftwood.
12[15,18,21] in Solan Goose.
8[10,12,14]g in Golden Plover.
6[7,8,10]g in Mountain Hare.

**Classic Version Moss:**
325[350,375,400] in Bogbean.
40[50,60,70]g each in Corncrake & Machair.
25[30,35,40]g in Mara.

1 pair 2.75mm & 3mm needles. 1 set of double-pointed or short circular 2.5mm needles for neckband. 2 Stitch holders. Stitch markers. Tapestry needle.

## Tension

27 Sts and 40 rows to 10cm measured over St.St. using 3mm needles. To make an accurate tension swatch, cast on 31 sts and work 42 rows. Pin the swatch on a flat surface and measure tension using a ruler.

## Back Cropped Version

• With 2.75mm needles and Spindrift/Corncrake cast on 104[113,122,131] sts.
**Row 1 (RS):** Knit. **Rows 2 (WS):** Purl.
**Row 3 (RS):** With Spindrift/Corncrake k2;
* with Solan Goose/Bogbean make knot (MK) thus: k the next st then sl the st back to the left needle and k into the front then back of the st twice, thus forming 4 sts; sl the first 3 sts over the last st made; with Spindrift/Corncrake k2, stranding the yarn across the WS; rep from * to end of row. Break off Solan Goose/Bogbean.
**Rows 4 & 6 (WS):** With Spindrift/Corncrake, purl.
**Row 5 (RS):** With Spindrift/Corncrake, knit.
**Row 7 (RS) – Make Ridge:** Pick up the first cast on loop from the WS and place it on the left needle tip then k the loop tog with the first st; continue in this manner picking up each cast on loop and k tog with its corresponding st along the whole row.
**Row 8 (WS):** With Spindrift/Corncrake knit.
**Row 9 (RS):** With Spindrift/Corncrake purl. Break off yarn.
Transfer sts back to left needle so that RS is facing for next row.
**+ Rows 10 & 12 (RS):** With Fulmar/Machair knit. **Row 11 (WS):** With Fulmar/Machair purl. Break off yarn.
**Row 13 (WS):** With Solan Goose/Bogbean purl. Break off yarn.
**Row 14 (RS):** With Fulmar/Machair knit.
**Row 15 (WS):** With Fulmar/Machair purl.
**Row 16 (RS):** With Fulmar/Machair work knot row as row 3, working knots in Golden Plover/Mara.
**Rows 17 & 19 (WS):** With Fulmar/Machair purl. **Row 18 (RS):** With Fulmar/Machair knit.
**Row 20 (RS) – Make Ridge**
With Fulmar/Machair, k each st tog with the corresponding WS loop of Solan Goose/Bogbean row (13) working along the whole row.
**Row 21 (WS):** With Fulmar/Machair knit.
**Row 22 (RS):** With Fulmar/Machair purl. Break off yarn. Transfer sts back to left needle so that RS is facing for next row. **++**
With Driftwood/Mara instead of Fulmar/Machair, Mountain Hare/Machair for knots and Solan Goose/Bogbean for row 13, rep from **+** to **++.**
With Fulmar/Machair and Golden Plover /Mara for knots and Solan Goose/Bogbean for row 13 rep from **+** to **++.**

With Spindrift/<u>Corncrake</u>, Solan Goose/<u>Bogbean</u> for knots and for row 13 rep from **+** to **++**. ●
With Fulmar/<u>Bogbean</u> and RS facing k1 row. Inc on next WS row as follows –
**First & Third Sizes:** P1; * m1; p51[60]; m1; rep from * once more; m1; p1. 107[125] Sts.
**Second Size:** P1; *m1; k37; rep from * to the last st; m1; p1. 117 Sts.
**Fourth Size:** P1; m1; p to the last st; m1; p1. 133 Sts.
**All Sizes:** Change to 3mm needles and work straight in St.St. for 4 rows.
■ **Next Row (RS) – First Inc:** K1; m1; k to the last st; m1; k1. 109[119,127,135] Sts.
Work 7 rows in St. St.
**Next Row (RS) – Second Inc:** K 36[39,41,43]; m1; k 37[41,45,49]; m1; k 36[39,41,43]. 111[121,129,137] Sts. Work 7 rows in St. St.
**Next Row (RS) – Third Inc:** As first inc. 113[123,131,139] Sts. Work 7 rows in St. St.
**Next Row (RS) – Fourth Inc:** K 38[41,43,45]; m1; k 37[41,45,49]; m1; k 38[41,43,45]. 115[125,133,141] Sts. Work 7 rows in St. St.
**Next Row (RS) – Fifth Inc:** As first inc. 117[127,135,143] Sts. Work 7 rows in St. St.
**Next Row (RS) – Sixth Inc:** K 40[43,45,47]; m1; k 37[41,45,49]; m1; k 40[43,45,47]. 119[129,137,145]Sts. Work 7 rows in St. St.
**Next Row (RS) – Seventh Inc:** As first inc. 121[131,139,147] Sts.
Continue straight in St.St. until piece measures 22.5[23,23.5,24]cm for cropped version and 39[40,41,42]cm for classic version, measured from hemline with RS facing for next row.
**Shape Armholes**
Cast off 5[6,6,6] sts at beg of next 2 rows. Cast off 3[3,4,4] sts at beg of next 2 rows. Dec 1st at each end of next 1[3,3,3] rows. Work 1 row without shaping then dec 1st at each end of next and every foll alt row until 89[93,97,101] sts remain. ●●
Continue straight without further shaping until armhole measures 16.5[17.5,18.5,19.5] cm with RS facing for next row.

**Shape Back Neck/Shoulders**
K 26[28,29,31] of right back shoulder; place the next 37[37,39,39] sts on a holder for back neck; place the rem 26[28,29,31]sts of left back shoulder on a spare needle.
Turn and shape right back neck as follows –
**+** Continue in St.St. and dec 1st at neck edge of the next 2 rows. Work 1 row without

shaping then dec 1st at neck edge of next row. 23[25,26,28] Sts rem. Work 1 row without shaping, thus ending with RS facing for next row.
**Shape Shoulder**
Cast off 7[8,8,9] sts at beg next row. Cast off 8[8,9,9] sts at beg of next alt row. Work 1 row then cast off the rem 8[9,9,10] sts. **++**
With RS facing, rejoin yarn to sts of left back shoulder and k to end of row. Work as right back neck and shoulder from **+** to **++**, except work 2 rows without shaping after the last neck dec row, thus having WS facing for shoulder shaping.

*Front Cropped Version*

As back from ● to ●●.
Continue straight until armhole measures 9.5[10.5,11,12]cm with RS facing for next row.
**Shape Neck**
K 35[37,38,40] of left side of neck; place the next 19[19,21,21] sts on a holder; place the rem 35[37,38,40] sts of right side of neck on a spare needle. Turn and shape left side of neck as follows —
* Dec 1st at neck edge of next 2 rows. Work 1 row without shaping then dec neck edge of next and foll alt row. 31[33,34,36] Sts rem. Work 2 rows without shaping then dec 1st at neck edge of next and every foll third row until 23[25,26,28] sts rem. **
Work 3[3,5,5] rows without shaping thus ending with RS facing for next row and armhole matching back in length at first shoulder cast-off. Shape shoulder as given for right back. Rejoin yarn to sts of right side of neck and k to end of row. Work as left side from * to **.
Work 4[4,6,6] rows without shaping after the last neck dec row, thus ending with WS facing for next row. Cast off shoulder sts as left back.

*Back Classic Version*

▲ With 2.75mm needles and Spindrift/<u>Corncrake</u>, cast on 122[131,140,149] Sts. Work the first 9 rows in chosen colourway as given in cropped version back. Transfer sts back to left needle so that RS is facing for next row. Change to 3mm needles and with Fulmar/<u>Bogbean</u> k1 row.
**Next Row (WS) – First & Third Sizes** P 60[69]; p2tog; p60[69]. 121[139] Sts.
**Next Row (WS) – Second Size:** Purl.
**Next Row (WS) – Fourth Size:** P48; p2tog; p49; p2tog; p48. 147 Sts.

## All Sizes

Continue straight in St.St. for 6[6,8,8] rows.

**Next Row (RS) – First Dec:** K1; k2tog; k to the last 3 sts; ssk k1. 119[129,137,145] Sts. Work 7 rows in St. St.

**Next Row (RS) – Second Dec:** K 39[42,44,46]; ssk; k 37[41,45,49]; k2tog; k 39[42,44,46]. 117[127,135,143] Sts. Work 7 rows in St. St.

**Next Row (RS) – Third Dec:** As first dec. 115[125,133,141] Sts. Work 7 rows in St. St.

**Next Row (RS) – Fourth Dec:** K 37[40,42,44]; ssk; k 37[41,45,49]; k2tog; k 37[40,42,44]. 113[123,131,139] Sts. Work 7 rows in St. St.

**Next Row (RS) – Fifth Dec:** As first dec. 111[121,129,137] Sts. Work 7 rows in St. St.

**Next Row (RS) – Sixth Dec:** K 35[38,40,42]; ssk; k 37[41,45,49]; k2tog; k 35[38,40,42]. 109[119,127,135] Sts. Work 7 rows in St. St.

**Next Row (RS) – Seventh Dec:** As first dec. 107[117,125,133] Sts.

Continue straight in St. St. for 17 rows, ending with RS facing for next row.

Continue and complete back as given for cropped version from ■.

## Front Classic Version

As classic version back, from ▲ then as cropped version back from ■ to ••.

Complete as given for cropped version front.

## Sleeves

With 2.75mm needles and Spindrift/Corncrake, cast on 53[56,59,62] sts and work the cuff as cropped version back from **Row 1** to ●.

Change to 3mm needles and with Fulmar/Bogbean work as follows –

**First & Third Sizes:** Beg with a RS row and work straight in St.St. for 14[12] rows.

**Second & Fourth Sizes:** K 1 RS row. **Next Row (WS):** P 28[31]; m1; p 28[31]. 57[63] Sts. Work 12[10] rows in St.St.

**All Sizes – Next Row (RS)**

**Beg Sleeve Shaping**

K1; m1; k to the last st; m1; k1. Work 7 rows without shaping then inc 1st as set at each end of next and every foll 8th row until there are 83[87,91,95] sts. Continue straight in St.St. until sleeve measures 44[44,45,45] cm from hemline with RS facing for next row.

**Beg Cap Shaping**

Cast off 5[6,6,6] sts at beg of next 2 rows. Cast off 3[3,4,4] sts at beg of next 2 rows. Dec 1st at each end of next row. Patt 2 rows without shaping then dec 1st at each end of next and every foll 3rd row until 59[57,55,59] sts rem. Patt 1 row without shaping then dec 1 st at each end of next and every foll alt row until 29 sts rem. Work 1 row without shaping then dec at each end of next and every foll row until 13 sts rem. Cast off sts.

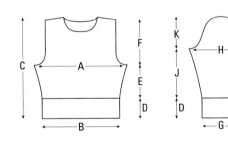

A = 44.75[48.5, 51.25, 54.25]cm
B = 39.5[43.25, 46.25, 49.25]cm
C = 40.5[42, 43.5, 45]cm
D = 7.5cm
E = 15[15.5, 16, 16.5]cm
F = 18[19, 20, 21]cm
G = 19[20, 20.5, 21]cm

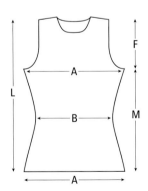

H = 30.75[32.25, 33.75, 35]cm
J = 36.5[36.5, 37.5, 37.5]cm
K = 13[14, 15, 16]cm
L = 57[59, 61, 63]cm
M = 39[40, 41, 42]cm

## Finishing

Darn in all loose ends. Block out pieces to measurements shown on schematic. Cover with damp towels and leave to dry away from direct heat. Sew back to fronts at shoulder seams and press seams very lightly on WS using a warm iron and damp cloth.

### Neckband

With RS facing, set of double-pointed or circular 2.5mm needles and Fulmar/Bogbean, beg at right shoulder seam and knit up 11 sts along neck edge to back neck holder; pick up and knit up 37[37,39,39] sts from holder; knit up 11 sts along neck edge to left shoulder seam; knit up 33[33,34,34] sts evenly along left side of neck to front neck holder; pick up and k the 19[19,21,21] sts from holder; knit up 33[33,34,34] sts evenly along right neck edge to complete the rnd. 144[144,150,150] Sts.

Place a marker at beg of rnd, and joining in and breaking off colours as required, patt as follows –

**Rnds 1 & 2:** With Spindrift/Corncrake, k.
**Rnd 3:** * With Spindrift/Corncrake k2; with Solan Goose/Bogbean MK; rep from * to end of rnd.
**Rnds 4,5 & 6:** With Spindrift/Corncrake, k.
**Rnd 7:** With Spindrift/Corncrake, make ridge by ktog into each st and its corresponding WS loop of the Fulmar/Bogbean pick up rnd.
**Rnds 8 & 9:** With Spindrift/Corncrake, p.
**Rnd 10:** With Fulmar /Machair, k.
**First & Second Sizes Rnd 11 – Dec:** With Fulmar/Machair, * k2tog; k10; rep from * to end of rnd. 132 Sts.
**Third & Fourth Sizes Rnd 11 – Dec:** With Fulmar/Machair, * k2tog; k10; k2tog k11; rep from * to end of rnd. 138 Sts.

**Rnd 12:** With Fulmar/Machair, k.
**Rnd 13:** With Solan Goose/Bogbean, k.
**Rnds 14 & 15:** With Fulmar/Machair, k.
**Rnd 16:** As rnd 3, but with Fulmar/Machair and Golden Plover/Mara for knots.
**Rnds 17, 18 & 19:** With Fulmar/Machair, k.
**Rnd 20:** With Fulmar/Machair, make ridge by working into each st and k tog with the corresponding WS loop of the Solan Goose/Bogbean rnd.
**Rnds 21 & 22:** With Fulmar/Machair, p.
**+ Rnds 23, 24 & 25:** With Driftwood/Mara, k.
**Rnd 26:** With Solan Goose/Bogbean, k.
**Rnds 27 & 28:** With Driftwood/Mara, k.
**Rnd 29:** As rnd 3, but with Driftwood /Mara and Mountain Hare/Machair for knots.
**Rnds 30, 31 & 32:** With Driftwood/Mara, k.
**Rnd 33:** With Driftwood/Mara as rnd 21.
**Rnds 34 & 35:** With Driftwood/Mara p. ++
**Rnd 36:** With Fulmar/Machair k.
**First & Second Sizes Rnd 37 – Dec:** With Fulmar/Machair, k4; * k2tog; k9; rep from * to the last 7 sts; k2tog; k5. 120 Sts.
**Third & Fourth Sizes Rnd 37 – Dec:** With Fulmar/Machair, k5; * k2tog; k9; k2tog; k10; rep from * to the last 18 sts; k2tog; k9; k2tog k5. 126 Sts.
**Rnds 38 through 48:** As rnds 12 through 22.
**Rnds 49 through 61:** With Spindrift/Corncrake instead of Driftwood/Mara and Solan Goose/Bogbean for knots work from + to ++.
With Spindrift/Corncrake, cast off purlwise. Darn in loose ends. Sew up side and sleeve seams and press seams on WS as before. Pin sleeve cast off edges to body at underarm cast-off, then pin centre top of sleeve at shoulder seam. Pin sleeves around armholes and sew sleeves to body. Press seams as before.

# The Raven Poncho

## Design Notes

Ravens are masters of the air. In stormy weather I can watch them from my studio as they suddenly rocket into view using the upcurrents around the clifftops to soar and plummet, forming kite-like shapes. I wanted to create a garment that would have the swagger and swing of the birds in flight and so I designed the poncho with its flattering curved and flaring shape to do just that.

I used two types of cast-on: the Knit Cast-on when elasticity is desired, and the firmer Cable Edge Cast-on. For illustrated descriptions of the cast-ons, see pages 264 and 265.

The poncho is worked in four pieces and the curved shaping is achieved by working short rows. To prevent gaps where the rows are shortened I have given instructions for wrapping the yarn around the base of the stitch next to the turning point. Once the short rows are complete you will knit across all of the stitches and you can either leave the wrap around the stitch which will show as a little horizontal bar, or you can pick up the wrap with the stitch and work them together so that the horizontal bar is eliminated. It is a matter of preference as I think both are attractive.

I wanted the poncho to have a dramatic shape: wide at the base but fitting snugly around the chest and neck. In order to effect this shape I worked decreases both at each side and also on either side of a straight centre panel on each piece. This involves decreasing at the sides on every fourth row and at each side of the centre panel (inner decs) on every sixth row. This means that the pairs of side decreases and the pairs of inner decreases are worked over a repeating 12-row sequence. Three out of four decrease pairs are worked on separate rows and one out of four decrease pairs are worked on the same row. This is a recipe for confusion and makes keeping track rather difficult. To eliminate this problem entirely, I devised a tabulated method to keep track of both side and inner pairs of decs as you work. I tried and tested my method when knitting both the ponchos shown here; it works very well and means that you can lay the work aside at any time, then pick it up and know exactly where you are. I found that it speeded up the knitting time significantly and made the poncho a very easy knit. Just remember to tick off each set of decs and rows as soon as you have completed them.

The poncho is worked in Hebridean 3 Ply with the collar worked in matching 2 Ply. The collar is worked in the round and placed over the Poncho neckline and then the neckband is worked in 3 Ply. You can work variations as I describe with the cardigan and furthermore, you can make the collar, with neckband, as a stunning neckwarmer.

*Sizes*

To fit small-medium [large, XL-XXL, XXXL].
Directions for larger sizes are given in square brackets.
Where there is only one set of figures, it applies to all
sizes.

*Knitted Measurements*

Width straight around widest point 220[231,242,253]cm.
Body Length (back neck to centre hemline) –
58[60.5,62,64]cm.
Side Panel Length (neckline to centre hemline) –
58[60.5,62,64]cm.

*Materials*

525[575,625,675]g **Alice Starmore® Hebridean 3 Ply**
shown in Storm Petrel and Driftwood.

For triple-layered feather collar –
125[140,150,175]g **Alice Starmore® Hebridean 2 Ply.**

For double-layered feather collar –
70[80,90,100g **Alice Starmore® Hebridean 2 Ply.**

2 pairs 4mm needles. Circular 60cm-long and 40cm-long
3.25mm needles. Circular 30cm-long 3.75mm needle.
Stitch holders. Stitch markers. Tapestry needle.

*Tension*

22 Sts and 30 rows to 10cm measured over St.St. using
4mm needles. To make an accurate tension swatch, cast
on 30 sts and work 40 rows. Pin the swatch on a flat
surface and measure tension using a ruler.

*Back Panel*

• **Lower Edging**
With pair of 4mm needles and 3 Ply Knit Cast-on
145[151,157,163] Sts.
**Row 1 (RS):** P1; k to the last st: p1. **Row 2 (WS):** K1; p
to the last st; k1. **Rows 3 & 4:** As rows 1 & 2.
**Rows 5 & 6:** As row 1. **Row 7 (RS):** As row 2.
**Row 8 (WS):** As row 1. **Row 9 (RS):** K. Break off yarn.
With RS facing sl the last 85[89,93,97] sts pw to LHN.
Join yarn at this point and shape curved border as
follows –
**Row 1 (RS):** K 25[27,29,31]; wrap the next st (wrap1 RS)
thus – sl1pw to RHN; yf; then sl the st back to LHN. Turn.
**Row 2 (WS):** Yf (thus wrapping the yarn around the base
of the st on RHN); sl1pw; p 29[32,34,36]; wrap the next st
(wrap1 WS) thus – sl1pw; yb; sl the st back to LHN. Turn.
**Row 3:** Yb (thus wrapping the yarn around the base of
the st on RHN); sl1pw; k 34[38,40,42]; wrap1 RS. Turn.
**Row 4:** Yf; sl1pw; p 39[44,46,48]; wrap1 WS. Turn.
**Row 5:** Yb; sl1pw; k 44[50,52,54]; wrap1 RS. Turn.
**Row 6:** Yf; sl1pw; p 49[55,58,60]; wrap1 WS. Turn.

161

**Row 7 – Dec:** Yb; sl1pw; k 13[15,16,16]; ssk; k23[25,27,29]; k2tog; k 14[16,17,17]; wrap1 RS. Turn.

**Row 8:** Yf; sl1pw; p 57[63,68,70]; wrap1 WS. Turn.

**Row 9:** Yb; sl1pw; k 62[68,74,76]; wrap1 RS. Turn.

**Row 10:** Yf; sl1pw; p 67[73,79,82]; wrap1 WS. Turn.

**Row 11 - Dec:** Yb; sl1pw; k 13[14,15,16]; ssk; k 41[45,49,51]; k2tog; k 14[15,16,17]; wrap1 RS.Turn.

**Row 12:** Yf; sl1pw; p 75[81,87,92]; wrap1 WS. Turn.

**Row 13:** Yb; sl1pw; k 80[86,92,98]; wrap1 RS. Turn.

**Row 14:** Yf; sl1pw; p 85[91,97,103]; wrap1 WS. Turn.

**Row 15 - Dec:** Yb; sl1pw; k 13[14,15,16]; ssk; k 59[63,67,71]; k2tog; k 14[15,16,17]; wrap1 RS. Turn.

**Row 16:** Yf; sl1pw; p 93[99,105,111]; wrap1 WS. Turn.

**Row 17:** Yb; sl1pw; k 98[104,110,116]; wrap1 RS. Turn.

**Row 18:** Yf; sl1pw; p 103[109,115,121]; wrap1 WS. Turn.

**Row 19 – Dec:** Yb; sl1pw; k 13[14,15,16]; ssk; k 77[81,85,89]; k2tog; k 14[15,16,17]; wrap1 RS. Turn.

**Row 20:** Yf; sl1pw; p 111[117,123,129]; wrap1 WS. Turn.

**Row 21:** Yb; sl1pw; k 116[122,128,134]; wrap1 RS. Turn.

**Row 22:** Yf; sl1pw; p 121[127,133,139]; wrap1 WS. Turn.

**Row 23 – Dec:** Yb; sl1pw; k 13[14,15,16]; ssk; k 95[99,103,107]; k2tog; k 14[15,16,17]; wrap1 RS.Turn.

**Row 24:** Yf; sl1pw; p to end of row.

**Row 25 – Dec:** K 14[15,16,17]; ssk; k 103[107,111,115]; k2tog; k 14[15,16,17]. 133[139,145,151] Sts. Purl 1 WS row. Set aside.

### Upper Edging

With 4mm needles and 2 Ply Cable Edge Cast-on 141[147,153,159] sts. Work the first 3 rows as lower edging.

**Next Row (WS) – Dec:** K1; p 2[4,6,8]; (p2tog; p14) 3 times; p2tog; p 35[37,39,41]; (p2tog; p14) 3 times; p2tog; p 2[4,6,8]; k1. 133[139,145,151] Sts. Break off yarn.

### Join Upper Edging to Curved Border

With RS facing, place the needle with curved border behind the upper edging needle and holding the needles parallel in the left hand, with a third 4mm needle and 3 Ply, ktog a stitch from each needle all along the row. 133[139,145,151] Sts. Break off yarn.

With RS facing sl the last 79[83,87,91] sts to LHN. Join yarn at this point and shape as follows –

**Row 1 (RS):** K 25[27,29,31]; wrap1 RS. Turn.

**Row 2 (WS):** Yf; sl1pw; p 33[36,38,40]; wrap1 WS. Turn.

**Row 3:** Yb; sl1pw; k 42[46,48,50]; wrap1 RS. Turn.

Continue as set and work 9[10,10,10] more sts at the end of every row until all [67,109, all] sts are worked, including first sl1pw.

**Second & Third Sizes Only:** Continue as set and work 9 more sts at the end of every row until all sts are worked.

**All Sizes:** P1 WS row.

**Next Row (RS) – Mark Centre Panel:** K 54[56,58,60]; mark the next st; k 23[25,27,29]; mark the next st; k 54[56,58,60]. P1 WS row.

**Next row (RS) – Set Side and Inner Decs:** K1; k2tog; k 49[51,53,55]; ssk;
k 25[27,29,31]; k2tog; k 49[51,53,55]; ssk; k1. 129[135,141,147] Sts.
Draw up a table as shown here –

## 12 ROW DECREASE SEQUENCE: BACK & FRONT

| | | | | | | | | | |
|---|---|---|---|---|---|---|---|---|---|
| 3 rows St.St.<br>4th row: side decs | | | | | | | | | |
| P1 WS row<br>6th row: inner decs | | | | | | | | | |
| P1 WS row<br>8th row: side decs | | | | | | | | | |
| 3 rows St.St.<br>12th row: side & inner decs | | | | | | | | | END 3rd & 4th sizes |

END 1st & 2nd sizes

| | | | | | | | | | |
|---|---|---|---|---|---|---|---|---|---|
| Total no. of sts decreased | 10 | 20 | 30 | 40 | 50 | 60 | 70 | 80 | 86 |
| Total no. of rows worked | 12 | 24 | 36 | 48 | 60 | 72 | 84 | 96 | 104 |

Beg at the top of the first column on the left, working 3 rows in St.St. and
mark in the adjacent box when done, then dec 1st at each side thus – k1;
k2tog; k to the last 3 sts; ssk; k1; and mark in the same box when done.
Continue and work down to the bottom of the column, working the first
inner dec immediately before the first marked st and the second inner dec
immediately after the second marked st, marking each instruction on the
table as done, thus decreasing 10 sts and working 12 rows after working
through the first column, as shown in the table directly below. Then repeat
from the top, marking off the rows and decs in the second column and
so on, until 80[80,86,86] sts have been decreased and 96[96,104,104]
tabled rows are worked in total. The inner decs are now completed with
49[55,55,61] sts rem. ••
Work 3 rows without shaping then dec 1st at each side of next and every
foll 4th row until 37[39,41,43] sts rem. Break off yarn and place sts on a
holder.

*Front Panel*

As back panel from • to ••.
Work 3 rows without shaping then dec 1st as set at each side of next and
every foll 4th row until 43[45,47,49] sts rem. Work 3 rows without shaping.
**Next Row (RS) – Beg Neck Shaping**
K1; k2tog; k7; place the next 23[25,27,29] sts on a holder for front neck;
place the rem 10 sts on a spare needle.
Turn and shape left side of neck as follows –
**Row 1 (WS):** P2tog; p7. **Row 2 (RS):** K6; k2tog. **Row 3 (WS):** P2tog; p5.
**Row 4 (RS):** (K1; k2tog) twice. **Row 5 (WS):** P4. **Row 6 (RS):** K2; k2tog.
**Row 7 (WS):** P3. **Row 8 (RS):** DD. Fasten off.
With RS facing, rejoin yarn to the 10 sts of right neck and shape as follows:
**Row 1 (RS):** K7; ssk; k1. **Row 2 (WS):** P7; p2togtbl. **Row 3 (RS):** Ssk; k6.
**Row 4 (WS):** P5; p2togtbl. **Row 5 (RS):** (Ssk; k1) twice. **Row 6 (WS):** P4.
**Row 7 (RS):** Ssk; k2. **Row 8 (WS):** P3. **Row 9 (RS):** DD. Fasten off.

*Side Panels (Make 2)*

## Lower Edging

With 4mm needles and 3 Ply Knit Cast-on
117[123,129,135] sts. Work the first 9 rows as back panel.
Break off yarn.
With RS facing sl the last 67[71,75,79] sts to LHN. Join
yarn at this point and shape curved border as follows –
**Row 1 (RS):** K 17[19,21,23]; wrap1 RS. Turn.
**Row 2 (WS):** Yf; sl1pw; p 21[23,25,27]; wrap1 WS. Turn.
**Row 3:** Yb ; sl1pw; k 26[28,30,32]; wrap1 RS. Turn.
**Row 4:** Yf; sl1pw; p 31[33,35,37]; wrap1 WS. Turn.
**Row 5:** Yb; sl1pw; k 36[38,40,42]; wrap1 RS. Turn.
**Row 6:** Yf; sl1pw; p 40[43,45,47]; wrap1 WS. Turn.
**Row 7:** Yb; sl1pw; k 44[48,50,52]; wrap1 RS. Turn.
**Row 8:** Yf; sl1pw; p 48[53,55,57]; wrap1 WS. Turn.
**Row 9:** Yb; sl1pw; k 52[58,60,62]; wrap1 RS. Turn.
**Row 10:** Yf; sl1pw; p 56[62,65,67]; wrap1 WS. Turn.
**Row 11 – Dec:** Yb; sl1pw; k 10[12,13,13]; ssk;
k 35[37,39,41]; k2tog; k 11[13,14,14]; wrap1 RS. Turn.
**Row 12:** Yf; sl1pw; p 62[68,73,75]; wrap1 WS. Turn.
**Row 13:** Yb; sl1pw; k 66[72,78,80]; wrap1 RS. Turn.
**Row 14:** Yf; sl1pw; p 70[76,82,85]; wrap1 WS. Turn.
**Row 15 – Dec:** Yb; sl1pw; k 8[9,10,11]; ssk; k 53[57,61,63];
k2tog; k 9[10,11,12]; wrap1 RS. Turn.
**Row 16:** Yf; sl1pw; p 76[82,88,93]; wrap1 WS. Turn.
**Row 17:** Yb; sl1pw; k 80[86,92,98]; wrap1 RS. Turn.
**Row 18:** Yf; sl1pw; p 84[90,96,102]; wrap1 WS. Turn.
**Row 19 – Dec:** Yb; sl1pw; k 8[9,10,11] ssk; k 67[71,75,79];
k2tog; k 9[10,11,12]; wrap1 RS. Turn.
**Row 20:** Yf; sl1pw; p 90[96,102,108]; wrap1 WS. Turn.
**Row 21:** Yb; sl1pw; k 94[100,106,112]; wrap1 RS. Turn.
**Row 22:** Yf; sl1pw; p 98[104,110,116]; wrap1 WS. Turn.
**Row 23:** Yb; sl1pw; k 102[108,114,120]; wrap1 RS. Turn.
**Row 24:** Yf; sl1pw; p to end of row.
**Row 25 – Dec:** K 9[10,11,12]; ssk; k 89[93,97,101]; k2tog;
k 9[10,11,12]. 109[115,121,127] Sts.
Purl 1 WS row. Set aside.

## Upper Edging

With double-pointed 4mm needles and 2 Ply, Cable Edge
Cast-on 115[121,127,133] sts. Work the first 3 rows as
lower edging.
**Next Row (WS) – Dec:** K1; p 4[6,8,10]; (p2tog; p16)
twice; p2tog; p 29[31,33,35]; (p2tog; k16) twice; p2tog;
p 4[6,8,10]; k1. 109[115,121,127] Sts. Break off yarn.
Join Upper Edging to Curved Border as given for back
panel. 109[115,121,127] Sts. Break off yarn.
With RS facing sl the last 61[65,69,73] sts to RHN. Rejoin
yarn at this point and shape as follows –
**Row 1 (RS):** K 13[15,17,19] wrap1 RS. Turn.
**Row 2 (WS):** Yf; sl1pw; p 20[23,25,27]; wrap1 WS. Turn.
**Row 3:** Yb; sl1pw; k 28[32,34,36]; wrap1 RS. Turn. Continue
as set and work 8[9,9,9] more sts at the end of every row
until all [51,89, all] sts are worked, including first sl1pw.

**Second & Third Sizes Only:** Continue as set and work 8 more sts at the end of every row until all sts are worked.

**All Sizes:** 109[115,121,127] Sts. Work 3 rows in St.St.

**Next Row (RS) – Work Side Decs:** K1; k2tog; k to the last 3 sts; ssk; k1. Work 3 rows in St.St. Continue and dec 1st as set at each side of next and every foll 4th row until 91[93,103,105] sts rem. P1 WS row.

**Next Row (RS) – Mark Centre Panel:** K 43[43,47,47]; mark the next st; k 3[5,7,9]; mark the next st; k 43[43,47,47]. P1 WS row.

**Next row (RS) – Set Side and Inner Decs:** K1; k2tog; k 38[38,42,42]; ssk; k 5[7,9,11]; k2tog; k 38[38,42,42]; ssk; k1. 87[89,99,101] Sts.

Draw up a table as shown here –

## 12 ROW DECREASE SEQUENCE: SIDE PANELS

| | | | | | | |
|---|---|---|---|---|---|---|
| 3 rows St.St.<br>4th row: side decs | | | | | | |
| P1 WS row<br>6th row: inner decs | | | | | | |
| P1 WS row<br>8th row: side decs | | | | | | |
| 3 rows St.St.<br>12th row: side & inner decs | | | | | END 1st &<br>2nd sizes | END 3rd &<br>4th sizes |
| Total no. of sts decreased | 10 | 20 | 30 | 40 | 50 | 60 |
| Total no. of rows worked | 12 | 24 | 36 | 48 | 60 | 72 |

Work the 12 row dec sequence as described for back and front panels, decreasing 50[50,60,60] sts and working a total of 60[60,72,72] tabled rows, thus ending with 37[39,39,41] sts rem.

Work 3 rows in St.St. then work **both side and inner decs** on next and every foll 4th row until 13[15,15,17] sts rem. Break off yarn and place sts on holder.

*Finishing*

Darn in loose ends. Block all pieces RS up to measurements shown on schematic. Ensure that lower and upper edgings are allowed to curl up so that purl side is facing. Cover with damp towels and leave to dry away from direct heat.

Sew up seams on the WS leaving lower and upper edgings free. Then sew ends of edgings together on the RS and allow to curl up. Press seams lightly on WS using a warm iron and damp cloth.

**Neckband**

With RS facing, 30cm-long 3.75mm circular needle and 3 Ply, beg at right back neck and pick up and k the 37[39,41,43] sts from holder; pick up and k the 13[15,15,17] sts of left side panel; knit up 7 sts along left side of neck; pick up and k the 23[25,27,29] sts from front neck holder; knit up 7 sts along right side of neck; pick up and k the 13[15,15,17] sts of right side panel. 100[108,112,120] Sts.

**First & Second Sizes:** K1 rnd.

**Third & Fourth Sizes: Next Rnd – Dec**
* K 26[18]; k2tog; rep from * 4[6] times.
108[114] sts.
**All Sizes:** Set aside.

*Collar*

**Note:**
The feather layers are arranged and decs worked so that the centre of each feather is in line with the edge of the feathers in the following layer. Consequently, for the triple-layered collar it is important to change the beg of rnd postion as described at the end of working the first layer. For a double-layered collar, work the second layer and top layer of feathers and join the second layer of feathers together as given but do not break off yarn; work from ▲ to ▲▲, then k the first 3 sts of the next rnd and place the marker on the next st for positioning the top layer.

**Feathers – First Layer**
With 4mm needle and 2 Ply Knit Cast-on 39 sts.
**Row 1 (RS):** P18; DD; p18.
**Row 2 (WS):** P17; PDD; p17.
**Row 3 (RS):** K16; DD; k16.
**• Row 4 (WS):** P15; PDD; p15.
**Row 5 (RS):** K14; DD; k14.
**Row 6 (WS):** P13; PDD; p13.
**Row 7 (RS):** K12; DD; k12.
**Row 8 (WS):** P11; PDD; p11. 23 Sts rem.
**Next Row (RS);** K10; * DD; slpw the rem st from DD and the next st on the RHN to the LHN; rep from * until 1st rem. Fasten off. Make 20[21,21,22] feathers. ••
**Feathers – Second Layer**
Knit Cast-on 35 sts as first layer.
**Row 1 (RS):** P16; DD p16. Work and complete as first layer feathers from • **(Row 4)** to ••.
**Feathers -Top Layer**
Knit Cast-on 29 sts as first layer.
**Row 1 (RS):** P13; DD p13.

**Row 2 (WS):** P12; PDD: p12.
**Row 3 (RS):** K11; DD k11.
**Row 4 (WS):** P10; PDD: p10.
**Row 5 (RS):** K9; DD; k9.
**Next Row (WS):** P8; * PDD; slpw the rem st from PDD and the next st on RHN to LHN; rep from * until 1st rem. Fasten off.
Make 20[21,21,22] feathers.
Block all feathers in their separate layer groups by laying them out on a flat surface, right side down. Pin down at each cast-on end and centre of top, then stretch the feather fully and pin down at the tip. First layer feathers measure 11cm from centre top to tip, second layer, 9.5cm and top layer 7.5cm. Cover with a damp towel and leave to dry away from direct heat.

**Join First Layer Feathers**
With circular 60cm long 3.25mm needle, 2 Ply and RS of each feather facing, knit up 10 sts evenly along the top end of each of the 20[21,21,22] 39-St feathers. 200[210,210,220] Sts. Place a marker at beg of rnd making sure the sts and feathers are not twisted, k6 rnds.
**Next Row – Dec:** K4; * k2tog; k8; rep from * to the last 6 sts; k2tog; k4. 180[189,189,198] Sts. K4 rnds. K the next rnd to the last st and move the beg of rnd marker to this st to mark it as the first st of next rnd.
**Next Rnd – Dec:** * K2tog; k7; rep from * to end of rnd. 160[168,168,176] Sts. With 40cm-long 3.25mm needle, k1 rnd then k the first 4 sts of next rnd (this is the position to begin joining in the second layer of feathers) and set aside.

**Join Second Layer Feathers**
With 60cm long 3.25mm needle and RS of each feather facing, knit up 8 sts along the top end of each of the 20[21,21,22] 35-St feathers. 160[168,168,176] Sts. Break off yarn. With RS facing, place the second layer of feathers in front of the first layer and holding

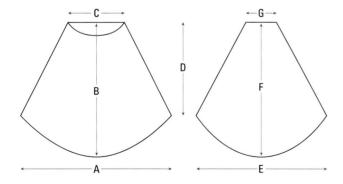

A = 60.5[63.25, 66, 68.5]cm
B = 58[60.5, 62, 64]cm
C = 17[17.75, 18.5, 19.5]cm
D = 46[48.5, 50, 52]cm
E = 49.5[52.25, 55, 58]cm
F = 58[60.5, 62, 64]cm
G = 6[6.75, 6.75, 7.75]cm

the needles parallel in the left hand, with the circular 3.25mm needle holding the first layer, ktog a stitch from each layer all along the rnd. 160[168,168,176] Sts. **NB:** Now place the beg of rnd marker on the 4th last st (back to its original position).
▲ K5 rnds.
**Next Rnd – Dec:** K3; * k2tog; k6; rep from * to the last 5 sts; k2tog; k3. 140[147,147,154] Sts. K2 rnds.
**Next Rnd – Dec:** * K2tog; k5: rep from * to end of rnd. 120[126,126,132] Sts. K1 rnd. Set aside. ▲▲

### Join Top Layer Feathers
With 60cm long 3.25mm needle and RS of each feather facing, knit up 6 sts evenly along the top end of each of the 20[21,21,22] 29-St feathers.120[126,126,132] Sts. With RS facing, place the needle with the top layer of feathers in front of the needle with the first two layers and holding the needles parallel in the left hand, with the circular 3.25mm needle holding the first two layers, ktog a stitch from each layer. 120[126,126,132] Sts.

### Next Rnd – Dec
**First, Second & Third Sizes:** K2 * k2tog; k 4[5,5]; rep from * to the last 4[5,5] sts; k2tog; k2[3,3]. 100[108,108] Sts.
**Fourth Size:** * (K2tog; k5) twice; k2tog k6; rep from * to end of rnd. 114 Sts.
**All Sizes:** Set aside.

### Edging
With 4mm needle and 2 Ply, Cable Edge Cast-on 110[120,120,126] sts. Beg with a k row and work in St.St. for 3 rows.
**Next Row (WS) – Dec:** P 0[0,0,6];
* p2tog; p 9[8,8,8]; rep from * to end of row. 100[108,108,114] Sts. With RS facing, place the needle with the edging in front of the needle holding the feathered collar and holding the needles parallel in the left hand ktog a stitch from each to join the edging to the collar. 100[108,108,114] Sts. Break off yarn.

### Join Collar to Body Neckband
Place the collar RS out over the neckband needle and holding the needles parallel in the left hand, with the 3 Ply neckband yarn and the 3.75mm neckband needle, ktog a st from collar and neckband to join collar to body. Place a marker at beg of rnd. * P3 rnds; k3 rnds; rep from * 4 times in all (24 rnds). P2 rnds. Cast off purlwise. Darn in all loose ends and sew ends of edging together.

167

# The Raven Cardigan

## Design Notes ——————————

A pair of ravens nest on the cliffs at the foot of my croft and so I am privileged to observe them at work and play on a daily basis without even having to leave my studio. They habitually sit on fence posts and preen themselves, or each other when they are feeling amorous. They use their massive bills to smooth their feathers into a sleek profile which contrasts with their bristling throat feathers. These are the features that I focused on to create the Raven Cardigan.

I based the rounded-feather lower border on the feathers I created for the chest of the costume. Once these feathers are joined up, the cardigan body is made in one piece, working back and forth in rows of Stocking Stitch. The body is lightly shaped with strategic decreases to the waist and increases to the bustline. The sleeve cuffs are steeply shaped with short rows and decreases echoing the distinctive curving wedge shape of the raven's tail. The pointed collar feathers are a take on their bearded throat feathers.

I have used three types of cast-on for specific purposes; the Long Tail Cast-on for the right amount of give and the appearance of the rounded feathers; the Knit Cast-on to provide the required blocking stretch for the collar feathers, and the firmer Cable Edge Cast-on for the curled purl edgings. For illustrated descriptions of the cast-ons, see pages 264 and 265.

The feathered collar leaves lots of room for improvisation: you can make it triple, double (see the poncho) or single, and work in colours at will. The Mara cardigan collar feathers are outlined in Strabhann. You may notice that the third feather on the left side is worked in Strabhann with a Mara outline. Individual feathers, or layers can be worked in any combination of colours.

I knitted and felted the buttons in Strabhann. As an added optional decoration I made four extra feathers, and then knitted and felted three little flower heads. I assembled them into a corsage, which can be worn according to your fancy.

To fit small [medium, large, X large].
Directions for larger sizes are given in square
brackets. Where there is only one set of figures,
it applies to all sizes.

## Knitted Measurements

Underarm (buttoned) 91[98,104.5,111]cm.
Waist 81[87.5,94.25,101]cm.
Length 48[50,52.5,54.5]cm.
Sleeve seam (top of cuff to underarm)
38[38,39,39]cm.
Centre hemline of cuff to underarm
50.5[51,52,52]cm.

## Materials

For cardigan with three-layered feather collar –
Of **Alice Starmore® Hebridean 2 Ply**
375[425,475,525]g shown in Solan Goose.
For cardigan with one-layer feather collar with
contrast feather trim –
Of **Alice Starmore® Hebridean 2 Ply**
325[375,425,475]g shown in Mara.
Plus 12g in Strabhann.

3 X 3mm needles and 1 long circular 3mm
needle.1 Pair 2.75mm, 3.25mm & 4mm needles.
Stitch holders. Stitch markers. Tapestry needle.
11 Buttons.

## Tension

27 Sts and 40 rows to 10cm measured over
St.St. using 3mm needles. To make an accurate
tension swatch, cast on 31 sts and work 42
rows. Pin the swatch on a flat surface and
measure tension using a ruler.

## Body

### Hemline Feathers
With 3mm needles and using Long Tail method,
cast on 13 sts.
**Row 1 (RS):** K1; p11; k1. **Row 2 (WS):** Purl.
**Row 3:** (K1; ssk) twice; k1; (k2tog; k1) twice.
9 Sts. **Row 4:** P1; p2tog; p3; p2togtbl; p1. 7 Sts.
**Row 5:** K2; DD; k2. 5 Sts.
**Row 6:** P2tog; p1; p2togtbl. 3 Sts.
Place the rem 3 sts on a holder. Make
25[27,29,31] feathers in total.
### Join Feathers
Place the 3 sts of one feather on a 3mm needle
with RS facing. Beg at cast on edge and with
second 3mm needle knit up 3 sts evenly along
right edge of feather; k the 3 sts from needle;

knit up 3 sts evenly along left edge of feather.
9 Sts in total. Continue in this manner over all
25[27,29,31] feathers. 225[243,261,279] Sts in
total. P1 WS row. K1 RS row on to a long circular
3mm needle. Break off yarn and set aside.
### Edging
With 3mm needles Cable Edge Cast-on
225[243,261,279] sts.
**Rows 1 & 3 (RS):** K. **Rows 2 & 4 (WS):** P.
### Join Feathers to Edging
With RS facing, place the needle with feathers
behind the edging needle and holding the
needles parallel in the left hand, with a third
3mm needle ktog a stitch from each needle all
along the row.
**Next Row (WS):** P1; k to the last st; p1.
**Next Row (RS):** K1; p to the last st; k1.
**Next Row (WS):** P1; k to the last st; p1.
Work 6[8,10,12] rows in St.St.
**Next Row (RS) – First Dec:** K 12[13,16,17];
k2tog; k 81[87,91,97]; ssk; k 31[35,39,43]; k2tog;
k 81[87,91,97]; ssk; k 12[13,16,17].
221[239,257,275] Sts. Work 7 rows in St.St.
**Next Row (RS) – Second Dec:**
K 51[55,60,64]; ssk; k1 and mark this st for
centre right underarm; k2tog; k 109[119,127,137];
ssk; k1 and mark this st for centre left underarm;
k2tog; k 51[55,60,64]. 217[235,253,271] Sts.
Work 5 rows in St.St.
**Next Row (RS) – Third Dec:** K 12[13,16,17];
k2tog; k 77[83,87,93]; ssk; k 31[35,39,43];
k2tog; k 77[83,87,93]; ssk; k 12[13,16,17].
213[231,249,267] Sts. Work 5 rows in St.St.
**Next Row (RS) – Fourth Dec:** Dec 1st as
set at each side of marked underarm sts.
209[227,245,263] Sts. Work 13 rows in St.St.
**Next Row (RS) – First Inc:** K 50[54,59,63];
m1; k marked st; m1; k 107[117,125,135]; m1; k
marked st; m1; k 50[54,59,63]. 213[231,249,267]
Sts. Work 9 rows in St.St.
**Next Row (RS) – Second Inc:** K 12[13,16,17];
m1; k 79[85,89,95]; m1; k 31[35,39,43];
m1; k 79[85,89,95]; m1; k 12[13,16,17].
217[235,253,271] Sts. Work 9 rows in St.St.
**Next Row (RS) – Third Inc:** Inc 1st as
set at each side of marked underarm sts.
221[239,257,275] Sts. Work 9 rows in St.St.
**Next Row (RS) – Fourth Inc:** K 12[13,16,17];
m1; k 83[89,93,99]; m1; k 31[35,39,43];
m1; k 83[89,93,99]; m1; k 12[13,16,17].
225[243,261,279] Sts. Work 9 rows in St.St.
**Next Row (RS) – Fifth Inc:** Inc 1st as set at
each side of marked underarm sts.

229[247,265,283] Sts. Work 9 rows in St.St.
**Next Row (RS) – Sixth Inc:** K 12[13,16,17]; m1; k 87[93,97,103]; m1; k 31[35,39,43]; m1; k 87[93,97,103]; m1; k 12[13,16,17]. 233[251,269,287] Sts. Work 9 rows in St.St.
**Next Row (RS) – Seventh Inc:** Inc 1st as set at each side of marked underarm sts. 237[255,273,291]Sts. Continue straight in St.St. until piece measures 27[28,29,30]cm from first St.St. row, with RS facing for next row.

**Divide for Armholes**
K 52[55,60,63] (right front) and place sts on holder; cast off the next 11[13,13,15] sts; k 111[119,127,135] (back) and place sts on a holder; cast off the next 11[13,13,15] sts; k 52[55,60,63] (left front). Turn and work left front as follows –
**Next Row (WS):** Purl. **Next Row (RS):** Cast off 3; k to end of row. P1 WS row.
Dec 1st at armhole edge of next 3 rows. 46[49,54,57] Sts rem. P1 WS row. Dec 1st at armhole edge of next and every foll alt row until 40[42,45,47] sts rem. Continue straight without further shaping until armhole measures 11[12,13,14]cm from underarm cast-off with RS facing for next row.

**Shape Front Neck**
K 35[37,39,40] place the rem 5[5,6,7] sts on a holder for front neck.
Turn and shape as follows –
**\*** Dec 1st at neck edge of next 2[2,3,2] rows. Work 1 row without shaping then dec 1st at neck edge of next and foll alt rows until 30[32,33,36] sts rem. Work 2 rows without shaping then dec 1st at neck edge of next and foll 3rd row until 28[30,31,34] sts rem. Work 3 rows without shaping then dec 1st at neck edge of next and every foll 4th row until 25[27,28,30] sts rem. On first, second and fourth sizes work 1 row without shaping. **\*\***

**Shape Shoulder**
**°** With RS facing cast off 8[9,9,10] sts at beg of next and foll alt row. P1 WS row. Cast off the rem 9[9,10,10] sts. **°°**

**Back**
With WS facing rejoin yarn to the 111[119,127,135] sts of back and shape armholes as follows –
Cast off 3 sts at beg of next 2 rows. Dec 1st at each end of next 3 rows. 99[107,115,123] Sts rem. P1 WS row. Dec 1st at each end of next and every foll alt row until 87[93,97,103] sts rem. Continue without further shaping until armholes

measure 17[18,19.5,20.5]cm with RS facing for next row (4 rows below first left front shoulder cast-off).

**Shape Back Neck/Shoulders**
K 27[29,30,32] of right back shoulder; place the next 33[35,37,39] sts on a holder for back neck; place the rem 27[29,30,32] sts of left back shoulder on a spare needle.
Turn and shape right back neck as follows –
Dec 1st at neck edge of the next and foll alt row. 25[27,28,30] Sts rem.
Shape shoulder as left front from **°** to **°°**.
With RS facing, rejoin yarn to sts of left back shoulder and k to end of row. Dec 1st at neck edge of the next and foll alt row. 25[27,28,30] Sts rem. K1 RS row.

**Shape Shoulder**
**+** With WS facing cast off 8[9,9,10] sts at beg of next and foll alt row. K1 RS row. Cast off the rem 9[9,10,10] sts. **++**

**Right Front**
With WS facing rejoin yarn to the 52[55,60,63] sts of right front and p1 row.
**Next Row (RS):** Knit.
**Next Row (WS):** Cast off 3; p to end of row.
Dec 1st at armhole edge of next 3 rows. 46[49,54,57] Sts rem. P1 WS row. Dec 1st at armhole edge of next and every foll alt row until 40[42,45,47] sts rem. Continue straight without further shaping until armhole measures 11[12,13,14]cm with WS facing for next row (right front matches left front in length to beg of front neck shaping).

**Shape Front Neck**
P 35[37,39,40] place the rem 5[5,6,7] sts on a holder for front neck. Turn and shape as left front neck from **\*** to **\*\***.
Shape shoulder as given for left back working from **+** to **++**.

*Sleeves*
---

**Cuff**
With 3mm needles Cable Edge Cast-on 83[87,89,91] sts.
**Row 1 (RS):** K. **Row 2 (WS):** P.
**Row 3:** K 38[40,41,42]; ssk; k3; k2tog; k 38[40,41,42]. 81[85,87,89] Sts. **Rows 4 & 5:** P.
**Row 6:** K. **Rows 7 & 8:** P. Break off yarn.
With RS facing, sl the first 30 sts pw to RHN. Beg at next st on LHN and patt as follows –
**Row 1 (RS):** K 9[11,12,13]; DD; k 9 [11,12,13]; wrap the next st (wrap1 RS) thus – sl1pw to RHN; yf then sl the st back to LHN. Turn.

**Row 2 (WS):** Yf (thus wrapping the yarn around the base of the st on RHN); sl1pw; p 21[25,27,29]; wrap the next st (wrap1 WS) thus – sl1pw; yb; sl the st back to LHN. Turn.

**Row 3:** Yb (thus wrapping the yarn around the base of the st on RHN); sl1pw; k 10[12,13,14]; DD; k 11[13,14,15]; wrap1 RS. Turn.

**Row 4:** Yf; sl1pw; p 25[29,31,33]; wrap1 WS. Turn.

**Row 5:** Yb; sl1pw; k 12[14,15,16]; DD; k 13[15,16,17]; wrap1 RS. Turn.

**Row 6:** Yf; sl1pw; p 29[33,35,37]; wrap1 WS. Turn.

**Row 7:** Yb; sl1pw; k 14[16,17,18]; DD; k 15[17,18,19]; wrap1 RS. Turn.

**Row 8:** Yf; sl1pw; p 33[37,39,41]; wrap1 WS. Turn.

**Row 9:** Yb; sl1pw; k 16[18,19,20]; DD; k 17[19,20,21]; wrap1 RS. Turn.

**Row 10:** Yf; sl1pw; p 37[41,43,45]; wrap1 WS. Turn.

**Row 11:** Yb; sl1pw; k 18[20,21,22]; DD; k 19[21,22,23]; wrap1 RS. Turn.

**Row 12:** Yf; sl1pw; p 41[45,47,49]; wrap1 WS. Turn.

**Row 13:** Yb; sl1pw; k 20[22,23,24]; DD; k 21[23,24,25]; wrap1 RS. Turn.

**Row 14:** Yf; sl1pw; p to end of row. Turn and with RS facing, dec over the rem 67[71,73,75] sts as follows –

**First Size:** K1; (ssk; k1) 3 times; ssk; k2; (ssk; k3) 3 times; ssk; k5; (k2tog; k3) 3 times; k2tog; k2; (k2tog; k1) 4 times. 51 Sts rem.

**Second & Third Sizes:** K1; (ssk; k1) twice; (ssk; k2) twice; (ssk; k3) 3 times; ssk; k7[9]; (k2tog; k3) 3 times; (k2tog; k2) twice; (k2tog; k1) 3 times. 55[57] Sts rem.

**Fourth Size:** K2; (ssk; k1) twice; (ssk; k2) twice; (ssk; k3) 3 times; ssk; k9; (k2tog; k3) 3 times; (k2tog; k2) twice; (k2tog; k1) twice; k2tog; k2. 59 Sts rem.

**All Sizes:** Set cuff aside.

**Edging**

With 3mm needles Cable Edge Cast-on 57[61,63,65] sts.

**Row 1 (RS):** (K1; ssk) twice; k to the last 6 sts (k2tog; k1) twice. 53[57,59,61] Sts rem. Break off yarn. Turn.

**Row 2 (WS):** Sl the first 5 sts pw; rejoin yarn and p 43[47,49,51]; wrap1 WS. Turn.

**Row 3 (RS):** Yb; sl1pw; k 18[20,21,22]; ssk; k1; k2tog; k 16[18,19,20]; wrap1 RS.

**Row 4 (WS):** Yf; sl1pw; p 34[38,40,42]. Break off yarn and sl the last 8 rem sts pw onto needle. 51[55,57,59] Sts in total.

Turn and place the edging in front of the cuff (RS of both facing) and holding the needles parallel, ktog the sts of edging and cuff all along the row thus joining the edging to the cuff. 51[55,57,59] Sts. Break off yarn.

With 3mm needles and WS facing, sl the first 28[31,33,35] sts pw to LHN. Turn, rejoin yarn at this point and work as follows –

**Row 1 (RS):** K5[7,9,11] (centre cuff sts); wrap1 RS. Turn.

**Row 2 (WS):** Yf; sl1pw; p 7[9,11,13]; wrap1 WS. Turn.

**Row 3:** Yb; sl1pw; k 10[12,14,16]; wrap1 RS. Turn.

**Row 4:** Yf; sl1pw; p 13[15,17,19]; wrap1 WS. Turn.

**Row 5:** Yb; sl1pw; k 16[18,20,22]; wrap1 RS. Turn.

**Row 6:** Yf; sl1pw; p 18[20,22,24]; wrap1 WS. Turn.

**Row 7:** Yb; sl1pw; k 20[22,24,26]; wrap1 RS. Turn. Continue as set and work 2 more sts at the end of every foll row until 45[47,49,51] sts have been worked in St.St. (including the first slpw st); wrap1 RS. Turn and with WS facing, dec as follows –

**Next Row (WS):** Sl1pw; p 43[45,47,49]; p2tog; wrap1 WS. Turn. **Next Row (RS):** Sl1pw; k 43[45,47,49]; k2tog; wrap1 RS. Turn. Rep these last 2 rows 1[2,2,2] more times.

**Next Row (WS):** Sl1pw; p 43[45,47,49]; p2tog; thus incorporating the last st on the WS. 46[48,50,52] Sts in total. Break off yarn.

With RS facing knit up 5 sts evenly along the top end of cuff working through the doubled cuff edging so that it remains curled up with p side out; k 44[46,48,50]; k2tog; knit up 5 sts into top end of cuff as before. 55[57,59,61] Sts. Continue in St.St. and inc 1st at each end of 6th row, then on every foll 10th row until there are 67 sts then continue and inc 1st at each end of every foll 8th row until there are 83[87,93,97] sts. Continue straight in St.St. until sleeve measures 38[38,39,39] cm from top of cuff (i.e. 5st knit-up row above cuff edging) and 50.5[51,52,52] cm from centre of curled cuff hemline, with RS facing for next row.

**Beg Cap Shaping**

Cast off 5[6,6,7] sts at beg of next 2 rows. Cast off 3[3,4,4] sts at beg of next 2 rows. Dec 1st at each end of next row. Patt 2 rows without shaping then dec 1st at each end of next and every foll 3rd row until 49[47,47,45] sts rem. Patt 1 row without shaping then dec 1st at each end of next and every foll alt row until 29 sts rem. Work 1 row without shaping then dec 1st at each end of next and every foll row until 13 sts rem. Cast off sts.

*Collar*

**Note:** For contrast-trimmed feathers, work the cast-on and the first row of each feather in a contrast shade, then change to the main colour. For a double layer of feathers work the second and top layers of feathers only and then follow the instructions from joining the second layer onwards. For a single layer of feathers, work the top layer feathers only and then follow the instructions from joining the top layer feathers onwards.

**Feathers – First Layer**
With 4mm needles Knit Cast-on 39 sts.
**Row 1 (RS):** P18; DD; p18. **Row 2 (WS):** P17; PDD; p17. **Row 3 (RS):** K16; DD; k16.
• **Row 4 (WS):** P15; PDD; p15.
**Row 5 (RS):** K14; DD; k14.
**Row 6 (WS):** P13; PDD; p13.
**Row 7 (RS):** K12; DD; k12.
**Row 8 (WS):** P11; PDD; p11. 23 Sts rem.
**Next Row (RS);** K10; * DD; slpw the rem st from DD and the next st on RHN to LHN; rep from * until 1st rem. Fasten off.
Make 21 feathers. ••

**Feathers – Second Layer**
With 4mm needles Knit Cast-on 35 sts.
**Row 1 (RS):** P16; DD; p16. Work and complete as first layer feathers from • to ••.

**Second Layer – Half Feathers**
Knit Cast-on 35 sts and work as second layer for 4 rows. 13 Sts rem at each side of PDD.
**Next Row (RS):** K12; * DD; slpw the rem st from DD and the next st on RHN to LHN; rep from * until 1st rem. Fasten off. Make 2 feathers.

**Feathers – Top Layer**
With 4mm needles Knit Cast-on 25 sts.
**Row 1 (RS):** P11; DD p11.
**Row 2 (WS):** P10; PDD: p10.
**Row 3 (RS):** K9; DD; k9.
**Row 4 (WS):** P8; PDD: p8.
**Next Row (RS):** K7; * DD; sl the rem st from DD and the next st pw to LHN; rep from * until 1 st rem. Fasten off. Make 21 feathers.
Darn in all loose ends. Block all feathers in their separate layer groups by laying them out on a flat surface, right side down. Pin down at each end of top, then stretch the feather fully and pin down at the tip. First layer feathers measure 11cm from centre top to tip, second layer, 9.5cm and top layer 7cm. Cover with a damp towel and leave to dry away from direct heat.

**Join First Layer Feathers**
With 3mm needles and RS of each feather facing, knit up 8 sts evenly along the top end of each of the 21 X 39-stitch feathers. 168 Sts. Begin with a p (WS) row and work 13 rows in St.St. thus ending with RS facing for next row.
**Next Row – Dec:** K7; * k2tog; k6; rep from * to the last 9 sts; k2tog; k7. 148 Sts. Set aside.

**Join Second Layer Feathers**
With 3mm needle and RS of each feather facing, knit up 4 sts evenly along the top of a half feather; knit up 7 sts evenly along the top end of each of the 20 X 35-stitch feathers; knit up 4 sts evenly along the top of the rem half feather. 148 Sts.
With RS facing, place the needle with the first layer of feathers behind the needle with the second layer and holding the needles parallel in the left hand, with a third 3mm needle, ktog a stitch from each layer all along the row. 148 Sts. Beg with a p (WS) row and work 3 rows in St.St. thus ending with RS facing for next row.
**Next Row – Dec:** K3; * k2tog; k5; rep from * to the last 5 sts; k2tog; k3. 127 Sts.
Work 3 rows in St.St. with RS facing for next row.
**Next Row – Dec:** K2tog; k3; * k2tog; k4; rep from * to the last 2 sts; k2tog. 105 Sts.
P1 WS row. Set aside.

**Join Top Layer Feathers**
With 3mm needle and RS of each feather facing, knit up 5 sts evenly along the top end of each of the 21 X 25-stitch feathers.105 Sts.
With RS facing, place the needle with the first two layers of feathers behind the needle with the top layer and holding the needles parallel in the left hand, with a third 3mm needle, ktog a stitch from each layer all along the row. 105 Sts.
P1 WS row. Set aside.

**Edging**
With 3.25mm needles Cable Edge Cast-on 112 sts. Change to 3mm needles and beg with a k row work in St.St. for 4 rows.
**Next Row (RS) – Dec:** K7; (k2tog; k14) 6 times; k2tog; k7. 105 Sts. P1 WS row.
With RS facing, place the needle with the feathered collar behind the needle with the edging and holding the needles parallel in the left hand, with a third 3mm needle, ktog a stitch from each layer all along the row. 105 Sts. P1 WS row.
**First Size – Dec (RS):** K2; * k2tog; k9; rep from * to the last 4 sts; k2tog; k2. 95 Sts. P1 WS row.

**Second & Third Sizes – Dec (RS):** K 14[20]; * k2tog; k13[19]; rep from * to the last 16[22] sts; k2tog; k 14[20]. 99[101]Sts. P1 WS row.

**Fourth Size:** Work 2 rows St.St.

**All Sizes:** Set collar aside.

*Finishing*

Darn in all loose ends on body and sleeves. Lay body out on a flat surface WS up and place damp towelling on back area then fold fronts over back at marked centre underarm sts, to measurements shown on schematic, ensuring that the inside towelling is flat and smooth. Block out sleeves and cover body and sleeves with damp towels and leave to dry away from direct heat. Sew back to fronts at shoulder seams and press seams very lightly on WS using a warm iron and damp cloth.

**Neckband**

With 2.75mm needle and RS of body facing, beg at left front and pick up and k the 5[5,6,7] sts from holder; knit up 33[34,34,35] sts evenly along right neck edge to back neck holder; pick up and k the 33[35,37,39] sts from holder; knit up 33[34,34,35] sts evenly along left side of neck; pick up and k the 5[5,6,7] sts from left front holder. 109[113,117,123] Sts. Change to 3mm needles and P1 WS row.

**Next Row – Dec:** K 2[4,5,1]; * k2tog; k 6[6,5,5]; rep from * to the last 3[5,7,3] sts; k2tog; k1[3,5,1]. 95[99,101,105] sts. Work 3 rows of St.St. thus ending with RS facing for next row.

**Join Collar to Neckband**

With RS facing, place the needle with neckband sts behind the needle with collar sts and and holding the needles parallel in the left hand, with a third 3mm needle, ktog a stitch from the neckband and collar all along the row. Continue to work the neckband as follows –

**Row 1 (WS):** P1; k to the last st; p1.

**Row 2 (RS):** K1; p to the last st; k1.

**Row 3 (WS):** As row 1. **Rows 4 & 6 (RS):** K.

**Row 5 (WS):** P. Rep rows 1 – 6 two more times, then work rows 1 & 2 once more, thus working 20 neckband rows ending with WS facing for next row. Cast off knitwise on the WS.

**Left Front Band**

With 2.75mm needle and RS facing beg at top of neckband and knit up 132[137,142,147] sts evenly to the bottom of the body curled edging, working through the doubled fabric of the curled collar and lower edgings thus sealing them in the curled position. Change to 3mm needles and work as neckband, repeating rows 1 – 6 twice. Then work rows 1 & 2 once more, thus working 14 rows and ending with WS facing for next row. Cast off sts knitwise on the WS.

**Right Front Band**

As left but beg at lower curled edge of body and knit up sts to top of neckband and work 11 buttonholes on row 8 (RS) as follows –

**First Size:** K1; p2; (cast off 2; p12; cast off 2; p11) 4 times; (cast off 2; p6) twice; cast off 2; p2; k1.

**Second Size:** K1; p3; (cast off 2; p12) 8 times; (cast off 2; p6) twice; cast off 2; p2; k1.

**Third Size:** K1; p4; (cast off 2; p13; cast off 2; p12) 4 times; (cast off 2; p6) twice; cast off 2; p2; k1.

**Fourth Size:** K1; p5; (cast off 2; p13) 8 times; (cast off 2; p6) twice; cast off 2; p2; k1.

Darn in loose ends. Sew buttons on to left front band.

Sew up sleeve seams from top of curved edging (i.e. 5-st knit up row) to underarm. Press seams gently on WS as before. Pin sleeves to body placing sleeve seam at centre underarm st of body and centre top of sleeve at shoulder seam. Pin sleeves evenly around armholes and sew sleeves to body. Press seams as before.

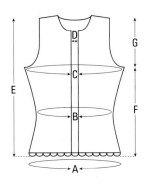

A = 83.5[90, 96.75, 103.5]cm
B = 77.5[84, 90.75, 97.5]cm
C = 87.5[94.5, 101, 107.5]cm
D = 3.5cm
E = 48[50, 52.5, 54.5]cm
F = 30[31, 32, 33]cm
G = 18[19, 20.5, 21.5]cm
H = 20.25[21, 21.75, 22.5]cm
I = 30.75[32.25, 34.5, 36]cm
J = 38[38, 39, 39]cm
K = 12.5[13, 13, 13]cm

# The
# Lapwing

## Design Notes ————

I took the colours, feathers and flowers from the costume and worked some curved shaping into this fine-knit pullover. The contrasting machair-coloured peplum and cuffs are shaped with short rows and then overlaid with a triple-feather pattern on the back and sleeves, whilst the front features an appliquéd flower arrangement.

I designed the feather pattern with right and left slanting increases and decreases placed to mimic the structure of individual feathers. These can be seen quite clearly in the charted patterns with Chart A for working the base of each of the three feathers and charts B & C for working the triple feather panel within the stocking stitch body and sleeves.

If you prefer, you can work the peplum with overlaid feathers on the front as on the back, instead of the flower arrangement. To do this, simply work the front as the back from the beginning (●) to the end of the armhole shaping (▲▲)

To fit small [medium, large, X large]. Directions for larger sizes are given in square brackets. Where there is only one set of figures, it applies to all sizes.

## Knitted Measurements

Underarm 88[95.5,104,112]cm.
Waist 73[80.5,88,95.5]cm.
Length (side to top of shoulder)42[44,46,48)cm.
Centre back hem to neckline 46[48,50,52]cm.
Sleeve length (wrist to underarm ex. cuff) 41[41.5,42,42.5]cm.

## Materials

Of **Alice Starmore® Hebridean 2 Ply –**
275[300,325,350]g in Lapwing.
50g in Machair. 7g in Clover.
1 pair 3mm needles. 1 Set of double-pointed or circular 2.75mm needles for neckband. Stitch holders. Stitch markers. Tapestry needle.

## Tension

27 Sts and 40 rows to 10cm measured over Stocking Stitch (St. St). To make an accurate tension swatch, cast on 33 sts and work 48 rows. Pin the swatch on a flat surface and measure tension using a ruler.

## Back

### Peplum

● With 3mm needles and Machair cast on 109[119,129,139] sts. Join in Lapwing and stranding the yarns on the WS on rows 1 & 2, work lower border as follows –
**Row 1 (RS):** * K1 Lapwing; k1 Machair; rep from * to the last st; k1 Lapwing.
**Row 2 (WS):** As row 1 but yf after working each st to strand the yarns on the WS.
Break off Lapwing. **Rows 3 & 4:** With Machair k. Break off yarn. With RS facing sl the first 45[49,54,56] sts pw to RHN. Rejoin Machair at this point and shape as follows –
**Row 1 (RS):** K 19[21,21,27]; wrap the next st (wrap 1 RS) thus – sl1pw to RHN; yf; then sl the st back to LHN. Turn.
**Row 2 (WS):** Yf (thus wrapping the yarn around the base of the st on RHN); sl1pw; p 23[26,26,33]; wrap the next st (wrap 1 WS) thus – sl1pw; yb; sl the st back to LHN. Turn.
**Row 3:** Yb (thus wrapping the yarn around the base of the st on RHN); sl1pw; k 28[32,32,40]; wrap1 RS. Turn.
**Row 4:** Yf; sl1pw; p 33[38,38,47]; wrap1 WS. Turn.
**Row 5:** Yb; sl1pw; k 38[44,44,54]; wrap1 RS. Turn.

**Row 6:** Yf; sl1pw; p 43[50,50,60]; wrap1 WS. Turn.
**Row 7:** Yb; sl1pw; k 48[56,56,66]; wrap1 RS. Turn.
**Row 8:** Yf; sl1pw; p 53[62,62,72]; wrap1 WS. Turn.
**Row 9:** Yb; sl1pw; k 58[68,68,78]; wrap1 RS. Turn.
There are now 25[25,30,30] unworked sts rem at each side. Continue as set and work 5[5,6,6] more sts at the end of every row until all sts are worked, thus ending with WS facing for next row. Break off Machair and with Lapwing p 1 WS row. Place sts on a spare needle. ● ●

### Centre Feathers

■ With 3mm needles and Lapwing cast on 1st and k this st. Turn.
**Next Row (WS):** K into the front then p into the back of the st. 2 Sts.
**Next Row (RS):** K1; k into the front then into the back of the st. 3 Sts.
**Next Row (WS):** K1; p1; k1.
Beg at row 1 of chart A and reading all RS (odd-numbered) rows from right to left, and all WS (even-numbered) rows from left to right, work the 10 rows of chart and inc 1st at each side of centre st on every RS row as indicated. 13 Sts in total. Break off yarn, place sts on a holder and work another 2 identical feathers leaving the yarn attached to the last feather.

### Join Feathers

**Next Row (RS):** Working the last feather, k4; * k2tog; M1R (see key); k1; M1L (see key); ssk; k3; ktog the next st with the first st of next feather; k3; rep from * once more; k2tog; M1R; k1; M1L; ssk; k4. 37 Sts.
**Next Row (WS):** (K1; p11) 3 times; k1.
With RS facing, set chart B as follows –
**Row 1 (RS):** Reading from right to left, rep the 12 patt sts 3 times; k the last st as indicated.
**Row 2 (WS):** Reading from left to right, k the first st as indicated; rep the 12 patt sts 3 times. Continue as set and dec on row 5 as indicated. 31 Sts rem. Work through row 6. Break off yarn and place sts on a spare needle. ■ ■

### Side Borders

With 3mm needles and Lapwing cast on 39[45,49,55] sts.
+ Join in Machair and stranding the yarns on the WS on rows 1 & 2, work border as follows –
**Row 1 (RS):** * K1 Machair; k1 Lapwing; rep from * to the last st; k1 Machair.
**Row 2 (WS):** As row 1 but yf after each st to strand on the WS. Break off Machair.
**Rows 3 & 4:** With Lapwing k.
Break off yarn. Place sts on a spare needle. Make a second identical border but do not break off yarn. ++

## CHART A

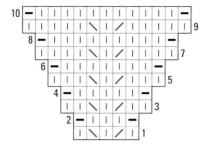

## CHART B

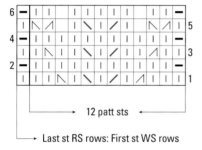

→ 12 patt sts ←

→ Last st RS rows: First st WS rows

## CHART C

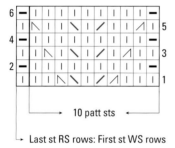

→ 10 patt sts ←

→ Last st RS rows: First st WS rows

**Join Borders and Centre Feather Panel**
**First & Third Sizes:** With RS facing, 3mm
needles and Lapwing k across the 39[49] sts
of current border; with RS facing and reading
from right to left, work row 1 of chart C over the
31 sts of feathers, repeating the 10 patt sts 3
times, then work the last st as indicated; with
RS facing k across the 39[49] sts of rem border.
109[129] Sts.
**Second & Fourth Sizes:** With RS facing,
3mm needles and Lapwing k1; k2tog; k 42[52]
over the sts of current border; with RS facing
and reading from right to left, work row 1 of
chart C over the 31 sts of feathers, repeating
the 10 patt sts 3 times, then work the last st
as indicated; with RS facing k 42[52]; k2tog; k1
over the sts of rem border. 119[139] Sts.

## KEY FOR LAPWING

☐ k on RS rows; p on WS rows.

⟋ M1R (make 1 right) thus: insert RHN tip through
the loop of the st below the next st on LHN, from front
to back, and k a new st.

⟍ M1L (make 1 left) thus: insert LHN tip through the
loop below the last st worked on RHN, from back to
front; k into the front of the loop, thus twisting it to
make a new st.

▬ p on RS rows; k on WS rows.

⟋ k2tog.    ⟍ ssk.    ☐ no stitch.

---

▲ **All Sizes –**
**Join Peplum to Feathered Border**
With WS of peplum facing, place it in front of
WS of bordered feather panel, and with 3mm
needle and Lapwing, p tog the first 39[44,49,54]
sts of peplum with border sts; work the next 31
sts of peplum and chart C sts tog in patt as row
2 of chart C – i.e. k the first st as indicated; (p9;
k1) 3 times; – p tog the last 39[44,49,54] sts of
peplum with border sts. 109[119,129,139] Sts.
Reading all odd-numbered rows (RS) from right
to left, and all even-numbered rows (WS) from
left to right, set the patt as follows –
**Next Row (RS):** K 39[44,49,54]; work row 3 of
chart C as set over the 31 centre sts;
k 39[44,49,54].
**Next Row (WS):** P 39[44,49,54]; work row 4 of
chart C as set over the centre 31 sts;
p 39[44,49,54].
Continue as set and work 2 more rows. Then
repeating the 6 rows of chart C over the centre
31 sts as set, shape as follows –
**Next Row (RS) – Work First Dec:** K1; ssk;
k 36[41,46,51]; work chart C over the next 31 sts;
k 36[41,46,51]; k2tog; k1. 107[117,127,137] Sts.
Work 3 rows without shaping.
**Next Row (RS) – Work Second Dec:**
K 36[41,46,51]; k2tog; work chart C over the next
31 sts; ssk; k 36[41,46,51]. 105[115,125,135] Sts.
Work 3 rows without shaping.
**Next Row (RS) – Work Third Dec:** K1; ssk;
k 34[39,44,49]; work chart C over the next 31
sts; k 34[39,44,49]; k2tog; k1. 103[113,123,133]
Sts. Work 13 rows without shaping.
**Next Row (RS) – First Inc:** K1; m1; patt as
set to the last st; m1; k1. 105[115,125,135] Sts.
Work 5 rows without shaping.

**Next Row (RS) – Second Inc:** K 36[41,46,51]; m1; k1; work chart C over the next 31 sts; k1; m1; k 36[41,46,51]. 107[117,127,137] sts.
Work 5 rows without shaping.
* On next row inc 1st at each side of back as first inc; work 5 rows without shaping; on next row inc 1st at each side of the centre 33 sts as second inc; work 5 rows without shaping; ** rep from * to ** thus inc as set on every foll 6th row until there are 46[51,57,62] sts in St.St. at each side of the centre 31 sts. 123[133,145,155] Sts in total.
Continue as set without further shaping until back measures 29[30,31,32]cm from centre of peplum hemline with RS facing for next row.

## Shape Armholes

Cast off 5[6,6,7]sts at beg of next 2 rows. Cast off 3[3,4,4] sts at beg of next 2 rows. Dec 1st at each end of next 3 rows. Work 1 row without shaping then dec 1st at each end of next and every foll alt row until 89[95,101,107] sts rem. ▲▲
Continue in patt without further shaping until armholes measure 16.5[17.5,18.5,19.5]cm from first armhole cast off row, with RS facing for next row.

## Shape Back Neck/Shoulders

K 27[29,31,33] of right back shoulder; place the next 35[37,39,41] sts on a holder for back neck; place the rem 27[29,31,33] sts of left back on a spare needle.
Turn and shape right back neck as follows –
+ Continue in St.St. and dec 1st at neck edge of the next 2 rows. Work 1 row without shaping then dec 1st at neck edge of next row. 24[26,28,30] Sts rem. Work 1 row without shaping, thus ending with RS facing for next row.

## Shape Shoulder

Cast off 8[8,9,10] sts at beg next and foll alt row. Work 1 row.
Cast off the rem 8[10,10,10] Sts. ++
With RS facing, rejoin yarn to sts of left back shoulder and k to end of row. Work as right back neck and shoulder from + to ++, except work 2 rows without shaping thus having WS facing for shoulder cast-off.

## *Front*

As back from ● to ●●.

## Main Body Border

With 3mm needes and Lapwing cast on 109[119,129,139] sts.
Join in Machair and stranding the yarns on the WS on rows 1 & 2, work border as follows –
**Row 1 (RS):** * K1 Machair; k1 Lapwing; rep from

* to the last st; k1 Machair.
**Row 2 (WS):** As row 1 but yf after each st to strand on the WS. Break off Machair.
**Rows 3 & 4:** With Lapwing, k.
Set the main patt as follows –
**Row 1 (RS):** K 39[44,49,54]; reading from right to left work row 1 of chart C over the next 31 sts; repeating the 10 patt sts 3 times, then work the last st as indicated; k 39[44,49,54].
Work as back from ▲ to ▲▲ joining peplum on next row.
Continue as set until armholes measure 12[13,14,15]cm with RS facing for next row.

## Shape Front Neck

Keeping continuity of patt as far as possible throughout, patt 36[38,40,42] sts; place the next 17[19,21,23] sts on a holder for front neck; place the rem 36[38,40,42] sts on a spare needle. Turn and shape left side as follows –
° Dec 1st at neck edge of next 4 rows. Patt 1 row without shaping then dec 1st at neck edge of next and every foll alt row until 28[30,32,34] sts rem. Work 2 rows without shaping then dec 1st at neck edge of next and every foll 3rd row until 24[26,28,30] sts rem. °° Work 1 WS row.

## Shape Shoulder

Cast off 8[8,9,10] sts at beg next and foll alt row. Work 1 row then cast off the rem 8[10,10,10] Sts.
With RS facing rejoin yarn to the 36[38,40,42] sts of right side and work as left from ° to °°. Work 1 RS row. With WS facing shape shoulder as given for left side.

## *Sleeves*

## Cuff

With 3mm needles and Machair cast on 73[73,77,77] sts. Join in Lapwing and work 4 rows of lower border as back.
With RS facing sl the first 27sts pw to RHN. Rejoin Machair at this point and shape as follows –
**Row 1 (RS):** K 19[19,23,23]; wrap1 RS. Turn.
**Row 2 (WS):** Yf; sl1pw; p 21[21,25,25]; wrap1 WS. Turn.
**Row 3:** Yb; sl1pw; k 24[24,28,28]; wrap1 RS. Turn.
**Row 4:** Yf; sl1pw; p 27[27,31,31]; sl1pw; yb; wrap1 WS. Turn.
Continue as set working 3 more sts at the end of every row until all sts are worked, thus ending with WS facing for next row. Break off Machair and with Lapwing, p 1 WS row. Place sts on a spare needle. Work centre feathers as back from ■ to ■ ■.

### Side Borders

With 3mm needles and Lapwing cast on 21[21,23,23] sts and work side borders as back Side Borders from **+** to **++**.

### Join Borders and Centre Feather Panel

With RS facing, 3mm needles and Lapwing k the 21[21,23,23] sts of current side border; with RS facing and reading from right to left, work row 1 of chart C over the 31 sts of feather panel, repeating the 10 patt sts 3 times, then work the last st as indicated; with RS facing k the 21[21,23,23] sts of rem border. 73[73,77,77] Sts.

### Join Cuff

With WS of cuff facing, place it in front of WS of bordered feathers, and with 3mm needles and Lapwing p tog the first 21[21,23,23] sts of cuff with border sts; work the next 31 sts of cuff and border tog in patt as row 2 of chart C – i.e. k the first st as indicated; (p9; k1) 3 times; – p tog the last 21[21,23,23] sts of cuff with border sts. Continue as set and work St. St. over the first and last 21[21,23,23] sts and work rows 3 and 4 of chart C over the centre 31 sts.

**Next Row (RS):** K 1[1,2,2]; (ssk; k6) twice; ssk; k 2[2,3,3]; work row 5 of chart C over the next 31 sts; k 2[2,3,3]; (k2tog; k6) twice; k2tog; k 1[1,2,2]. 67[67,71,71] Sts.

**Next Row (WS):** P 18[18,20,20]; work row 6 of chart C over the next 31 sts; p 18[18,20,20].

**Next Row (RS):** K 4[4,5,5]; ssk; k4; ssk; k 6[6,7,7]; work row 1 of chart C over the next 31 sts; k 6[6,7,7]; k2tog; k4; k2tog; k 4[4,5,5]. 63[63,67,67] Sts. Patt 1[1,1,5] rows as set without shaping.

### First, Second & Third Sizes Only –

**Next Row (RS):** K 1[1,2]; ssk; k 10[10,11]; ssk; k1; work row 3 of chart C over the next 31 sts; k1; k2tog; k 10[10,11]; k2tog; k 1[1,2]. 59[59, 63] sts. Patt 1[3,3] rows without shaping.

### First Size Only – Next Row (RS):

K3; ssk; k4; ssk; k3; work row 5 of chart C over the next 31 sts; k3; k2tog; k4; k2tog; k3. 55 Sts. Patt 1 WS row.

**All Sizes:** Place a marker at each end of next row. Rep the 6 chart C rows over the centre 31 sts throughout and work 8 rows.

### Next Row (RS) – Beg Sleeve Shaping:

K1; m1; patt as set to the last st; m1; k1. Work 7 rows without shaping, working inc sts into St.St. Then inc 1st as set at each side of sleeve on next and every foll 8th row until there are 65[69,73,77] sts. Work 9 rows without shaping then inc 1st as set at each side of sleeve on next and every foll 10th row until

there are 87[91,97,101] sts. Continue as set without further shaping until sleeve measures 41[41.5,42,42.5]cm from marked row, with RS facing for next row.

### Shape Cap

Cast off 5[6,6,7] sts at beg of next 2 rows. Cast off 3[3,4,4] sts at beg of next 2 rows. Dec 1st at each end of next and every foll 3rd row until 63[63,65,65] sts rem. Patt 1 row without shaping then dec 1st at each end of every foll alt row until 29[27,29,27] sts rem. Dec 1st at each end of every foll row until 13 sts rem. Cast off.

### *Finishing*

Darn in all loose ends. Sew inner ends of side borders to edge of feather panel on back and sleeves. Block all pieces, right side up, to measurements shown on schematic. Cover with damp towels and leave to dry away from direct heat. Sew back and fronts together at shoulder seams. Press seams lightly on WS using a warm iron and damp cloth.

### Neckband

With RS facing, set of double-pointed or circular 2.75mm needles and Lapwing, beg at right shoulder seam and knit up 10 sts evenly along right back neck edge to back neck holder; pick up and dec from back neck holder thus – k 6[7,8,9]; (DD; k7) twice; DD; k 6[7,8,9] – 29[31,33,35] sts rem from holder; knit up 10 sts evenly along left back neck edge to left shoulder seam; knit up 25 sts evenly along left front neck edge to front neck holder; pick up and dec from front neck holder thus – k 7[8,9,10]; DD; k 7[8,9,10] – 15[17,19,21] sts rem from front holder; knit up 25 sts evenly along left front neck edge to right shoulder seam. 114[118,122,126] Sts. Place a marker at beg of rnd and joining in and breaking off colours as required and stranding yarns on the WS on two-colour rnds, patt as follows –

**Rnd 1:** K. **Rnd 2:** P. **Rnd 3:** * K1 Lapwing; k1 Machair; rep from * to end of rnd.

**Rnd 4:** * P1 Lapwing; p1 Machair; rep from * to end of rnd. **Rnd 5:** With Lapwing, k.

**Rnd 6:** With Lapwing, p. **Rnd 7:** With Machair, k.

**Rnd 8:** With Machair, p.

**Rnds 9 & 10:** As rnds 3 & 4.

**Rnd 11:** With Machair, k.

With Machair cast off purlwise.

If you are applying the appliqued decoration to the front peplum, then make and attach before sewing up the side seams. Sew up side and sleeve seams, sewing peplum seams and main body and sleeve border seams separately so that the main borders overlay the peplums, and press all seams as before. Pin centre top of sleeves to shoulder seams and underarm seams together and then pin and sew sleeves into armholes. Press seams as before.

## Felted Appliqué

I created the appliquéd decoration by knitting then felting the elements separately. Once dry, I stitched the elements together to form the piece before stitching on to the garment. See page 268 for the felting process.

### Stems (make 2)

With 3mm needles and Lapwing, cast on 21 sts. Cast off the sts and using the yarn tails, oversew the cast-on and cast-off edges together to form a solid tube. To felt and shape roll each stem between the palms of your hands making sure that you roll evenly along the length: it will become thinner and longer with rolling. Once the stems are felted bend them into S shapes and plunge into cold water before rinsing in warm water. Re-shape if necessary and leave to dry on a towel.

### Leaves (make 2)

With 3mm needles and Lapwing, make a Knit Cast-on (see page 264) of 17 sts.
**Row 1 (WS):** P2tog; p to the last 2 sts; p2togb. 15 Sts. Break off yarn.
**Row 2 (RS):** With Machair, ssk; k4; DD; k4; k2tog. 11 Sts. **Row 2 (WS):** P4; PDD; p4. 9 Sts.
**Row 3 (RS):** K3; * DD; slpw the rem st from DD and the next st on RHN to LHN; rep from * until 1 centre st remains. Fasten off. Thread the Lapwing cast-on tail into a darner and sew cast on ends together on WS, then thread darner with Machair cast-off end and bring through to the WS and fasten off. Allow the cast on edge to curl inward to the RS of the leaf.

### Petals (make 3)

Make exactly as leaves but with 2 Ply Clover (or desired colour) instead of Lapwing.
To felt the leaves and petals roll each one lengthwise between the palms and once felted, shape by spreading the top end out and then rolling the tip gently to a point. The fabric is very malleable at this stage and can be shaped at will. I further shaped the leaves by pinching on one side, near the tip and then bending the tip to point upward. If you do this, remember to reflect the shape so that the leaves will be symmetrical in the finished piece. Plunge in cold water and rinse, re-shape as necessary and leave to dry.

### Centre Ball

With 3mm needles and Lapwing cast on 3 sts. P1 WS row.
**Row 1 (RS):** K1; (m1; k1) twice. 5 sts.
**Row 2:** P5. **Row 3:** K2tog; k1; ssk.
**Row 4:** P3tog. Fasten off and stuff the cast-on tail and additional tiny yarn scraps into the centre of the piece and sew the sides to form a ball. Felt by rolling between the palms until the ball feels solid. Plunge in cold water, rinse and leave to dry.

Once the pieces are dry assemble into shape on a flat surface. With Clover, stitch the top ends of the three petals together with one in the centre and one at each side, then stitch the Lapwing ball on top. With Lapwing, stitch a leaf to one end of the stems, then stitch the other end of the stems to the WS of the petals, one at each side of the centre petal. Pin the piece to the centre front of the front peplum as shown in the photograph. With Machair catch stitch in postition on the WS. It is not necessary to sew every part of the appliqué to the garment, but just enough to hold all of the elements in place.

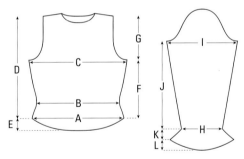

A = 40[44, 47, 50]cm
B = 36.5[40.25, 44, 47.75]cm
C = 44[47.75, 52, 56]cm
D = 42[44, 46, 48]cm
E = 5cm
F = 24[25, 26, 27]cm
G = 18[19, 20, 21]cm
H = 19[20.5, 22, 23.5]cm
I = 30.75[32.25, 34.5, 36]cm
J = 41[41.5, 42, 42.5]cm
K = 4.5cm
L = 4.5cm

# The Cailleach

## Design Notes

The *Cailleach* design comes straight from the front cover of her *Book of Future Possibilities*. This was an exercise in creating a pattern that would speak of the moorland landscape but at the same time be small in scale and therefore easy to memorise and knit. I felt my *Cailleach* would appreciate this, and also the classic stranded technique of working in the round with steeks. The end result aims to be beautiful, practical and flattering for all ages and shapes.

The coloured garter stitch border pattern is worked in the round at the hemline and cuffs, and then back and forth in rows on the neckband and front bands. This means that every alternate round is purled. On the neckband and borders every row is worked in knit stitch. Make sure that you always strand the yarns evenly across the wrong side on all two-colour rnds and rows.

The chart pattern is worked in the round throughout, except for the sleeve caps which are worked back and forth in rows on right and wrong sides. All rnds are read from right to left and worked in k throughout. All rows are worked in k

on RS and p on WS. On two-colour rnds, the yarn not in immediate use is stranded evenly across the WS.

The steeks are worked at the front, armholes and neck and later cut up centre to form openings. Each steek is worked over 8 sts and k in alt colours on every st and rnd – i.e. on first rnd (k1 patt colour, k1 background colour) 4 times: on alt rnds (k1 background, k1 patt) 4 times. Do not weave in newly joined in and broken off yarns at the centre of front steek. Instead leave a (approx) 5cm tail when joining in and breaking off yarns.

Edge stitches are worked at each side of steeks and are knit in background colours throughout. Sts for the front band are knitted up from edge sts and sleeve caps are sewn in along the armhole edge sts.

All steeks are finished by working cross stitch over the trimmed steeks. To do this thread the yarn into a tapestry needle and over-cast the raw edges of trimmed steeks to strands on WS. After sewing to end, reverse to form cross stitches.

## Sizes

To fit small [medium, large, X large].
Directions for larger sizes are given in square brackets. Where there is only one set of figures, it applies to all sizes.

## Knitted Measurements

Underarm (buttoned) 90.5[99,107.5,116]cm.
Length 62[64,66,67.75]cm.
Sleeve length (cuff to underarm) 43[44,44,45cm.

## Materials

Of **Alice Starmore® Hebridean 2 Ply** –
125[150,175,200]g in Calluna. 100[125,150,175]g each in Bogbean, Lapwing and Mountain Hare. 50[62,75,87]g each in Sea Anemone, Clover, Sundew & Corncrake. 25[37,50,62]g in Limpet. 1 Set of double-pointed or circular 3mm & 3.25mm needles. 1 Set of short 3mm & 3.25mm double-pointed needles (for lower sleeve). 1 Stitch holder. Stitch markers. Tapestry needle. 11[11,11,12] Buttons.

## Tension

28 Sts and 32 rows to 10cm, measured over chart patt using 3.25mm needles. To make an accurate tension swatch, cast on 37 sts on 1 double-pointed or circular needle and reading all rows from right to left, rep the 12 chart patt sts 3 times, then patt the last st. Work as a flat piece, **knitting on the RS only**, breaking off the yarn at the end of every row. Using a warm iron and damp cloth, press the swatch lightly on the WS. Measure tension of swatch on a flat surface using a ruler.

## Body

With double-pointed or circular 3mm needles cast on 241[265,283,305] sts. Place a marker at beg of rnd and making sure cast on edge is not twisted, join in and break off colours as required and stranding the yarns across the WS on all rnds, work steek, edge sts and lower border as follows –
**Rnd 1:** With alt Calluna and Clover k4 steek sts; with Calluna k1 edge st; * k1 Clover; k1 Calluna; rep from * to the last 6 sts; k1 Clover; with Calluna k1 edge st; with alt colours k4 steek sts.
**Rnd 2:** With alt Clover and Calluna k4 steek sts; with Calluna k1 edge st; * p1 Clover; p1 Calluna rep from * to the last 6 sts; k1 Clover; with Calluna k1 edge st; with alt colours k4 steek sts.
**Rnd 3:** With Lapwing k to end of rnd.

**Rnd 4:** With Lapwing k5; p to the last 5 sts; k5.
**Rnd 5:** With alt Bogbean and Sundew k4 steek sts; with Bogbean k1 edge st; * k3 Bogbean; k3 Sundew; rep from * to the last 8 sts; k3 Bogbean; with Bogbean k1 edge st; with alt colours k4 steek sts.
**Rnd 6:** With alt Sundew and Bogbean k4 steek sts; with Bogbean k1 edge st; * p3 Bogbean; p3 Sundew; rep from * to the last 8 sts; p3 Bogbean; with Bogbean k1 edge st; with alt colours k4 steek sts.
**Rnd 7:** With alt Bogbean and Sea Anemone k4 steek sts; with Bogbean k1 edge st; * k1 Bogbean; k1 Sea Anemone; rep from * to the last 6 sts; k1 Bogbean; with Bogbean k1 edge st; with alt colours k4 steek sts.
**Rnd 8:** With alt Bogbean and Sea Anemone k4 steek sts; with Bogbean k1 edge st; * p1 Bogbean; p1 Sea Anemone; rep from * to the last 6 sts; p1 Bogbean; with Bogbean k1 edge st; with alt colours k4 steek sts.
**Rnds 9 & 10:** Wth Sundew and Bogbean as rnds 5 & 6. **Rnds 11 & 12:** With Lapwing as rnds 3 & 4. **Rnds 13 & 14:** With Calluna and Clover as rnds 1 & 2.
**Rnds 15 & 16:** With Calluna as rnds 3 & 4.
**Next Rnd – Inc**
With Limpet k 8[6,6,8] * m1; k 25[28,18,17]; rep from * to the last 8[7,7,8]sts; m1; k 8[7,7,8]. 251[275,299,323] Sts.
Place a marker at beg of rnd. Change to 3.25mm needles. Joining in Sea Anemone, beg at rnd 1 of chart and set the patt as follows –
With alt colours k4 steek sts; with Limpet k1 edge st; reading from right to left rep the 12 patt sts 20[22,24,26] times; patt the last st as indicated; with Limpet k1 edge st; with alt colours k4 steek sts.
Joining in and breaking off colours as required and reading all rnds from right to left, continue as set, working edge sts in background (darker) colours throughout. Rep the 12 chart patt rnds and work 129[132,134,136] chart patt rnds in total thus ending on rnd 9[12,2,4] inclusive.
**Next Rnd –**
**Beg Armhole Steeks and Edge Sts**
With colours as for next rnd of chart, k4 steek sts and k1 edge st as set; keeping continuity, patt the next 54[59,64,69]sts (right front); with a separate length of background colour yarn, cast off the next 13[15,17,19] sts; with alt colours cast on 10 edge and steek sts; keeping continuity, patt the next 107[117,127,137] sts

## CHART

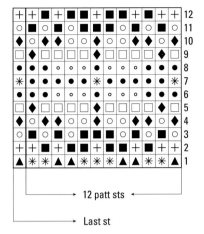

→ 12 patt sts ←

→ Last st

## KEY

| | |
|---|---|
| ▲ | LIMPET |
| ✳ | SEA ANEMONE |
| + | CLOVER |
| ■ | CALLUNA |
| ◆ | LAPWING |
| ○ | MOUNTAIN HARE |
| □ | SUNDEW |
| ● | BOGBEAN |
| ∘ | CORNCRAKE |

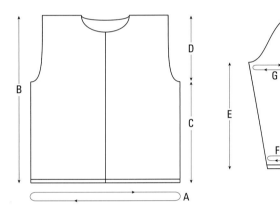

A = 90[98.5, 107, 115.5]cm
B = 62[64, 66, 67.75]cm
C = 44[45, 46, 46.5]cm
D = 18[19, 20, 21.25]cm
E = 42.5[43.5, 43.5, 44.5]cm
F = 21.5[22, 24.25, 25]cm
G = 32.75[34.25, 35.75, 38]cm

(back); with separate yarn as before, cast off the next 13[15,17,19] sts; with alt colours cast on 10 edge and steek sts; keeping continuity, patt the next 54[59,64,69] sts (left front); k1 edge st and k4 steek sts as set.

**Next Rnd:** With colours as next rnd of chart, k4 steek sts and k1 edge st; keeping continuity patt the next 52[57,62,67] sts of right front; k2tog; k1 edge st; k8 steek sts; k1 edge st; ssk; keeping continuity, patt the next 103[113,123,133] sts of back; k2tog; k1 edge st; k8 steek sts; k1 edge st; ssk; keeping continuity, patt the rem 52[57,62,67] sts of left front; k1 edge st; k4 steek sts.

Continue and dec 1st at chart patt side of armhole edge sts as set on next 3[4,5,5] rnds. Patt 1 rnd without shaping then dec as set on next and every foll alt rnd 5[5,6,7] times in all. 45[49,52,56] Chart patt sts rem on each front and 89[97,103,111] chart patt sts rem on back.

Then continue in patt as set without further shaping until 161[167,173,177] chart patt rnds have been worked in total thus ending on rnd 5[11,5,9] inclusive of chart.

**Next Rnd –**
**Beg Front Neck Steek and Edge Sts**
With alt colours as for next rnd of chart, cast off the first 4 steek sts and 1 edge st; patt as set to the last 5 sts of rnd and cast off 1 edge st and 4 steek sts. Break off yarns.

**Next Rnd:** Place the first 9[10,11,12] sts on a holder; with alt colours as for next rnd of chart, cast on 4 steek sts and mark the first st cast on for beg of rnd; with background colour cast on 1 edge st; keeping continuity, patt as set to the last 9[10,11,12] sts of rnd and place these sts on a holder; with background colour cast on 1 edge st; with alt colours cast on 4 steek sts. Work front neck steek and edge sts as set and keeping continuity, shape front neck by decreasing 1st at chart patt side of front neck edge sts on next 4 rnds. 32[35,37,40] Chart patt sts rem on each front. Continue as set and patt 1 rnd without shaping, then dec 1st at each side of front neck as set on the next and every foll alt rnd 7[7,7,8] times in all. 25[28,30,32] Chart patt sts rem on each front and ending on rnd 1[7,1,7] inclusive of chart.

**Next Rnd –**
**Beg Back Neck Steek and Edge Sts**
Keeping continuity, work straight without shaping to the 89[97,103,111] chart patt sts of back; patt the first 26[29,31,33] sts; place the next 37[39,41,45] sts on a holder; with background colour cast on 1 edge st; with alt colours cast on 8 steek sts; with background colour cast on 1 edge st; keeping continuity, patt the rem 26[29,31,33] chart patt sts of back, then continue straight without shaping to end of rnd.

Work back neck steek and edge sts as set and keeping continuity, dec 1st at chart patt side of back and front neck edge sts on next rnd. Patt 1 rnd without shaping then dec 1st at chart patt side of back neck steeks on next rnd. 24[27,29,31] Chart patt sts rem on each shoulder. Patt 1 rnd without shaping and cast off **all** steek sts on this rnd (rnd 6[12,6,12] of chart).

With Bogbean [Limpet, Bogbean, Limpet] graft shoulder sts together including edge sts.

*Sleeves*

With short double-pointed 3mm needles and Calluna, cast on 54[57,63,66] sts. Place a marker and beg of rnd and joining in and breaking off colours as required, work border as follows –
**Rnd 1:** * K1 Calluna; k1 Clover; rep from * to end [last st, last st, end]; k 0[1,1,0] Calluna.
**Rnd 2:** As rnd 1 but p all sts.
**Rnd 3:** With Lapwing k. **Rnd 4:** As rnd 3 but p all sts. **Rnd 5:** K3 Bogbean; k3 Sundew; rep from * to end [last 3 sts; last 3 sts; end]; k 0[3,3,0] Bogbean. **Rnd 6:** As rnd 5 but p all sts.
**Rnd 7:** * K1 Bogbean; k1 Sea Anemone; rep from * to end [last st, last st, end]; k 0[1,1,0] Bogbean. **Rnd 8:** As rnd 7 but p all sts.
**Rnds 9 & 10:** As rnds 5 & 6.
**Rnds 11 & 12:** As rnds 3 & 4.
**Rnds 13 & 14:** As rnds 1 & 2.
**Rnds 15 & 16:** With Calluna as rnds 3 &4.

**Next Rnd – Inc**
**First Size:** With Bogbean * m1; k9; rep from * to end of rnd. 60 Sts.
**Second, Third & Fourth Sizes:** With Bogbean [Calluna, Calluna], k 2[1,1]; * m1; k 13[15,21]; rep from * to the last 3[2,2] sts; m1; k3[2,2]. 62[68,70] Sts.
**All Sizes:** Place a marker at beg of rnd. Change to 3.25 mm needles and set chart patt as follows –
With Bogbean [Bogbean, Lapwing, Bogbean] k1 (seam st); beg at rnd 7[7,9,8] of chart, join in colour as required and patt the last 5[0,3,4] sts of 12st rep; rep the 12 patt sts 4[5,5,5] times; patt the first 6[1,4,5] sts of rep.
Joining in and breaking off colours as required continue as set, and working all inc sts into patt, inc 1st at each side of seam st on 7th[7th, 9th, 5th] chart patt rnd worked and then on every foll 7th rnd until there are 92[96,100,106] sts. Continue straight in patt until 123[126,126,129] chart patt rnds have been worked in total thus ending on rnd 9[12,2,4] inclusive.

**Next Rnd – Beg Cap Shaping**
With colours as for next rnd of patt, cast off seam st and next 6[7,8,9] patt sts; continue in patt as set to the last 6[7,8,9] sts and cast off these sts. Break off yarns.
With RS facing and working back and forth in rows from now on, keep continuity of patt and dec 1st at each end of next 5 rows. 69[71,73,77] Sts rem. Patt 1 row without shaping then dec 1st at each end of next and every foll alt row until 45 sts rem. Then continue and dec at each end of next and every foll row until 19 sts rem. Keeping continuity of patt, cast off 3 sts at beg of next 2 rows. Cast off the rem 13 sts.

**Neckband**
Cut open front, and front and back neck steeks up centre between 4th and 5th steek sts.
With RS facing, 3mm needles and Calluna, pick up and k the 9[10,11,12] sts from right front holder; knit up 28[29,30,30] sts along right neck edge to back neck holder, working into loop of edge st next to chart patt sts; pick up and k the 37[39,41,45] sts from back neck holder; knit up 28[29,30,30] sts along left neck edge working into edge st as before; pick up and k the 9[10,11,12] sts from left front holder. 111[117,123,129] Sts.
Joining in and breaking off colours as required,

work back and forth in rows, stranding the yarn on the WS on all two-colour rows, as follows –

**Row 1 (WS):** With Calluna p1; k to the last st; p1.
**Row 2 (RS):** * K1 Clover; k1 Calluna; rep from * to the last st; k1 Clover.
**Row 3 (WS):** P1 Clover; * k1 Calluna; k1 Clover; rep from * to the last 2 sts; k1 Calluna; p1 Clover.
**Row 4 (RS):** With Lapwing, k.
**Row 5 (WS):** With Lapwing as row 1.
**Row 6 (RS):** K3 Bogbean; * k3 Sundew; k3 Bogbean; rep from * to end of row.
**Row 7 (WS):** With Bogbean p1; k2; * k3 Sundew; k3 Bogbean; rep from * to the last 6 sts; k3 Sundew; with Bogbean k2; p1.
**Row 8 (RS):** * K1 Bogbean; k1 Sea Anemone; rep from * to the last st; k1 Bogbean.
**Row 9 (WS):** P1 Bogbean; * k1 Sea Anemone; k1 Bogbean; rep from * to the last 2 sts; k1 Sea Anemone; p1 Bogbean.
**Row 10 (RS):** As row 6.
**Row 11 (WS):** As row 7.
**Row 12 (RS):** As row 4.
**Row 13 (WS):** As row 5.
**Row 14 (RS):** As row 2.
**Row 15 (WS):** As row 3.
**Row 16 (RS):** With Calluna, k.
With Calluna, cast off all sts knitwise on WS.

## Left Front Band

With RS facing, 3mm needles and Calluna beg at top of neckband and knit up 159[165,171,177] sts evenly to cast on edge, working into loop of edge st next to chart patt sts. Work 16 rows of border patt as given for neckband.

## Right Front Band

As left but beg at cast on edge and knit up sts to top of neckband and work 11[11,11,12] buttonholes on row 8 (RS) as follows –

**First, Third & Fourth Sizes**
Patt 4[6,7]; * cast off 2; patt 13[14,13]; rep from * to the last 5 sts; cast off 2; patt 3.
**Second Size:** Patt 5; * cast off 2; patt 13; cast off 2 patt 14; rep from * to the last 5 sts; cast off 2; patt 3.
With colours as set, continue in patt and cast on 2 sts over those cast off on the previous row. Complete as left front band.

*Finishing*

Cut open armhole steeks up centre between 4th and 5th steek sts. Trim front and neck steeks to a 2st width and with Calluna, cross stitch steeks in position. Darn in all loose ends on sleeves. Using a warm iron and damp cloth, press body and sleeves very lightly on the WS. Pin centre top of sleeve caps to body at grafted shoulder seam. Pin sleeve cast-off edges to body at underarm cast off, then pin cap edges of sleeves around armholes along armhole edge sts. Sew sleeves to body. Trim armhole steeks to a 2st width and with Calluna, cross stitch steeks to body. Press lightly on WS. Sew buttons on to left front band.

# The
# Eagle Wrap

## Design Notes ——————

I based the Eagle Wrap on the tail pieces for the costume but made them wing-shaped. This is a very versatile design which can be worn in lots of ways. It is made from side-to-side in two separate, reflecting pieces. Each piece begins with 3 sts at the short end and is worked by gradually increasing sts and rows, section, by section, to the longest length at the centre back. Every section within each piece is worked in stocking stitch with short rows, and finished with two rows of reverse stocking stitch which I refer to as purl ridges.

Every section is essentially a repeat of the second section worked for each piece, but with more stitches and rows added, and so it becomes easy and rhythmic to work: it's a matter of keeping your eye on stitch counts and short-row positions as I have laid out in the pattern. The two pieces are grafted together after blocking, and then a curved cabled band is worked and sewn on along the top edge of the wrap.

The large wrap has eighteen sections in each piece whilst the smaller wrap is made by working the first 10 sections of each piece. You can easily vary the size by working the desired (but equal) number of sections in each piece.

I added some optional decorations for the small wrap in the form of a 2 Ply knitted edging, cords and French Knots worked along the purl ridges. The edging pattern is worked over a multiple of 12 sts (decreasing to 8) and so if you wish to add the edging to a larger wrap then be sure to expand the number of stitches by a multiple of 12 for casting on. Likewise, to make the cabled band for a different size, work the appropriate number of charted row repeats (rows 21-32) to fit along the top edge of the wrap.

I curved each end of the cabled band using short rows at one side. You will see on the chart that I have made symbols to denote the actions for the short rows which are explained in the key. The H symbol stands simply for "hold": in other words the stitch in question stays where it is on the needle and is not worked on the rows where it appears as an H. Like the blank squares (which are place holders on the chart for stitches that are increased at the beginning of chart A and decreased at the end of chart B), you can simply ignore them as they require no action.

## Knitted Measurements

**Large Wrap** – Centre back length 78cm. Width along top edge of curved band 144cm.
**Small Wrap** – Centre back length 39cm. Width along top band 62cm.

## Materials

Large Wrap:
Of **Alice Starmore® Hebridean 3 Ply** 425g shown in Tormentil.

Small Wrap:
Of **Alice Starmore® Hebridean 3 Ply** 125g shown in Golden Plover.

Optional Decorations:
Of **Alice Starmore® Hebridean 2 Ply** 12g each in Whin, Golden Plover, Sundew, & Mountain Hare. 1 pair 3.75mm needles for optional edging.

1 pair 4mm & 5mm needles.
1 Cable needle. 1 Tapestry needle.

## Tension

19 Sts and 29 rows to 10cm measured over St.St. (k RS rows; p WS rows) using 5mm needles.

## LARGE WRAP

*Right Side*

With 5mm needles and 3 Ply cast on 3 sts.
**First Section**
**Row 1 (RS):** K2; k into front then back of st. 4 Sts. **Row 2 (WS):** K1; p3. **Row 3 (RS):** K3; k into front then back of st. 5 Sts.
**Row 4 (WS):** K1; p4. **Row 5 (RS):** K4; k into front then back of st. 6 Sts.
**Row 6 (WS):** K1; p5. **Row 7 (RS):** K5; k into front then back of st. 7 Sts.
**Work Short Rows**
**Row 1 (WS):** K1; p to the last 2 sts; wrap1 WS thus – sl1pw; yb; sl the st back to the LHN. Turn.
**Row 2 (RS):** Yb (thus wrapping the yarn around the base of the slipped st on the RHN); sl1pw; k to the last st; k into front then back of st. 8 Sts total.
**Row 3 (WS):** K1; p to the last 4 sts; wrap1 WS. Turn. **Row 4 (RS):** As row 2. 9 Sts total.
**Row 5 (WS):** K1; p to the last 6 sts; wrap1 WS. Turn. **Row 6 (RS):** As row 2. 10 Sts total.
**Next Row (WS):** K1; p9 picking up and purling

the wrap tog with the st on the 3 wrapped sts.
**Next Row (RS):** K1; p8; p into front then k into back of st. 11 Sts.
**Next Row (WS):** Cast off 3 knitwise; k7; p1. 8 Sts.

**Second Section**
**Main Rows**
**Row 1 (RS):** K to the last st; k into front then back of st. **Row 2 (WS):** K1; p to end of row. Rep these 2 rows once more. 10 Sts. Work row 1 once more. 11 Sts.
**Work Short Rows**
**Row 1 (WS):** K1; p to the last 2 sts; wrap1 WS. Turn.
**Row 2 (RS):** Yb; sl1pw; k to the last st; k into front then back of st. 12 Sts total.
**Row 3 (WS):** K1; p to the last 4 sts; wrap1 WS. Turn. **Row 4 (RS):** As row 2. 13 Sts total.
**Row 5 (WS):** K1; p to the last 6 sts; wrap1 WS. Turn. **Row 6 (RS):** As row 2. 14 Sts total.
**Row 7 (WS):** K1; p to the last 8 sts; wrap1 WS. Turn. **Row 8 (RS):** As row 2. 15 Sts total.
**Last 3 Main Rows**
**Next Row (WS):** K1; p to end picking up and purling the wrap tog with the st on each wrapped st.
**Next Row (RS):** K1; p to the last st; p into front then k into back of st. 16 Sts.
**Next Row (WS):** Cast off 4 knitwise; k to the last st; p1. 12 Sts.

* After working the second section, all following sections follow the same format but with higher stitch counts and gradually altered short row positions, additional rows and numbers of sts cast-off. The main rows, which include all sts in the section, are worked at the beginning of each section and are repeated the number of times specified in each section. There are also 3 main rows worked at the end of each section; the first being where all the sts are worked after the short rows are complete; the second last main row is a purl ridge row and is also the last inc row of the section; the third and last main row is also a purl ridge row where sts are cast off at the beginning. The short rows are all worked over fewer sts within each section. Sts are increased in every section at the rate of 1st on every alt row, so that each following section will have more sts than the last. Based on the second section, all following sections are worked with row and stitch counts as set out.

### Third Section

Rep the first 2 main rows and work a total of 5 rows. 15 Sts.

Work 8 short rows, working to the last 3 sts on row 1; the last 6 sts on row 3; the last 9 sts on row 5; the last 12 sts on row 7 and inc 1st as given on row 2 and every foll alt row through row 8. 19 Sts in total. Work the last 3 main rows with 20 sts after last inc row. 16 Sts rem on completion of last main row.

### Fourth Section

Work as third section but with st counts as follows –

19 Sts on completion of first 5 main rows. 23 Sts on completion of 8 short rows. 24 Sts after last inc row. 20 Sts on completion of last main row.

### Fifth Section

Work as third section but with st counts as follows –

23 Sts on completion of first 5 rows. 27 Sts on completion of 8 short rows. Work a further 2 short rows, working to the last 15 sts and inc at the end of the 10th row. 28 Sts in total. 29 Sts after last inc row. 25 Sts on completion of last main row.

### Sixth Section

Work the first 5 rows as third section. 28 Sts. Work 10 short rows, working to the last 4 sts on row 1; the last 8 sts on row 3; the last 12 sts on row 5; the last 16 sts on row 7; the last 20 sts on row 9 and inc 1st as given on row 2 and every foll alt row through row 10. 33 Sts in total. Work the next 2 main rows with 34 sts on completion of last inc row. Cast off 5 sts at beg of last main row. 29 Sts rem.

### Seventh Section

Rep the first 2 main rows 3 times then work row 1 once more, thus working 7 rows. 33 Sts. Work 12 short rows, working to the last 4 sts on row 1; the last 9 sts on row 3; the last 14 sts on row 5; the last 19 sts on row 7; the last 24 sts on row 9; the last 29 sts on row 11 and inc 1st as given on row 2 and every foll alt row through row 12. 39 Sts in total. Work the next 2 main rows with 40 sts on completion of last inc row. Cast off 5 sts at beg of last main row. 35 Sts rem.

### Eighth Section

Rep the first 2 main rows 3 times then work row 1 once more, thus working 7 rows. 39 Sts Work 12 short rows, working to the last 5 sts on row 1; the last 10 sts on row 3; the last 15 sts on row 5; the last 20 sts on row 7; the last 25 sts on row 9; the last 30 sts on row 11 and inc 1st as given on row 2 and every foll alt row through row 12. 45 Sts in total. Work the next 2 main rows with 46 sts on completion of last inc row. Cast off 5 sts at beg of last main row. 41 Sts rem.

### Ninth Section

Rep the first 2 main rows 3 times then work row 1 once more, thus working 7 rows. 45 Sts. Work 12 short rows as eighth section. 51 Sts in total. Work next 2 main rows with 52 sts on completion of last inc row. Cast off 5 sts at beg of last main row. 47 Sts rem.

### Tenth Section

Rep the first 2 main rows 4 times, then work row 1 once more, thus working 9 rows. 52 Sts. Work 12 short rows, working to the last 5 sts on row 1; the last 10 sts on row 3; the lst 15 sts on row 5; the last 21 sts on row 7; the last 27 sts on row 9; the last 33 sts on row 11 and inc 1st as given on row 2 and every foll alt row through row 12. 58 Sts in total. Work next 2 main rows with 59 sts on completion of last inc row. Cast off 5 sts at beg of last main row. 54 Sts rem.

### Eleventh Section

Rep the first 2 main rows 4 times, then work row 1 once more, thus working 9 rows. 59 Sts. Work 12 short rows, working to the last 6 sts on row 1; the last 12 sts on row 3; the lst 18 sts on row 5; the last 24 sts on row 7; the last 30 sts on row 9; the last 36 sts on row 11 and inc 1st as given on row 2 and every foll alt row through row 12. 65 Sts in total. Work next 2 main rows with 66 sts on completion of last inc row. Cast off 5 sts at beg of last main row. 61 Sts rem.

### Twelfth Section

As eleventh section with 66 sts on completion of first 9 rows; 72 sts on completion of 12 short rows; 73 sts on completion of last inc row. Cast off 5 sts at beg of last main row. 68 Sts rem.

## KEY FOR EAGLE WRAP

|I| k on RS rows; p on WS rows.

|−| p on RS rows; k on WS rows.

|☐| no stitch.

|V| (k1b, k1) into same st, then insert left hand needle point between the vertical strand that runs down between the 2 sts just made and k into this strand, making the third st of the group.

|M| make 1 st thus: insert the needle tip into the loop of the st below the next st to be worked and k into this loop to make a new st.

|ᵛ| (p1, yo, p1) into same st, making 3 sts in the group.

|H| hold – leave the st unworked on needle.

|⊃| wrap 1 thus: yf; sl1pw; yb; sl the st back to LHN; turn to RS; yb, thus wrapping the yarn round the base of the st.

|−/|||  sl first st to cn and hold at back; k2; p1 from cn.

|||\−|  sl first 2 sts to cn and hold at front; p1; k2 from cn.

|SL| slip the st purlwise.

|||−|||  sl first 3 sts to cn and hold at back; k2; sl the p st from cn back onto left needle and p it; k2 from cn.

|K| make knot thus – (k1, p1) twice into same st, then sl the first 3 sts made over the last st made.

|⋀| k2 tog.

|⑤| sl decrease 5 sts tog thus – sl 3 knitwise, one at a time, with yarn at back, drop yarn, then * pass the second st on right hand needle over the first (centre) st; sl the centre st back to left hand needle and pass the next st on left hand needle over it **; sl the centre st back to right hand needle and rep from * to ** once more; p the centre st.

## CHART B

## CHART A

Rep rows 21 - 32

## Thirteenth Section
Rep the first 2 main rows 4 times, then work row 1 once more, thus working 9 rows. 73 Sts.
Work 12 short rows, working to the last 6 sts on row 1; the last 12 sts on row 3; the last 19 sts on row 5; the last 26 sts on row 7; the last 33 sts on row 9; the last 40 sts on row 11 and inc 1st as given on row 2 and every foll alt row through row 12. 79 Sts in total. Work next 2 main rows with 80 sts on completion of last inc row. Cast off 5 sts at beg of last main row. 75 Sts rem.

## Fourteenth Section
Rep the first 2 main rows 5 times, then work row 1 once more, thus working 11 rows. 81 Sts.
Work 12 short rows, working to the last 7 sts on row 1; the last 14 sts on row 3; the last 21 sts on row 5; the last 28 sts on row 7; the last 35 sts on row 9; the last 42 sts on row 11 and inc 1st as given on row 2 and every foll alt row through row 12. 87 Sts in total. Work next 2 main rows with 88 sts on completion of last inc row. Cast off 5 sts at beg of last main row. 83 Sts rem.

## Fifteenth Section
Rep the first 2 main rows 5 times, then work row 1 once more, thus working 11 rows. 89 Sts.
Work 12 short rows, working to the last 8 sts on row 1; the last 16 sts on row 3; the last 24 sts on row 5; the last 33 sts on row 7; the last 42 sts on row 9; the last 50 sts on row 11 and inc 1st as given on row 2 and every foll alt row through row 12. 95 Sts in total. Work next 2 main rows with 96 sts on completion of last inc row. Cast off 5 sts at beg of last main row. 91 Sts rem.

## Sixteenth Section
Rep the first 2 main rows 5 times, then work row 1 once more, thus working 11 rows. 97 Sts.
Work 12 short rows, working to the last 9 sts on row 1; the last 18 sts on row 3; the last 28 sts on row 5; the last 38 sts on row 7; the last 48 sts on row 9; the last 58 sts on row 11 and inc 1st as given on row 2 and every foll alt row through row 12. 103 Sts in total. Work next 2 main rows with 104 sts on completion of last inc row. Cast off 6 sts at beg of last main row. 98 Sts rem.

## Seventeenth Section
Rep the first 2 main rows 5 times, then work row 1 once more, thus working 11 rows. 104 Sts.
Work 12 short rows, working to the last 10 sts on row 1; the last 20 sts on row 3; the last 30 sts on row 5; the last 40 sts on row 7; the last 50 sts on row 9; the last 60 sts on row 11 and inc 1st as given on row 2 and every foll alt row through row 12. 110 Sts in total. Work next 2 main rows with 111 sts on completion of last inc row. Cast off 6 sts at beg of last main row. 105 Sts rem.

## Eighteenth Section
Rep the first 2 main rows 5 times, then work row 1 once more, thus working 11 rows. 111 Sts.
Work 12 short rows, working to the last 12 sts on row 1; the last 24 sts on row 3; the last 36 sts on row 5; the last 48 sts on row 7; the last 60 sts on row 9; the last 72 sts on row 11 and inc 1st as given on row 2 and every foll alt row through row 12. 117 Sts in total. Work next 2 main rows with 118 sts on completion of last inc row. Using a darning needle place the rem 118 sts on a long length of yarn so that the sts can be spread to the full length of the last section. **

## *Left Side*

With 5mm needles and 3 Ply cast on 3 sts.

## First Section
**Row 1 (RS):** K3. **Row 2 (WS):** P2; p into front then k into back of st. 4 Sts.
**Rows 3, 5 & 7 (RS):** K. **Row 4 (WS):** P3; p into front then k back of st. 5 Sts.
**Row 6 (WS):** P4; p into front then k back of st. 6 Sts.
**Row 8 (WS):** P5; p into front then k back of st. 7 Sts.
**Work Short Rows**
**Row 1 (RS):** K to the last 2 sts; wrap1 RS thus – sl1pw; yf; sl the st back to the LHN. Turn.
**Row 2 (WS):** Yf (thus wrapping the yarn around the base of the slipped st on the RHN); sl1pw; p to the last st; p into front then k into back of st. 8 Sts total.
**Row 3 (RS):** K to the last 4 sts; wrap1 RS. Turn.
**Row 4 (WS):** As row 2. 9 Sts total.
**Row 5 (RS):** K to the last 6 sts; wrap1 RS. Turn.
**Row 6 (WS):** As row 2. 10 Sts total.
**Next Row (RS):** K all sts, picking up and knitting the wrap tog with the st on the 3 wrapped sts.
**Next Row (WS):** P1; k8; k into front then into back of st. 11 Sts.
**Next Row (RS):** Cast off 3 pw; p7; k1. 8 Sts.

**Second Section**
**Main Rows**
**Row 1 (WS):** P to the last st; p into front then k into back of st. **Row 2 (RS):** K.
Rep these 2 rows once more. 10 Sts. Work row 1 once more. 11 Sts.
**Work Short Rows**
**Row 1 (RS):** K to the last 2 sts; wrap1 RS. Turn.
**Row 2 (WS):** Yf; sl1pw; p to the last st; p into front then k into back of st. 12 Sts total.
**Row 3 (RS):** K to the last 4 sts; wrap1 RS. Turn.
**Row 4 (WS):** As row 2. 13 Sts total.
**Row 5 (RS):** K to the last 6 sts; wrap1 RS. Turn.
**Row 6 (WS):** As row 2. 14 Sts total.
**Row 7 (RS):** K to the last 8 sts; wrap1 RS. Turn.
**Row 8 (WS):** As row 2. 15 Sts total.
**Last 3 Main Rows**
**Next Row (RS):** K all sts picking up and knitting the wrap tog with the st on each wrapped st.
**Next Row (WS):** P1; k to the last st; k into front then into back of st. 16 Sts.
**Next Row (RS):** Cast off 4 pw; p to the last st; k1. 12 Sts rem.
Continue as set and basing all following sections on the left side second section just completed, follow the st and row counts and short row positions as given for right side from * to **.

*Finishing*

Darn in loose ends. Rinse both pieces in lukewarm water. Roll in towels to remove excess water and then lay each piece on a large towel, right side up, and spread out in full. Beginning at longest section (eighteenth), raise up along the length of the purl ridge between the eighteenth and seventeenth section, then continue likewise with each following section in turn, to the first, so that the sections are folded in concertina fashion with the purl ridges all stacked together and leaning towards the longest edge. Leave both sections in this position for several hours or overnight. Then beginning at the short end (first section), gently open out each section just enough so that the purl ridges are still raised up but the knit sections are exposed enough to dry out. When completely dry, place the sts of each piece on 5mm needles with the tips at the bottom end. Thread a darner with 3 ply and hold the needles parallel with right sides of each piece together and graft the sts together on the WS. Darn in loose ends.

**Cabled Band**
With 4mm needles cast on 1st.
**Row 1 (RS):** K, then p into the front, then k into back of the st. 3 Sts. **Row 2 (WS):** K3.
**Row 3 (RS):** K1; p1; m1; k1. 4 Sts.
**Row 4 (WS):** K4. **Row 5 (RS):** K1; p2; k1.
**Row 6 (WS):** K1; m1; k3.
**Row 7 (RS):** K1; p3; k1. **Row 8 (WS):** K3; wrap1 thus – yf; sl1pw; yb; sl the st back to LHN. Turn.
**Row 9 (RS):** Yb; sl1pw; p1; m1; k1. 6 Sts.
**Row 10 (WS):** K6.
Reading all odd-numbered (RS) rows from right to left and all even-numbered rows (WS) from left to right, beg at row 1 and work the patt from chart A. Work through row 20. 15 Sts. Continue and rep rows 21 through 32, 33 times in total. Work row 21 through 30 once more.
Beg at row 1 (RS) and work the 20 rows of chart B. 6 Sts rem.
Complete band as follows –
**Row 1 (RS):** K1; p4; k1. **Row 2 (WS):** K4; wrap1. Turn. **Row 3 (RS):** Yb; sl1pw; p2; k1.
**Row 4 (WS):** K6.
**Row 5 (RS):** K1; p2; p2tog; k1. 5 Sts.
**Row 6 (WS):** K5.
**Row 7 (RS):** K1; p3tog; k1. 3 Sts.
**Row 8 (RS):** Sl2tog knitwise; k1; p2sso.
Fasten off.
Pin out the cabled band on a flat surface following the short row curve at each end. Cover with damp towels and allow to dry away from direct heat. Once dry, fold the band in half and mark the centre point of the longer curved edge.
Lay the wrap out on a flat surface RS up. With RS of band facing, pin the longer curving edge of the band at each end of the top edge of the wrap so that the edge st of the band is on top of the top edge st of the wrap. Then pin the centre point of the band on top of the centre top of the wrap, then stretching the band gently and evenly, pin it along the entire top edge of the wrap.
Sew the band to the wrap on the RS working small running stitches between the garter stitch "bumps" of the band. **Note:** If adding cords (see **Optional Decorations** ) lightly stitch them in place at the top centre of chosen sections and place the cabled band on top so that they are sewn in along with the band

## SMALL WRAP

As large wrap but working only the first 10 sections in each of right and left sides and ending tenth sections on last main inc row with 59 Sts in total. Graft sections together on WS as large wrap. Rinse and block out as large wrap. Make cabled band as large wrap but rep rows 21 through 32, 11 times in total instead of 33 times. Block out band and finish as large wrap.

### Optional Decorations
With 2 Ply colors as desired, embroider French Knots along purl ridges at will (see page 267 for making French Knots).

### Edging
With 3.75mm needles and 2 Ply Whin cast on 253 sts. Break off Whin.
**Row 1 (RS):** With 2 Ply Golden Plover k2tog; * k9; DD; rep from * to the last 11 sts; k9; ssk. 211 Sts.
**Row 2 (WS):** P1; k to the last st; p1.
Break off Golden Plover.
**Row 3 (RS):** With 2 Ply Sundew k2tog; * k7; DD; rep from * to the last 9 sts; k7; ssk. 169 Sts.
**Row 4 (WS):** P1; k to the last st; p1.
Break off Sundew.
**Row 5: (RS):** With 2 Ply Mountain Hare k2tog; * k5; DD; rep from * to the last 7 sts; k5; ssk. 127 Sts.
**Row 6: (WS):** P1; k to the last st; p1.
Break off Mountain Hare.
**Row 7: (RS):** Golden Plover, k.
Cast off purlwise. Block out edging and pin out the DD points to emphasise them. Cover with damp towels and leave to dry. Mark the centre point of the edging cast off and pin it at the centre top back of the wrap, then pin at each end and along the top edge of the wrap. Sew the cast-off edge lightly along the top edge st of the wrap before sewing the cabled band in place on top, as described for the large wrap.

### Cords
Cords can be made in various lengths using colours as desired. I made two 25cm-long Sundew cords and placed them at the centre of the tenth sections at each side of the centre back grafted purl ridge; then two 20cm-long Mountain Hare cords at centre of the ninth sections and two 15cm-long cords at the centre of each 8th section.

For each cord cut two lengths of 2 Ply yarn, each 140[120,100]cm long for finished cords of roughly 25[20,15] cm. To make each cord, fold the two lengths in half and loop over a peg (I use a warping peg clamped to a table), tie the open ends in an overhand knot so that the yarns are now in a closed loop, with the mid-point from the knotted end placed around the peg. Place

a pencil inside the loop at the knotted end and pinch the threads so that the pencil is tightly held between the knot and your fingers. Twirl the pencil round in one direction until the yarns are twisted very tightly (the more you twirl, the tighter the cord). Then carefully remove the pencil while pinching the knotted end to maintain the twist. Fold the twisted cord in half

and lift off the peg, allowing the cord to twist around itself to half its length. Knot the looped and the knotted end together, above the original knot and trim the end. Place the unknotted ends of the cords at top edge of wrap at the centre of chosen sections and stitch in position.

# The Selkie Cardigan

## Design Notes ——————

I designed the Selkie cardigan as an extension of the stranded pattern I designed for the lining of the collar and cuffs of the costume. My idea was to further explore the element in which the Selkie excels and how it changes from its limited movements on shore to a creature of balletic grace in water. So it casts off its coat of stone and becomes at one with the underwater world. Sea colours, ripples and the perpetual motion of kelp forests were my themes.

The design is worked in the round with steeks at all openings, except for the sleeve caps which are worked back and forth in rows. See page 196 for a word on steeks. The body has subtle shaping within the vertical "seaweed" panels (charts B & D) and so these patterns shrink in size to the waist and are then turned upside-down and expanded again to complete the body. So this is a design that requires expertise and concentration; be especially careful when setting out the chart patterns above the rib.

You will see that I have numbered the rounds of charts B & D for working both ways, and though the method of numbering may look peculiar at first glance, I have done this to make working easier as all of the charts are synchronised so that you will always be working the same round number of all charts at the same time.

Like the costume, I knitted, embroidered and felted the buttons. This is optional and you may well prefer to button the cardigan in a more conventional manner.

## Sizes

To fit small [medium, large, X large].
Directions for larger sizes are given in square brackets. Where there is only one set of figures, it applies to all sizes.

## Knitted Measurements

Underarm (buttoned) 90[96,101.5,107.5]cm.
Waist (buttoned) 81.5[87.5,93,99]cm.
Length 58[60,62,64]cm.
Sleeve length (cuff to underarm)
42.5[43.5,44.5,45.5]cm.

## Materials

Of **Alice Starmore® Hebridean 2 Ply** –
160[180,200,225]g in Summertide.
100[120,135,150]g in Storm Petrel.
50[62,75,87]g in each of Limpet, Lapwing & Witchflower. 37[50,62,75]g in each of Kelpie & Calluna. 25[32,37,50]g in each of Strabhann & Shearwater. 15[20,25,30]g in Mara.
1 Set of double-pointed or circular 3.25mm needles. 1 Set of short 2.75mm & 3.25mm double-pointed needles (for lower sleeve).
1 Stitch holder. Stitch markers. Tapestry needle. 12 Buttons.

## Tension

28 Sts and 32 rows to 10cm, measured over chart A patt using 3.25mm needles. To make an accurate tension swatch, cast on 36 sts on 1 double-pointed or circular needle and reading all rows from right to left, work the first 4 sts of chart A, then rep the 4 patt sts 7 times; then work the last 4 sts. Work as a flat piece, **knitting on the RS only**, breaking off the yarn at the end of every row. Using a warm iron and damp cloth, press the swatch lightly on the WS. Measure tension of swatch on a flat surface using a ruler.

## Body

With double-pointed or circular 3.25mm needles and Shearwater, cast on 247[263,279,295] sts. Place a marker at beg of rnd and making sure cast on edge is not twisted, join in and break off colours as required and set front steek, edge sts and 2/2 rib as follows –
**Rnd 1:** With alt Shearwater and Calluna k4 steek sts; with Shearwater k1 edge st; * (k2 Calluna, p2 Shearwater) 29[31,33,35] times; k2 Calluna; ** p1 Shearwater (centre back) rep from * to ** once more; k2 Calluna;

with Shearwater, k1 edge st; with alt colours k4 steek sts.
**Rnd 2:** As set but substitute Summertide for Shearwater.
**Rnds 3 & 4:** As set but substitute Lapwing for Calluna.
**Rnd 5:** As set but substitute Storm Petrel for Lapwing.
**Rnd 6:** As set but substitute Strabhann for Summertide.
**Rnd 7:** As set but substitute Summertide for Strabhann.
**Rnds 8 & 9:** As set but substitute Limpet for Storm Petrel.
**Rnd 10:** As set but substitute Witchflower for Summertide.
**Next Rnd – Inc**
With alt Kelpie and Witchflower, k4 steek sts; with Witchflower k1 edge st; • (k2 Kelpie; k2 Witchflower) 6[7,7,8] times; with Kelpie k1; m1; k1; (k2 Witchflower; k2 Kelpie) 8[8,9,9] times; with Witchflower k1; m1; k1; (k2 Kelpie; k2 Witchflower); 8[8,9,9] times; with Kelpie k1; m1; k1; (k2 Witchflower; k2 Kelpie) 6[7,7,8] times; •• k1 Witchflower (centre back st); rep from • to •• once more; with Witchflower k1 edge st; with alt colours k4 steek sts. 253[269,285,301] Sts. Place a marker at beg of rnd. Beg at rnd 1 of charts and reading all charts from right to left, set the patt as follows –
With alt colours k4 steek sts; with Mara k1 edge st; ▲ work the first 4 sts of chart A as indicated; rep the 4 patt sts 2[3,3,4] times; work the last 4 sts as indicated, thus having worked chart A over 16[20,20,24] sts; work chart B1 over the next 19 sts; work the first 4 sts of chart C as indicated; rep the 4 patt sts 2[2,3,3] times; work the last 4 sts as indicated thus having worked chart C over 16[16,20,20] sts; work chart D1 over the next 19 sts; work the first 4 sts of chart A as indicated; rep the 4 patt sts 2[2,3,3] times; work the last 4 sts as indicated thus having worked chart A over 16[16,20,20] sts; work chart B1 over the next 19 sts; work the first 4 sts of chart C as indicated; rep the 4 patt sts 2[3,3,4] times; work the last 4 sts as indicated thus having worked chart C over 16[20,20,24] sts; ▲▲ k1 Mara (centre back st); rep from ▲ to ▲▲ once more; with Mara k1 edge st; with alt colours k4 steek sts. Joining in and breaking off colours as required continue as set, working edge sts and centre back st in lighter colours throughout, and work through rnd 17 of charts.

### Next Rnd – Dec Chart D1

Patt rnd 18 of charts as set to the first chart D1 panel; patt the first 6 sts; with Storm Petrel k2tog (the 2 sts are indicated by the symbol above); patt the next 3 sts; with Storm Petrel ssk the next 2 sts as indicated; patt the rem 6 sts - there are now 17 sts in the panel; patt rnd 18 of charts as set to the second chart D1 panel and dec 2 sts as before; patt as set to end of rnd. 249[265,281,297] Sts rem.

Continue as set and reading from right to left, beg on rnd 19 and work chart D2 over the 17 sts of both chart D panels and work through rnd 23 of all charts.

### Next Rnd – Dec Chart B1

Patt rnd 24 and work chart A as set; patt the first 6 sts of chart B1; with Witchflower k2tog as indicated; patt the next 3 sts; with Witchflower ssk the next 2 sts as indicated; patt the rem 6 sts of panel - there are now 17 sts in the panel; patt rnd 24 of charts to the next chart B1 panel and dec 2 sts as before; continue as set thus dec 2 sts on each of the four chart B1 panels and patt as set to end of rnd. 241[257,273,289] Sts rem.

Continue as set and working rnd 1 of all charts (rep the 24 rnds of charts A and C throughout) work chart B2 over the 17 sts of each of the four chart B panels and work through rnd 11 of all charts.

### Next Rnd – Dec Chart D2

Patt rnd 12 of charts as set to the first chart D2 panel; patt the first 5 sts; with Calluna k2tog as indicated; patt the next 3 sts; with Calluna ssk the next 2 sts as indicated; patt the rem 5 sts - there are now 15 sts in the panel; patt rnd 12 of charts to the second chart D2 panel and dec 2sts as before; patt as set to end of rnd. 237[253,269,285] Sts rem.

Continue as set and reading from right to left, beg on rnd 13 and work chart D3 over the 15 sts of both chart D panels and work through rnd 23 of all charts.

### Next Rnd – Dec Chart B2

Patt rnd 24 and work chart A as set; patt the first 3 sts of chart B2 panel; with Kepie k2tog as indicated; patt the next 7 sts; with Kelpie ssk the next 2 sts as indicated; patt the rem 3 sts - there are now 15 sts in the panel; patt rnd 24 of charts to the next chart B2 panel and dec 2sts as before; continue as set, thus dec 2 sts on each of the four chart B2 panels. 229[245,261,277] Sts rem.

Continue as set and beg at rnd 1 of all charts, work chart B3 over the 15 sts of each chart B panel and work through rnd 13 of all charts.

### Next Rnd – Inc Chart D3 Panels

Work rnd 14 of charts A, B3 and C as set to the first Chart D3 panel; turn chart D2 upside down and reading from right to left, beg at rnd 14 and patt the first 5 sts; with Calluna k1; m1 (these are the next 2 sts above the first indicator symbol) patt 3; with Calluna m1; k1 (the 2sts above second indicator symbol); patt the rem 5 sts - there are now 17 sts in chart D2 panel; patt rnd 14 of panels as set to the second chart D3 panel and work chart D2 and inc 2sts as before; patt as set to end of rnd. 233[249,265,281] Sts. Continue as set through rnd 24 of all charts. Work rnd 1 of all charts.

### Next Rnd – Inc Chart B3 Panels

Patt rnd 2 and work chart A as set; turn chart B2 upside down and reading from right to left, beg at rnd 2 and patt the first 3 sts; with Kelpie k1; m1 as indicated; patt 7; with Kelpie m1; k1 as indicated; patt the rem 3 sts - there are now 17 sts in chart B2 panel; patt rnd 2 of all chart panels as set and inc 2 sts as before over the rem three chart B panels. 241[257,273,289] Sts. Continue as set through rnd 7 of all charts.

### Next Rnd – Inc Chart D2 Panels

Work rnd 8 of charts A, B2 and C as set to the first Chart D2 panel, then turn chart D1 upside down and reading from right to left, beg at rnd 8 and patt the first 6 sts; with Storm Petrel k1; m1 as indicated; patt 3; with Storm Petrel m1; k1 as indicated; patt the rem 6 sts - there are now 19 sts in chart D1 panel; continue and work rnd 8 of panels as set to the second chart D2 panel then work chart D1 and inc 2sts as before; patt as set to end of rnd. 245[261,277,293] Sts. Continue as set through rnd 24 of all charts. Work rnd 1 of all charts.

### Next Rnd – Inc Chart B2 Panels & Work Chart D4

Patt rnd 2 and work chart A as set; turn chart B1 upside down and reading from right to left, beg at rnd 2 and patt the first 6 sts; with Witchflower k1; m1 as indicated; patt 3; with Witchflower m1; k1 as indicated; patt the rem 6 sts - there are now 19 sts in chart B1 panel; patt rnd 2 of all panels, and turn chart D4 upside down and reading from right to left, beg at rnd 2 and work over the 19 sts of both chart D3 panels, and working chart B1, inc 2 sts over the rem 3 chart B2 panels. 253[269,285,301] Sts.

## CHART A

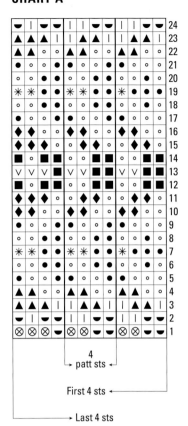

4
patt sts

First 4 sts

Last 4 sts

## CHART B1

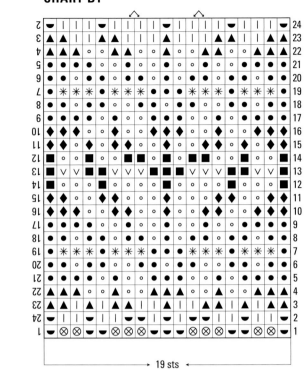

19 sts

## CHART C

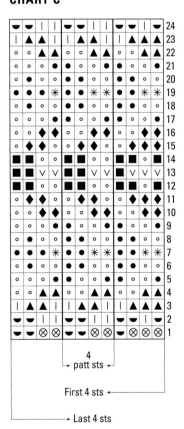

4
patt sts

First 4 sts

Last 4 sts

## CHART D1

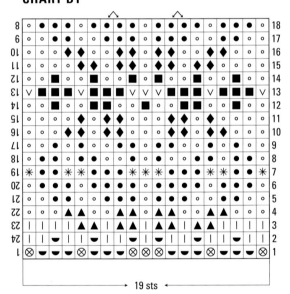

19 sts

224

## CHART D2

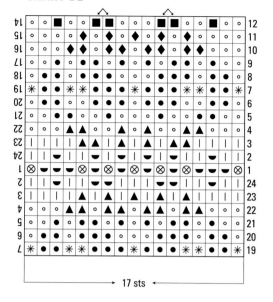

17 sts

|  |  |
|---|---|
| ⌣ | KELPIE |
| ⊗ | MARA |
| I | WITCHFLOWER |
| ▲ | LIMPET |
| ○ | SUMMERTIDE |
| ● | STORM PETREL |
| ✳ | STRABHANN |
| ◆ | LAPWING |
| ■ | CALLUNA |
| V | SHEARWATER |

## CHART B2

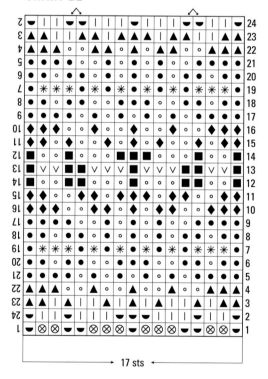

17 sts

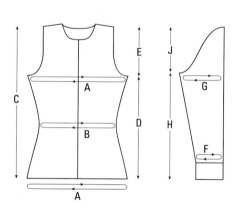

A = 90[96, 101.5, 107.5]cm
B = 81.5[87.5, 93, 99]cm
C = 58[60, 62, 64]cm
D = 40[41, 42, 43]cm
E = 18[19, 20, 21]cm
F = 20[21.5, 23, 24.25]cm
G = 32.75[34.25, 35.75, 38]cm
H = 42.5[43.5, 44.5, 45.5]cm
J = 14[14.75, 15.75, 17]cm

**CHART D3**

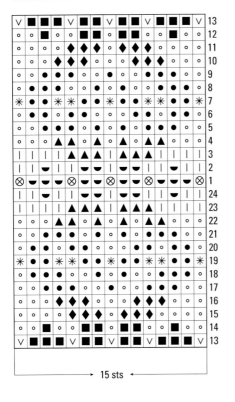

15 sts

**CHART B3**

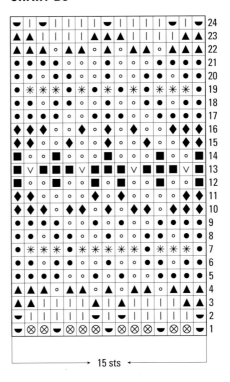

15 sts

**CHART D4**

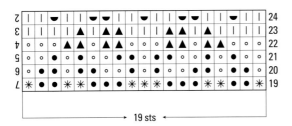

19 sts

| ⏺ | KELPIE |
|---|---|
| ⊗ | MARA |
| I | WITCHFLOWER |
| ▲ | LIMPET |
| ○ | SUMMERTIDE |
| ● | STORM PETREL |
| ✳ | STRABHANN |
| ◆ | LAPWING |
| ■ | CALLUNA |
| V | SHEARWATER |

Continue as set and rep the rnds of charts A, B1 and C panels. Work through rnd 7 of chart D4 then work chart D1 upside down and reading from right to left, beg at rnd 8 and work through rnd 1 thus repeating the patt panels every 24 rnds.

Continue as set working 115[118,121,124] chart patt rnds in total, thus ending on rnd 19[22,1,4] inclusive of all charts.

**Next Rnd –**
**Beg Armhole Steeks and Edge Sts**

With colours as for next rnd of chart, k4 steek sts and k1 edge st as set; keeping continuity, patt the next 54[57,60,63] sts (right front); with a separate length of the darker colour, cast off the next 13[15,17,19] sts; with alt colours cast on 10 edge and steek sts; keeping continuity, patt the next 109[115,121,127] sts (back); with separate yarn as before, cast off the next

226

13[15,17,19] sts; with alt colours cast on 10 edge and steek sts; keeping continuity, patt the next 54[57,60,63] sts (left front); k1 edge st and k4 steek sts as set.

**Next Rnd:** With colours as next rnd of chart, k4 steek sts and k1 edge st; keeping continuity patt the next 52[55,58,61] of right front; k2tog; k10 edge and steek sts; ssk; keeping continuity, patt the next 105[111,117,123] sts of back; k2tog; k10 edge and steek sts; ssk; keeping continuity, patt the rem 52[55,58,61] sts of left front; k1 edge st; k4 steek sts.

Continue and dec 1st at chart patt side of armhole edge sts as set on next 4[4,5,5] rnds and then on every foll alt rnd until 43[46,48,50] chart patt sts rem on each front and 87[93,97,101] chart patt sts rem on back. Then continue straight in patt as set without further shaping until 148[154,158,164] chart rnds have been worked in total thus ending on rnd 4[10,14,20] inclusive of charts.

**Next Rnd –**

### Beg Front Neck Steek and Edge Sts

With alt colours as for next rnd of charts, cast off the first 4 steek sts and 1 edge st; patt as set to the last 5 sts of rnd and cast off the last edge st and 4 steek sts. Break off yarns.

**Next Rnd:** Place the first 9[10,10,11] sts on a holder; with colours as for next rnd of chart, cast on 4 steek sts and mark the first st cast on for beg of rnd; with lighter colour cast on 1 edge st; keeping continuity, patt as set to the last 9[10,10,11] sts of rnd and place these sts on a holder; with lighter colour cast on 1 edge st; with alt colours cast on 4 steek sts.

Work front neck steek and edge sts as set and keeping continuity, shape front neck by dec 1st at chart patt side of front neck edge sts on next 4 rnds. 30[32,34,35] Chart patt sts rem on each front. Continue as set and patt 1 rnd without shaping, then dec 1st at each side of front neck as set on the next and every foll alt rnd 7[7,8,8] times in all. 23[25,26,27] Chart patt sts rem and ending on rnd 24[6,12,18] inclusive of charts.

**Next Rnd –**

### Beg Back Neck Steek and Edge Sts

Keeping continuity, work without shaping to the 87[93,97,101] chart patt sts of back; patt the first 24[26,27,28] sts; place the next 39[41,43,45] sts on a holder; cast on 10 edge and steek sts; keeping continuity, patt the rem 24[26,27,28] chart patt sts of back, then continue without shaping to end of rnd.

Work back neck steek and edge sts as set and keeping continuity, dec 1st at chart patt side of back and front neck edge sts on next rnd. Patt 1 rnd without shaping then dec 1st at chart patt side of back neck steeks on next rnd. 22[24,25,26] Chart patt sts rem on each shoulder. Patt 1 rnd without shaping and cast off **all** steek sts on this rnd (rnd 5[11,17,23] of charts).

With Summertide [Summertide, Summertide, Witchflower] graft shoulder sts together including edge sts.

*Sleeves*

With short double-pointed 2.75mm needles and Shearwater cast on 56[60,64,68] sts. Making sure cast on edge is not twisted, place a marker at beg of rnd, and joining in and breaking off colours as required work 2/2 rib as follows –

**Rnds 1 & 2:** * K2 Calluna; p2 Shearwater; rep from * to end of rnd.

**Rnd 3:** * K2 Calluna; p2 Summertide; rep from * to end of rnd.

**Rnds 4 & 5:** * K2 Lapwing; p2 Summertide; rep from * to end of rnd.

**Rnds 6,7 & 8:** * K2 Storm Petrel; p2 Summertide; rep from * to end of rnd.

**Rnds 9 & 10:** * K2 Storm Petrel; p2 Strabhann; rep from * to end of rnd.

**Rnds 11,12 & 13:** As rnds 6,7 & 8.

**Rnds 14 & 15:** * K2 Limpet; p2 Summertide; rep from * to end of rnd.

**Rnds 16 & 17:** * K2 Limpet; p2 Witchflower; rep from * to end of rnd.

**Rnds 18 & 19:** * K2 Kelpie p2 Witchflower; rep from * to end of rnd.

**Rnd 20:** * K2 Kelpie; p2 Mara; rep from * to end of rnd.

Change to 3.25 mm needles and set the chart patt panels as follows –

With Mara k1 (seam st); beg at rnd 1 of chart C, and patt the last 2[0,2,0] sts of 4st patt rep; rep the 4 patt sts 3[4,4,5] times; patt the last 4 sts of chart C; beg at rnd 1 of chart D1 and patt the 19 sts; patt the first 4 sts of chart A then rep the 4 patt sts 3[4,4,5] times; patt the first 2[0,2,0] sts of 4 st rep once more.

Joining in and breaking off colours as required, continue as set, and working all inc sts into 4st patt rep of charts C and A, inc 1st at each side of seam st on 6th rnd and every foll 6th rnd until there are 92[96,100,106] sts in total. AT THE SAME TIME, work through rnd 18 of chart

D1 then work rnds 19 through 24 of chart D4, then rep the 24 rnds of all chart panels as set. Continue in patt without further shaping until 115[118,121,124] chart patt rnds have been worked in total thus ending on rnd 19[22,1,4] inclusive of chart.

### Next Rnd – Beg Cap Shaping

With colours as for next rnd of patt, cast off seam st and next 6[7,8,9] patt sts; continue in patt as set to the last 6[7,8,9] sts and cast off these sts. Break off yarns.

With RS facing and working back and forth in rows from now on, keep continuity of patt and dec 1st at each end of next 5 rows. 69[71,73,77] Sts rem. Patt 1 row without shaping then dec 1st at each end of next and every foll alt row until 47 sts rem. Then continue and dec 1st at each end of next and every foll row until 19 sts rem. Keeping continuity of patt, cast off 3 sts at beg of next 2 rows. Cast off the rem 13 sts.

### Neckband

Cut open front and back neck steeks up centre between 4th and 5th steek sts. With RS facing, 3.25mm needles and Witchflower, pick up and k the 9[10,10,11] sts from right front holder; knit up 29[29,30,30] sts along right neck edge to back neck holder, working into loop of edge st next to chart patt sts; pick up and k the 39[41,43,45] sts from back neck holder and dec 1st at centre back neck during pick up; knit up 29[29,30,30] sts along left neck edge working into edge st as before; pick up and k the 9[10,10,11] sts from left front holder. 114[118,122,126] Sts.

Joining in and breaking off colours as required, work 2/2 rib back and forth in rows, stranding the yarns on the WS throughout, as follows –

**Row 1 (WS):** * P2 Limpet; k2 Witchflower; rep from * to the last 2 sts; p2 Limpet.

**Row 2 (RS):** * K2 Limpet; p2 Summertide; rep from * to the last 2 sts; k2 Limpet.

**Row 3 (WS):** * P2 Storm Petrel; k2 Summertide; rep from * to the last 2 sts; p2 Storm Petrel.

**Row 4 (RS):** * K2 Storm Petrel; p2 Strabhann; rep from * to the last 2 sts; k2 Storm Petrel.

**Row 5 (WS):** * P2 Storm Petrel; k2 Summertide; rep from * to the last 2 sts; p2 Storm Petrel.

**Row 6 (RS):** * K2 Lapwing; p2 Summertide; rep from * to the last 2 sts; k2 Lapwing.

**Row 7 (WS):** * P2 Lapwing; k2 Summertide; rep from * to the last 2 sts; p2 Lapwing.

**Row 8 (RS):** * K2 Calluna; p2 Summertide; rep from * to the last 2 sts; k2 Calluna.

**Row 9 (WS):** * P2 Calluna; k2 Shearwater; rep from * to the last 2 sts; p2 Calluna.

With RS facing and Shearwater, cast off knitwise.

### Left Front Band

With RS facing, 3.25mm needles and Limpet beg at top of neckband and knit up 150[154,158,162] sts to cast on edge, working into loop of edge st next to chart patt sts. Joining in and breaking off colours as required, and stranding yarns across the WS throughout, work 9 rows of 2/2 rib as neckband. With RS facing and Shearwater, cast off knitwise.

### Right Front Band

As left but beg at cast on edge and knit up sts to top of neckband and work 12 buttonholes on row 5 (WS) as follows –

**First & Fourth Sizes:** Patt 2[3]; * cast off 2; patt 11[12] rep from * to the last 5 sts; cast off 2; patt 3.

**Second & Third Sizes:** Patt 2; (cast off 2; patt 11) 7[3] times; (cast off 2; patt 12) 4[8] times; cast off 2; patt 3.

**All Sizes:** With colours as set, continue in patt and cast on 2 sts over those cast off on the previous row. Complete as left front band.

*Finishing*

Cut open armhole steeks up centre between 4th and 5th steek sts. Trim front and neck steeks to a 2st width and with Storm Petrel, cross stitch steeks in position. Darn in all loose ends on sleeves. Using a warm iron and damp cloth, press body and sleeves very lightly on the WS, omitting 2/2 ribs. Pin centre top of sleeve caps to body at grafted shoulder seam. Pin sleeve cast off edges to body at underarm cast off, then pin cap edges of sleeves around armholes along armhole edge sts. With Summertide, sew sleeves to body. Trim armhole steeks to a 2st width and with Shearwater, cross stitch steeks to body. Press lightly on WS. Sew buttons on to left front band.

### Optional Felted Buttons

I made 12 buttons as those I made for the Mountain Hare jacket, using the Selkie colours randomly. See page 143 **Felted Buttons** for directions on making the buttons. Each button is embroidered with a small star in a contrast colour before felting. For notes on embroidering stars and felting see pages 266 and 268.

# The
# Damselfly

## Design Notes ───

Damselflies come in many colours and given enough space and time I could work just as many variations on the theme. For this collection I have confined myself to just two colourways – the Emerald shown opposite, and the Northern Blue shown on page 251. The latter is a rare Scottish Highland species which I saw often as a child but which is no longer here in Lewis.

This is an interesting project for an adventurous knitter. The body and sleeves are worked as flat pieces; the patterning is quite straightforward, based closely on the centre back panel of the costume. For the yoke, I stylised the abstract wing pattern that I created for the costume front panels so that it could be repeated for a number of sizes and reflected at the centre back and front. Once the body is knitted and blocked, the yoke border is worked and then the body and border are knitted together so that the border is overlaid. The yoke is then worked in the round with steeks at the front, armholes and neck so that the yoke pattern is worked on the right side throughout. See page 196 for a word on steeks. One very important point to bear in mind is that the stitch tension must be the same on both the St.St. body area as on the stranded yoke, so make sure that you achieve this with your swatches before beginning.

Note also that when knitting up sts for the front bands, the ratio for knitting up the sts along the rows is different along the stranded yoke than along the lower body. This is because the row tension on the stranded yoke and the body pattern is different. For the stranded yoke area, knit up 1st into 7 consecutive rows then miss 1 row and repeat. On the lower body, knit up 1st into 2 consecutive rows and then miss 1 and repeat. I have placed buttons from the yoke border to the neckband only, but if you prefer you can work button holes from the hemline to the neckband. The directions for the all the colours used in the Emerald colourway are stated first and the Northern Blue colours are stated second and <u>underlined</u>. Where only one colour is stated, it is used in both colourways.

232

## Sizes

To fit petite [small, medium, large, X large]. Directions for larger sizes are given in square brackets. Where there is only one set of figures, it applies to all sizes.

## Knitted Measurements

Underarm (buttoned) 80[86,92,98,103.5]cm.
Waist 74[80,86,92,98]cm.
Length 53.75[57.25,59.5,61.5,63.75]cm.
Sleeve seam 42[44,44.5,45,45.5]cm.

## Materials

Of **Alice Starmore® Hebridean 2 Ply – Emerald Colourway:**
100[113,125,140,150]g in Mountain Hare.
75[87,100,113,125]g in Golden Plover.
50[63,75,87,100]g in Machair & Sundew.
40[50,60,70,80]g in Bogbean & Witchflower.
30[40,50,60,70]g in Lapwing.
25[30,35,40,45]g in Mara.

**Northern Blue Colourway:**
100[113,125,140,150]g in Summertide.
75[87,100,113,125]g in Mara.
50[63,75,87,100]g in Machair & Strabhann.
40[50,60,70,80]g in Golden Plover, Sundew & Mountain Hare.
15[20,25,30,35]g in Whin.

1 Pair 3mm & 3.25mm needles. Circular 3mm & 3.25mm needles. Stitch holders. Stitch markers. Tapestry needle. 7[7,8,8,8] Buttons.

## Tension

27 Sts and 40 rows to 10cm measured over St.St. using 3mm needles. To make an accurate tension swatch, cast on 31 sts and work 42 rows.
27 Sts and 32 rows to 10cm measured over chart patt using 3.25mm needles. To make an accurate tension swatch, cast on 36 sts and work 34 rows. Reading all rows from right to left, work the 18 patt sts of chart A twice, working as a flat piece on RS only, breaking off the yarns at the end of every row. Pin the swatches on a flat surface and measure tension using a ruler.

## Body

With pair of 3mm needles and Mara/Sundew cast on 225[241,257,273,289] sts. Joining in and breaking off colours as required throughout, work lower border as follows –
**Row 1 (RS):** * K1 Machair; k3 Mara/Sundew;
rep from * to the last st; k1 Machair.
**Row 2 (WS):** As row 1 but after working each colour, yf to strand across the WS.
**Rows 3 & 4:** As rows 1 & 2 but substitute Lapwing/Mountain Hare for Mara/Sundew.
**Rows 5 & 6:** With Witchflower/Whin, k.
**Row 7 (RS):** * K1 Bogbean/Golden Plover; k1 Witchflower/Whin; rep from * to the last st; k1 Bogbean/Golden Plover.
**Row 8 (WS):** As row 7 but after working each colour, yf to strand across the WS.
**Rows 9 & 10:** With Bogbean/Golden Plover k. Place markers at centre underarms as follows – With Golden Plover/Mara, k 55[59,63,67,71] (right front); k the next st and mark it (centre right underarm); k 113[121,129,137,145] (back); k the next st and mark it (centre left underarm); k the rem 55[59,63,67,71] sts of left front. P the next WS row then continue in St. St. for a further 6[6,8,8,8] rows, thus working 8[8,10,10,10] St. St. rows in total.
**Next Row (RS) – First Dec**
K 53[57,61,65,69]; k2tog; k right underarm st; ssk; k 109[117,125,133,141]; k2tog; k left underarm st; ssk; k 53[57,61,65,69]; 221[237,253,269,285] Sts.
Work 5[7,7,7,7] rows in St.St.
**Next Row (RS) – Second Dec**
K 14[16,18,20,22]; k2tog; k 79[83,87,91,95]; ssk; k 27[31,35,39,43]; k2tog; k 79[83,87,91,95]; ssk; k 14[16,18,20,22]. 217[233,249,265,281] Sts.
P1 WS row. Break off yarn.
▲ Work Machair band (Machair is used here in both colourways and therefore stated just once) as follows –
**Rows 1 & 2:** With Machair k.
**Row 3 (RS):** * K1 Machair; k1 Lapwing/Mountain Hare; rep from * to the last st; k1 Machair.
**Row 4 (WS):** As row 3 but after working each colour, yf to strand across the WS.
**Rows 5 & 6:** With Machair k.
Break off yarns. ▲▲
With Mountain Hare/Summertide St.St. 2 rows.
**Next Row (RS) – Third Dec**
Dec 1st as set at each side of underarm sts. 213[229,245,261,277] Sts. Work 5[7,7,7,7] rows in St.St.
**Next Row (RS) – Fourth Dec**
K 14[16,18,20,22]; k2tog; k 75[79,83,87,91]; ssk; k 27[31,35,39,43]; k2tog; k 75[79,83,87,91]; ssk; k 14[16,18,20,22]. 209[225,241,257,273] Sts.
Work 5 rows in St.St.

## CHART A

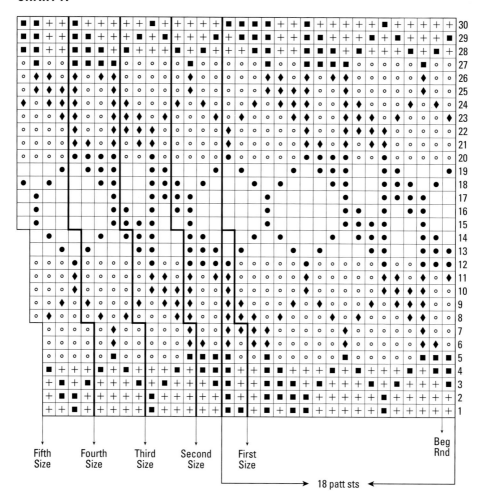

Fifth Size    Fourth Size    Third Size    Second Size    First Size    Beg Rnd

18 patt sts

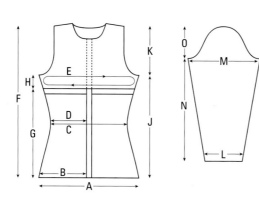

A = 42.5[45.25, 48.25, 51.25, 54]cm
B = 20.5[22, 23.5, 25, 26.5]cm
C = 36.5[39.5, 42.25, 45.25, 48.25]cm
D = 17.5[19, 20.5, 22, 23.5]cm
E = 80[86, 92, 98, 103.5]cm
F = 53.75[57.25, 59.5, 61.5, 63.75]cm
G = 28[30, 30.5, 31, 31.5]cm
H = 8.75[9.25, 10, 10.5, 11.25]cm
J = 36.75[39.25, 40.5, 41.5, 42.75]cm
K = 17[18, 19, 20, 21]cm
L = 17[18.5, 19.25, 20, 21.5]cm
M = 29.25[31.5, 33, 35, 36.5]cm
N = 42[44, 44.5, 45, 45.5]cm
O = 13.5[14.5, 15.5, 16.5, 17.5]cm

## CHART B

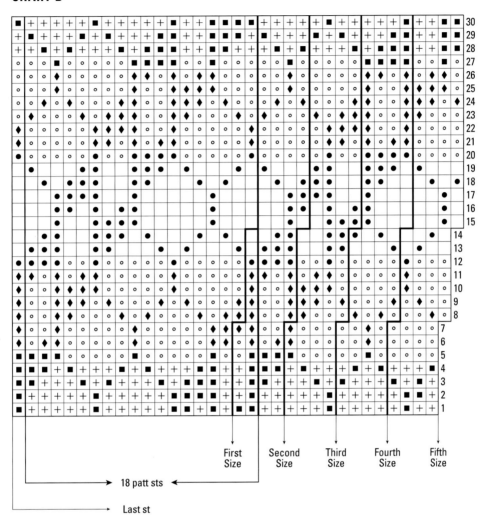

First Size  Second Size  Third Size  Fourth Size  Fifth Size

18 patt sts

Last st

**KEY: EMERALD**

| | |
|---|---|
| + | SUNDEW |
| ■ | LAPWING |
| ○ | MOUNTAIN HARE |
| ◆ | BOGBEAN |
| | GOLDEN PLOVER |
| ● | WITCHFLOWER |

**KEY: NORTHERN BLUE**

| | |
|---|---|
| + | MARA |
| ■ | SUNDEW |
| ○ | SUMMERTIDE |
| ◆ | MOUNTAIN HARE |
| | STRABHANN |
| ● | GOLDEN PLOVER |

**Next Row (RS) – Fifth Dec**
Dec 1st as set at each side of underarm sts.
205[221,237,253,269] Sts. P1 WS row.
Break off yarn.
With Machair and substituting Bogbean/Golden Plover for Lapwing/Mountain Hare, work the 6 rows of Machair band as given from ▲ to ▲▲. With Sundew/Strabhann work 2 rows in St.St.
**Next Row (RS) – Sixth Dec**
K 14[16,18,20,22]; k2tog; k 71[75,79,83,87]; ssk; k 27[31,35,39,43]; k2tog; k 71[75,79,83,87]; ssk; k 14[16,18,20,22]. 201[217,233,249,265] Sts.
Work 5 rows in St.St.
**Next Row (RS) – Seventh Dec**
Dec 1st as set at each side of underarm sts.
197[213,229,245,261] Sts.
Work 3[5,5,5,5] rows in St.St.
**Next Row (RS) – Eighth Dec**
K 14[16,18,20,22]; k2tog; k 67[71,75,79,83]; ssk; k 27[31,35,39,43]; k2tog; k 67[71,75,79,83]; ssk; k 14[16,18,20,22]. 193[209,225,241,257] Sts.
P1 WS row.
With Machair and substituting Witchflower/Whin for Lapwing/Mountain Hare, work the 6 rows of Machair band as given from ▲ to ▲▲. With Mountain Hare/Summertide work 10[10,10,12,14] rows in St.St.
**Next Row (RS) – First Inc**
K 14[16,18,20,22]; m1; k 69[73,77,81,85]; m1; k 27[31,35,39,43]; m1; k 69[73,77,81,85]; m1; k 14[16,18,20,22]. 197[213,229,245,261] Sts.
Work 3 rows in St.St.
With Machair and substituting Mara/Sundew for Lapwing/Mountain Hare work the 6 rows of Machair band as given from ▲ to ▲▲. With Golden Plover/Mara work 2 rows in St.St.
**Next Row (RS) – Second Inc**
K 48[52,56,60,64]; m1; k underarm st; m1; k 99[107,115,123,131]; m1; k underarm st; m1; k 48[52,56,60,64]. 201[217,233,249,265] Sts.
Work 9 rows in St.St.
**Next Row (RS) – Third Inc**
K 14[16,18,20,22]; m1; k 73[77,81,85,89]; m1; k 27[31,35,39,43]; m1; k 73[77,81,85,89]; m1; k 14[16,18,20,22]. 205[221,237,253,269] Sts.
Work 9[11,11,11,11] rows in St.St.
**Next Row (RS) – Fourth Inc**
Inc 1st at each side of underarm sts.
209[225,241,257,273] Sts.
P1 WS row. Darn in all loose ends. Transfer all sts onto a long length of contrast yarn. Lay body out on a flat surface and block out (measurements A,B,C,D & G on schematic)

placing damp towelling on back area, then fold fronts over back at marked centre underarm sts, ensuring that the inside towelling is flat and smooth. Cover with a damp towel and leave to dry away from direct heat. Once dry, place sts on 3mm circular needle.
**Yoke Border**
With pair of 3.25mm needles and Bogbean/Sundew cast on 209[225,241,257,273] sts. Joining in and breaking off colours as required, work border as follows –
**Row 1 (RS):** * K1 Bogbean/Sundew; k1 Lapwing/Machair; rep from * to the last st; k1 Bogbean/Sundew.
**Row 2 (WS):** As row 1 but after working each colour, yf to strand across the WS.
**Rows 3 & 4:** With Lapwing/Machair k.
**Rows 5 & 6:** With Machair/Mountain Hare k.
**Rows 7 & 8:** With Machair/Mountain Hare and Witchflower/Golden Plover as rnds 1 & 2.
**Rows 9 & 10:** With Witchflower/Golden Plover k.
Break off yarn.

**Join Yoke Border to Body**
With circular 3.25mm needles and Sundew/Mara cast on 5 sts; with RS of both yoke border and body facing, place yoke border needle in front of body needle and holding both needles parallel in the left hand, insert the 3.25mm circular needle with the 5 cast-on sts into the first st of both yoke and body and k these sts tog, then continue and k tog the border and body sts to end of row; cast on 5 sts.
219[235,251,267,283] Sts.
Place a marker at beg of rnd, join in Lapwing/Sundew and set the front steek, edge sts and chart patts as follows –
**First Size – Rnd 1:** With alt Sundew/Mara and Lapwing/Sundew k4 steek sts; with Sundew/Mara k1 edge st; reading from right to left, beg at second st of chart A as indicated, and patt the last 17 sts of the 18st rep; patt the 18st rep once, then patt the first 16 sts once more; with Sundew/Mara k1 and mark this st for centre right underarm; beg at indicated first size st of chart B and patt the last 16 sts of rep; patt the 18st rep twice; patt the last st as indicated; patt the 18st rep of chart A twice, then patt first 16 sts of rep once more; with Sundew/Mara k1 and mark this st for centre left underarm; beg at indicated first size st of chart B and patt the last 16 sts of the 18st rep; patt the 18st rep once, then patt the first 17 sts of rep once

more; with Sundew/Mara k1 edge st; with alt colours k4 steek sts.

## Second, Third, Fourth & Fifth Sizes

**Rnd 1:** With alt Sundew/Mara and Lapwing/Sundew k4 steek sts; with Sundew/Mara k1 edge st; reading from right to left, beg at second st of chart A as indicated, and patt the last 17 sts of the 18st rep; patt the 18st rep twice; patt the last 2[6,10,14] sts as indicated; with Sundew/Mara k1 and mark this st for centre right underarm; patt the first 2[6,10,14] sts of chart B as indicated; patt the 18st rep 3 times; patt the last st as indicated; patt the 18st rep of chart A 3 times; patt the last 2[6,10,14] sts as indicated; with Sundew/Mara k1 and mark this st for centre left underarm; patt the first 2[6,10,14] sts of chart B as indicated; patt the 18st rep twice, then patt the first 17 sts of rep once more; with Sundew/Mara k1 edge st; with alt colours k4 steek sts.

## All Sizes

Joining in and breaking off colours as required, continue as set and inc 1st at each side of marked underarm sts on rnd 8 and on rnd 15 as indicated on charts. 227[243,259,275,291] Sts. Continue in patt as set and work 28[30,32,34,36] chart patt rnds in total thus ending on rnd 28[30,2,4,6] inclusive.

## Next Rnd –

## Beg Armhole Steeks and Edge Sts

With colours as for next rnd of chart, k4 steek sts and k1 edge st as set; keeping continuity, patt the next 49[52,55,58,61] sts (right front); with a separate length of background colour yarn, cast off the next 9[11,13,15,17] sts; with alt colours cast on 10 edge and steek sts; keeping continuity, patt the next 101[107,113,119,125] sts (back); with separate yarn as before, cast off the next 9[11,13,15,17] sts; with alt colours cast on 10 edge and steek sts; keeping continuity, patt the next 49[52,55,58,61] sts (left front); k1 edge st and k4 steek sts as set.

**Next Rnd:** With colours as next rnd of chart, k4 steek sts and k1 edge st; keeping continuity patt the next 47[50,53,56,59] sts of right front; k2tog; k1 edge st; k8 steek sts; k1 edge st; ssk; keeping continuity, patt the next 97[103,109,115,121] sts of back; k2tog; k1 edge st; k8 steek sts; k1 edge st; ssk; keeping continuity, patt the 47[50,53,56,59] sts of left front; k1 edge st; k4 steek sts.

Continue and dec 1st at chart patt side of armhole edge sts as set on next 4[4,4,5,5] rnds

and then on every foll alt rnd 5[6,6,6,7] times in all. 39[41,44,46,48] Chart patt sts rem on each front and 81[85,91,95,99] chart patt sts rem on back.

Continue straight in patt as set without further shaping until 58[63,68,71,76] chart patt rnds have been worked in total, thus ending on rnd 28[3,8,11,16] inclusive of charts.

## Next Rnd –

## Beg Front Neck Steek and Edge Sts

With alt colours as for next rnd of chart, cast off the first 4 steek sts and 1 edge st; patt as set to the last 5 sts of rnd and cast off 1 edge st and 4 steek sts. Break off yarns.

**Next Rnd:** Place the first 5[6,7,7,7] sts on a holder; with alt colours as for next rnd of chart, cast on 4 steek sts and mark the first st cast on for beg of rnd; with background colour cast on 1 edge st; keeping continuity, patt as set to the last 5[6,7,7,7] sts of rnd and place these sts on a holder; with background colour cast on 1 edge st; with alt colours cast on 4 steek sts. Work front neck steek and edge sts as set and keeping continuity, shape front neck by decreasing 1st at chart patt side of front neck edge sts on next 4 rnds. 30[31,33,35,37] Chart patt sts rem on each front. Continue as set and patt 1 rnd without shaping, then dec 1st at each side of front neck as set on the next and every foll alt rnd 7[7,7,8,8] times in all. 23[24,26,27,29] Chart patt sts rem on each front and ending on rnd 18[23,28,3,8] inclusive of chart.

## Next Rnd –

## Beg Back Neck Steek and Edge Sts

Keeping continuity, work straight without shaping to the 81[85,91,95,99] chart patt sts of back; patt the first 24[25,27,28,30] sts; place the next 33[35,37,39,39] sts on a holder; with background colour cast on 1 edge st; with alt colours cast on 8 steek sts; with background colour cast on 1 edge st; keeping continuity, patt the rem 24[25,27,28,30] chart patt sts of back, then continue straight without shaping to end of rnd.

Work back neck steek and edge sts as set and keeping continuity, dec 1st at chart patt side of back and front neck edge sts on next rnd. Patt 1 rnd straight without shaping then dec 1st at chart patt side of back neck steeks on next rnd. 22[23,25,26,28] Chart patt sts rem on each shoulder. Patt 1 rnd without shaping and cast off **all** steek sts on this rnd (rnd 23[28,3,8,13] of charts).

239

With Mountain Hare/Summertide[Sundew/Mara, Sundew/Mara, Mountain Hare/Summertide, Golden Plover/Strabhann] graft shoulder sts together including edge sts.

## Sleeves

With pair of 3mm needles and Mara/Sundew cast on 43[47,49,51,55] Sts. Joining in and breaking off colours as required throughout, work cuff border as follows –
**Row 1 (RS):** K 3[3,0,3,3] Mara/Sundew; * K1 Machair; k3 Mara/Sundew; rep from * to the end [end; last st; end; end]; k 0[0,1,0,0] Machair.
**Row 2 (WS):** As row 1 but after working each colour, yf to strand across the WS.
Work 8 rows as lower body border working from row 3 through row 10.
With Golden Plover/Mara k 1 RS row.
**Next Row (WS) – Inc**
P 1[1,2,3,5]; * m1; p 8[9,9,9,9]; rep from * to the last 2[1,2,3,5] sts; m1; p 2[1,2,3,5]. 49[53,55,57,61] Sts.
Work a further 10 rows in St.St..
**Next Row (RS) – Beg Sleeve Shaping:** K1; m1; k to the last st; m1; k1. 51[55,57,59,63] Sts.
Work 9 rows in St.St. On next RS row inc 1st at each side of sleeve as set. 53[57,59,61,65] Sts.
P1 WS row. Break off Golden Plover/ Mara.
From now on shape sleeve by inc 1st at each side as set on every 10th row from last inc row until there are 79[85,79,77,81] sts. On third, fourth and fifth sizes only, continue to inc 1st at each end of every foll 8th row until there are 89[95,99] sts. **AT THE SAME TIME** work the colour/patt sequence as follows –
* with Machair and Lapwing/Mountain Hare, work 6 row band as body from ▲ to ▲▲; work 16[18,18,18,18] rows St.St. in Mountain Hare/ Summertide; with Machair and Bogbean/ Golden Plover, work band from ▲ to ▲▲; work 16[18,18,18,18] rows St.St. in Sundew/Strabhann; with Machair and Witchflower/Whin, work band as body from ▲ to ▲▲; work 16[18,18,18,18] rows St.St. in Mountain Hare/Summertide; with Machair and Mara/Sundew, work band as body from ▲ to ▲▲; with Golden Plover/Mara work 16[18,18,18,18] rows in St.St.; rep from * throughout entire sleeve.

Continue straight in colour/patt sequence with 79[85,89,95,99] sts until sleeve measures 42[44,44.5,45,45.5]cm from cast on edge with RS facing for next row.

## Beg Cap Shaping

Continue working in colour/patt sequence as set and cast off 4[5,6,7,8] sts at beg of next 2 rows. Cast off 3 sts at beg of next 2 rows. Dec 1st at each end of next row. Work 2 rows without shaping then dec 1st at each end of next and every foll 3rd row until 47[49,47,47,45] sts rem. Work 1 row without shaping then dec 1st at each end of next and every foll alt row until 29 sts rem. Work 1 row without shaping then dec 1st at each end of next and every foll row until 11[13,13,15,15] sts rem. Cast off sts.

## Finishing

Darn in all loose sleeve ends. Block out sleeves and cover with damp towels and leave to dry away from direct heat.
Cut open front yoke and front and back neck steeks up centre between 4th and 5th steek sts.

**Neckband**
With pair of 3mm needles, Bogbean/Golden Plover and RS of body facing, beg at left front and pick up and k the 5[6,7,7,7] sts from holder; knit up 31[31,31,32,34] sts evenly along right neck edge to back neck holder; pick up and k the 33[35,37,39,39] sts from holder; knit up 31[31,31,32,34] sts evenly along left side of neck; pick up and k the 5[6,7,7,7] sts from left front holder. 105[109,113,117,121] Sts.
**Row 1 (WS):** With Bogbean/Golden Plover k.
**Row 2 (RS):** * K1 Bogbean/Golden Plover; k1 Witchflower/Whin; rep from * to the last st; k1 Bogbean/Golden Plover.
**Row 3 (WS):** As row 2 but after working each colour, yf to strand across the WS.
**Rows 4 & 5:** With Witchflower/Whin, k.
**Rows 6 & 7:** * K1 Machair; k3 Lapwing/ Mountain Hare; rep from * to the last st; k1 Machair.
**Rows 8 & 9:** As rows 6 & 7 but substiute Mara/ Sundew for Lapwing/Mountain Hare.
**Row 10:** With Mara/Sundew, k.
Cast off knitwise on WS.

**Left Front Band**
With pair of 3mm needles, Bogbean/Golden Plover and RS facing beg at top of neckband and knit up 8 sts from top of neckband to top of steek; knit up 52[56,61,63, 68] sts evenly along stranded yoke edge, working into the loop of the first chart patt st next to the edge st;

knit up 8 sts along end of yoke border, working through both border and body edge; knit up 68[72,73,75,76] sts evenly along body edge to top of hemline border; knit up 7 sts along border end to cast-on. 143[151,157,161,167]. Sts in total. Work 10 rows of border as neckline except on first, second and fifth sizes, work rows 6 & 7 as follows –
* K3 Lapwing/<u>Mountain Hare</u>; k1 Machair; rep from * to the last 3 sts; k3 Lapwing/<u>Mountain Hare</u>.
**All Sizes:** Cast off sts knitwise on the WS.

### Right Front Band
As left but beg at cast on edge of body and knit up sts to top of neckband and work 7[7,8,8,8] buttonholes on row 6 (RS) as follows –
### First, Third, & Fourth Sizes
Patt 78[82,86]; * cast off 2; patt 8; rep from * to the last 5 sts; cast off 2; patt 3.
**Second Size:** Patt 83; (cast off 2 patt 9; cast off 2 patt 8) 3 times; cast off 2; patt 3.
**Fifth Size:** Patt 86; (cast off 2; patt 9) 6 times; cast off 2; patt 8; cast off 2; patt 3.
Trim front and neck steeks to a 2st width and with Mountain Hare/<u>Summertide</u> cross stitch steeks in postion. Cut open armhole steeks up centre between 4th and 5th steek sts. Press yoke, including yoke border and front bands, lightly on the WS using a warm iron and damp cloth. Sew up sleeve seams. Press seams gently on WS as before. Pin sleeves to body placing sleeve seam at centre underarm st of body and centre top of sleeve at grafted shoulder seam. Pin sleeves evenly around armholes enclosing the edge st of armholes all around and sew sleeves to body. Trim armhole steeks and cross stitch to body. Press seams as before. Sew buttons on to left front band.

# The
# Sea Anemone

## Design Notes

The upper body of the costume served as the main element in the design. This time I worked the embroidered shells in the same colour as the garment and – of course – these are optional as the pattern stands well undecorated. The neck and cuff surfles are also optional and based on the short-row structure I employed for the skirt part of the costume.

I have made the cuff surfles especially fulsome as I liked them covering the backs of the hands. This may not be too practical for everyday wear, in which case it is easy to use the shorter neckline surfle instructions to make short surfles for the cuffs instead.

Note that the textured pattern has a good deal of lateral give and should be carefully blocked to size so as not to stretch it out too much overall. The little hemline border has more width, though fewer stitches than the main body, and I have used that to allow gentle and gradual stretching of the lower part of the body to the measurements given in the schematic. The garment is shaped by decreasing and increasing at each side of the four chart B panels.

The skirt worn by the model is rather special; Jade designed and made it using fabric she created from one of my photographs – of a red beadlet anemone.

## Sizes

To fit small [medium, large, X large].
Directions for larger sizes are given in square brackets. Where there is only one set of figures, it applies to all sizes.

## Knitted Measurements

Underarm 88[94,100,106]cm.
Waist 76[82,88,94]cm.
Length 57[59,61,63]cm.
Sleeve length (wrist to underarm ex. surfle) 43[44,44,45]cm. Cuff Surfle length 9.5cm

## Materials

Of **Alice Starmore® Hebridean 2 Ply**
425[475,525,550]g shown in Red Deer.
1 pair 3mm & 3.25mm needles. 1 set of double-pointed or circular 2.75mm needles. 1 extra 2.75mm circular needle (for knitting up neck surfle sts). Stitch holders. Stitch markers. Tapestry needle.

## Tension

27 Sts and 40 rows to 10cm measured over St.St. using 3mm needles. To make an accurate tension swatch, cast on 31 sts and work 42 rows. Pin the swatch on a flat surface and measure tension using a ruler.

## Back

### • Picot Chain Edging

With 3.25mm needles make a picot chain cast on as follows –
Make a cast-on slip knot for the first st; * k into the st and transfer the new st from RHN to LHN; rep from * two more times. There are now 4 sts on LHN. K2 then cast off the first st; k the third st and then cast off the second st; k the fourth st and then cast off the third st. 1 St rem on RHN and 1 picot point completed. Transfer the rem st to the LHN and rep from first * and make a chain with 59[63,67,71] picot points.

### Knit Up Sts from Picot Chain

Change to 3mm needles and place the rem st from chain on to the RHN and counting this as the first st, knit up 118[126,134,142] sts along the straight edge of the chain, knitting up 2 sts for each picot point (1st into the long loop and 1st into the short, cast-off loop between each point). 119[127,135,143] Sts.

### Border

**Row 1 (WS):** P1; k to the last 2sts; p2tog. 118[126,134,142] Sts.

**Row 2 (RS):** K1; p to the last st; k1.
**Row 3 (WS):** Purl.
**Row 4 (RS):** K1; * Make Piques (MP) thus – p2 then sl the 2 sts back to the LHN purlwise; bring the yarn across the front of the 2 sts then to the back; sl the 2 sts back to the RHN purlwise; yf; rep from * to the last st, leaving the yarn at the back to k the last st.
**Row 5:** Purl. **Row 6:** As row 2.
**Row 7:** P1; k to the last st; m1; p1.
119[127,135,143] Sts.
**Set Chart Patts**
**Row 1 (RS):** K1; * reading from right to left, work chart A over the next 5 sts; work chart B over the next 23[25,27,29] sts; rep from * to the last 6 sts; work chart A over the next 5 sts; k1.
**Row 2 (WS):** P1; * reading from left to right, work chart A over the next 5 sts; work chart B over the next 23[25,27,29] sts; rep from * to the last 6 sts; work chart A over the next 5 sts; p1.
**Row 3 (RS):** K1; * reading from right to left, work chart A over the next 5 sts; work chart B over the next 23[25,27,29] sts inc to 25[27,29,31] sts at centre as indicated; rep from * to the last 6 sts; work chart A over the next 5 sts; k1. 127[135,143,151] Sts in total.
**Row 4 (WS):** P1; * reading from left to right, work chart A over the next 5 sts; work chart B over the next 25[27,29,31] sts inc to 27[29,31,33] sts at centre as indicated; rep from * to the last 6 sts; work chart A over the next 5 sts; p1.135[143,151,159] Sts in total.
Continue as set and work through row 12 of charts.
**Next Row – First Dec:** K1; * work row 1 of chart A over the next 5 sts; k2tog (first 2 sts of chart B); patt to the last 2 sts of row 13 of chart B; ssk; ** (work row 1 of chart A over the next 5 sts; work row 13 of chart B over the next 27[29,31,33] sts) twice; work from * to ** once more; work row 1 of chart A over the next 5 sts; k1. 131[139,147,155] Sts.
Continue working the charts as set, with 25[27,29,31] sts in first and last chart B panels and work 11 rows, thus working through row 24 of chart B.
**Next Row – Second Dec:** K1; work row 1 of chart A over the next 5 sts; work row 25 of chart B as set over the next 25[27,29,31] sts; work row 1 of chart A over the next 5 sts; * k2tog (first 2 sts of chart B); patt to the last 2 sts of row 25 of chart B; ssk; work row 1 of chart A over the next 5 sts; rep from * once more; work row 25

250

of chart B as set over the next 25[27,29,31] sts; work row 1 of chart A over the next 5 sts; k1. 127[135,143,151] Sts.

Continue working the charts as set, with 25[27,29,31] sts in all four chart B panels and work 7 rows, thus working through row 32 of chart B. Thereafter rep chart B rows from 9 through 32 as indicated and work through row 12 of next rep.

**Next Row – Third Dec:** K1; * work row 1 of chart A over the next 5 sts; k2tog (first 2 sts of chart B); patt to the last 2 sts of row 13 of chart B; ssk; ** (work row 1 of chart A over the next 5 sts; work row 13 of chart B over the next 25[27,29,31] sts) twice; work from * to ** once more; work row 1 of chart A over the next 5 sts; k1. 123[131,139,147] Sts.

Continue working the charts as set, with 23[25,27,29] sts in first and last chart B panels and work 11 rows, thus working through row 24 of chart B.

**Next Row – Fourth Dec:** K1; work row 1 of chart A over the next 5 sts; work row 25 of chart B as set over the next 23[25,27,29] sts; work row 1 of chart A over the next 5 sts; * k2tog (first 2 sts of chart B); patt to the last 2 sts of row 25 of chart B; ssk; work row 1 of chart A over the next 5 sts; rep from * once more; work row 25 of chart B as set over the next 23[25,27,29] sts; work row 1 of chart A over the next 5 sts; k1. 119[127,135,143] Sts.

Continue in patts as set with 23[25,27,29] sts in all four chart B panels and work 17[19,21,21] rows, thus working through row 18[20,22,22] of chart B.

**Next Row – First Inc:** K1; * work chart A as set over the next 5 sts; k1; m1; continue working row 19[21,23,23] of chart B as set over the next 21[23,25,27] sts; m1; k1; ** (work chart A as set over the next 5 sts; work row 19[21,23,23] of chart B as set over the next 23[25,27,29] sts) twice; work from * to ** once more; work chart A as set over the next 5 sts; k1. 123[131,139,147] Sts.

Continue working the charts as set, with 25[27,29,31] sts in first and last chart B panels and work 21 rows, thus working through row 16[18,20,20] of chart B.

**Next Row – Second Inc:** K1; work chart A as set over the next 5 sts; work row 17[19,21,21] of chart B as set over the next 25[27,29,31] sts; work chart A as set over the next 5 sts; * k1; m1; patt to the last st of chart B; m1; k1; work

chart A as set over the next 5 sts; rep from * once more; work chart B as set over the next 25[27,29,31] sts; work chart A over the next 5 sts; k1. 127[135,143,151] Sts.

Continue working the charts as set, with 25[27,29,31] sts in all four chart B panels and work 21 rows, thus working through row 14[16,18,18] of chart B.

**Next Row – Third Inc:** K1; * work chart A as set over the next 5 sts; k1; m1; continue working row 15[17,19,19] of chart B as set over the next 23[25,27,29] sts; m1; k1; ** (work chart A as set over the next 5 sts; work row 15[17,19,19] of chart B as set over the next 25[27,29,31] sts) twice; work from * to ** once more; work chart A as set over the next 5 sts; k1. 131[139,147,155] Sts.

Continue working the charts as set, with 27[29,31,33] sts in first and last chart B panels and work 21 rows, thus working through row 12[14,16,16] of chart B.

**Next Row – Fourth Inc:** K1; work chart A as set over the next 5 sts; work row 13[15,17,17] of chart B over the next 27[29,31,33] sts; work chart A as set over the next 5 sts; * k1; m1; patt to the last st of chart B; m1; k1; work chart A as set over the next 5 sts; rep from * once more; work chart B as set over the next 27[29,31,33] sts; work chart A over the next 5 sts; k1. There are now 27[29,31,33] sts in all four chart B panel and 135[143,151,159] sts in total.

Continue in patt without shaping and work a further 15[17,19,21] rows, thus working through row 28[32,12,14] of chart B with 148[152,156,158] chart rows worked in total.

**Shape Armholes**

Keeping continuity of patts as much as possible throughout, cast off 6[6,7,7] sts at beg of next 2 rows. Cast off 4 sts at beg of next 2 rows. Dec 1st at each end of next 3 rows. Patt 1 WS row without shaping, working first and last st in p, then dec 1st at each end of next and every foll alt row until 101[107,113,119] sts rem, working first and last st of all WS rows in p. ●●

Continue without further shaping and working the first and last sts in p on WS rows and in k on RS rows, patt a total of 68[72,76,82] rows from and including first armhole cast-off row, thus ending on row 24[32,16,24] inclusive of chart B with armholes measuring 17.5[18.5,19.5, 21]cm.

**Shape Back Neck/Shoulders**

Patt the first 26[28,30,32] sts of right shoulder; place the next 49[51,53,55] sts on a holder for

back neck; place the rem 26[28,30,32] sts of left shoulder on a spare needle.
Turn and shape right neck/shoulder as follows –
**Rows 1 & 3 (WS):** P2tog; keeping continuity patt to end of row. **Row 2 (RS):** Cast off 8[8,9,10] sts; patt to end of row.
**Row 4 (RS):** Cast off 8[9,9,10] sts; patt to end of row.
**Row 5 (WS):** Patt as set to end of row. Turn and cast off the rem 8[9,10,10] sts.
With RS facing, rejoin yarn to the 26[28,30,32] sts of left shoulder and keeping continuity, patt as set to end of row. Turn and shape left neck/shoulder as follows –
**Row 1 (WS):** Patt to the last 2 sts; p2togtbl.
**Rows 2 & 4 (RS):** Patt as set to end of row.
**Row 3 (WS):** Cast off 8[8,9,10] sts; patt to the last 2 sts; p2togtbl. **Row 5 (WS):** Cast off 8[9,9,10] sts; patt to end of row. **Row 6:** As rows 2 & 4. Turn and cast off the rem 8[9,10,10] sts.

*Front*

As back from • to ••.
Continue without further shaping and working the first and last sts in p on WS rows and in k on RS rows, work a total of 42[44,46,50] rows from and including first armhole cast-off row, thus ending on row 22[28,10,16] inclusive of chart B.
**Shape Front Neck**
**Next Row (RS):** Patt 39[42,45,47]; place the next 23[23,23,25] sts on a holder for front neck; place the rem 39[42,45,47] sts on a spare needle. Turn and work left neck/shoulder as follows –
**\*** Keeping continuity of patt, dec 1st at neck edge of next 4 rows. Patt 1 row without shaping then dec 1st at neck edge of next and every foll alt row until 25[27,29,30] sts rem. Patt 1 WS row ending on row 24[32,16,24] inclusive of chart B with armhole matching back in length. **\*\***
**First, Second & Third Sizes**
**Next Row (RS):** Cast off 8[8,9]; patt as set to the last 2 sts; k2tog.
**Fourth Size**
**Next Row (RS):** Cast off 10; patt to end of row.
**All Sizes:** Patt 1 WS row. Cast off 8[9,9,10] sts at beg of next row. Patt 1 WS row.
Cast off the rem 8[9,10,10] sts.
With RS facing rejoin yarn to the 39[42,45,47] sts of right front neck/shoulder and keeping continuity, patt as set to end of row. Work as left neck from **\*** to **\*\***.
Work 1 more RS row, then shape shoulder as

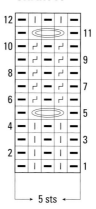

## CHART A

$\rightarrow$ 5 sts $\leftarrow$

## KEY FOR SEA ANEMONE

⊟ p on RS rows; k on WS rows.

Ⅰ k on RS rows; p on WS rows.

☐ no stitch.

Ⅴ (k1b, k1) into same st, then insert left hand needle point between the vertical strand that runs down between the 2 sts just made and k into this strand, making the third st of the group.

Ⅴ (p1, yo, p1) into same st, making 3 sts in the group.

⬯ **\*** yb; sl next 3 sts purlwise to right needle; pass yarn across back of the 3 sl sts; then yf and sl the 3 sl sts back to left needle; rep from **\*** once more; yb; sl the 3 sts purlwise to right needle.

⌐ k into back of st on RS rows; p into back of st on WS rows.

Ⅰ/Ⅰ WS: sl first st to cn and hold at back; p1; p1 from cn.

Ⅰ\Ⅰ WS: sl first st to cn and hold at front; p1; p1 from cn.

⊟/ⅠⅠ sl first st to cn and hold at back; k2; p1 from cn.

ⅠⅠ\⊟ sl first 2 sts to cn and hold at front; p1; k2 from cn.

**CHART B**

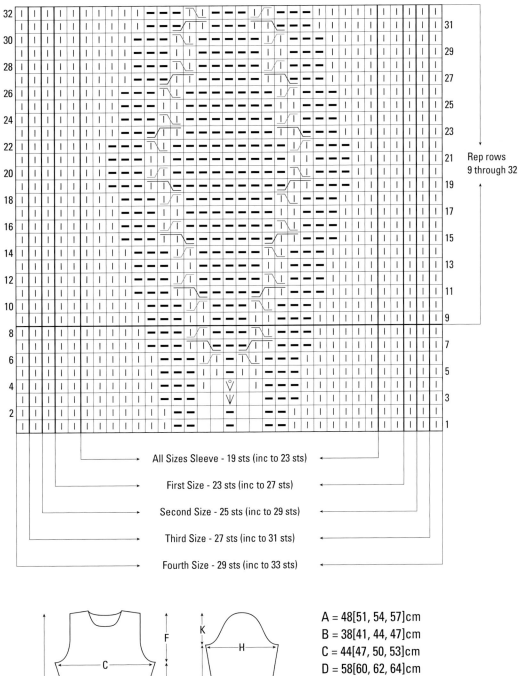

Rep rows
9 through 32

All Sizes Sleeve - 19 sts (inc to 23 sts)

First Size - 23 sts (inc to 27 sts)

Second Size - 25 sts (inc to 29 sts)

Third Size - 27 sts (inc to 31 sts)

Fourth Size - 29 sts (inc to 33 sts)

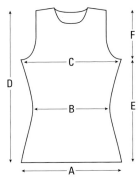

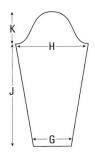

A = 48[51, 54, 57]cm
B = 38[41, 44, 47]cm
C = 44[47, 50, 53]cm
D = 58[60, 62, 64]cm
E = 39.5[40.5, 41.5, 42]cm
F = 18[19, 20, 21.5]cm
G = 20[20.5, 21.5, 22]cm
H = 32[33.5, 35.5, 37.5]cm
J = 43[44, 44, 45]cm
K = 14[15, 16, 17.25]cm

left side but cast off on WS rows and p2togtbl at end of first cast-off row on first, second and third sizes.

## Sleeves

With 3.25mm needles make a 26[27,29,30] point picot chain and knit up 52[54,58,60] sts into chain as worked for back and front. 53[55,59,61] Sts in total.

Change to 3mm needles and work 7 rows of border as back and front with 52[54,58,60] sts after working row 1 and 53[55,59,61] sts after working row 7.

### Set Chart Patts

**Row 1 (RS):** K 2[3,5,6]; * reading from right to left, work chart A over the next 5 sts; k5; work chart A over the next 5 sts; ** work chart B over the next 19 sts as indicated; work from * to ** once more; k 2[3,5,6].

**Row 2 (WS):** P 2[3,5,6]; * reading from left to right, work chart A over the next 5 sts; p5; work chart A over the next 5 sts; ** work chart B over the next 19 sts as indicated; work from * to ** once more; p 2[3,5,6].

Continue as set and inc 2 sts at centre of chart B on rows 3 & 4 as indicated. 57[59,63,65] Sts. Continue in patt as set and work through row 16 of chart B. Then shape sleeve by inc 1st at each end of next and every foll 6th row, working the inc sts into patt of chart A set between 5-st St.St. panels. Begin working new chart A patts at each side once there are 2 sts increased beyond each 5-st St.St. panel at each end of row, and wrap the centre 3 chart A sts only when there is 1st increased beyond the full 5 chart A sts. AT THE SAME TIME work the 32 rows of chart B once, then rep rows 9 through 32 as indicated, and continue to inc on every 6th row until there are 97[101,105,111] sts in total. Continue as set without further shaping until sleeve measures 43[44,44,45]cm from first border row above picot edging with RS facing for next row.

### Shape Cap

Keeping continuity of patt as far as possible throughout, cast off 6[6,7,7] sts at beg of next 2 rows. Cast off 4 sts at beg of next 2 rows. Dec 1st at each end of next and every foll third row until 65[67,67,73] sts rem. Patt 1 row without shaping then dec 1st at each end of next and every foll alt row until 43[47,43,45] sts rem. Dec 1st at each end of every foll row until 13[13,15,15] sts rem. Cast off sts.

### Cuff Surfle (Optional)

With 3mm needles, cast on 21 sts.
**Row 1 (RS):** K1; p to the last 2 sts; k2.
**Row 2 (WS):** P to the last st; (p1,p1b) into st. 22 Sts.
**Row 3:** K to the last 8 sts; wrap1 RS thus – sl next st pw; yf; sl the st back to LHN; turn.
**Row 4:** Yf; sl1pw; p to the last st; (p1,p1b) into st. 23 Sts.
**Row 5:** K to the last 12 sts; wrap1 RS; turn.
**Row 6:** As row 4. 24 Sts. **Row 7:** K9; wrap1 RS; turn. **Row 8:** As row 4. 25 Sts. **Row 9:** K25, picking up and knitting the wrap tog with the st on the 3 wrapped sts. **Row 10:** P25.
**Row 11:** K25. **Row 12:** P25. **Row 13:** As row 3.
**Row 14:** Yf; sl1pw; p to end of row.
**Row 15:** Ssk; k to the last 12 sts; wrap1RS; turn.
**Row 16:** As row 14.
**Row 17:** Ssk; k7; wrap1 RS; turn.
**Row 18:** As row 14. **Row 19:** Ssk; k to end of row, working wraps as row 9. 22 Sts. **Row 20:** P.
**Row 21:** Ssk; k to end of row. 21 Sts.
**Row 22 (WS):** P2; k to the last st; p1.
Rep rows 1 through 22, 8[8,9,9] times in total. Cast off purlwise on RS.

### Neck Surfle (optional)

With 3mm needles, cast on 9 sts.
**Row 1 (RS):** K1; p7; k1. **Row 2 (WS):** P to the last st; (p1,p1b) into st. 10 Sts.
**Row 3:** K to the last 3 sts; wrap1 RS; turn.
**Row 4:** Yf; sl1pw; p to the last st; (p1,p1b) into st. 11 Sts.
**Row 5:** K to the last 7 sts; wrap1 RS; turn.
**Row 6:** Yf; sl1pw; p to end of row.
**Row 7:** K11, picking up and knitting the wrap tog with the st on the 2 wrapped sts.
**Row 8:** P11. **Row 9:** As row 3. **Row 10:** As row 6.
**Row 11:** Ssk; k2; wrap1 RS; turn. 10 Sts.
**Row 12:** As row 6. **Row 13:** Ssk; k to end of row, working the wraps as row 7. 9 Sts.
**Row 14:** P1; k7; p1.
Rep rows 1 through 14, 33[34,35,36] times in total. Cast off purlwise on RS.

### *Finishing*

Block back, front and sleeves to measurements shown on schematic. Cover with damp towels and leave to dry away from direct heat. Immerse the cuff and neck surfles in hand-warm water. Gently squeeze (do not wring) and roll the surfles in a towel to remove excess water. Pleat each surfle by laying each purl ridge one on top of the other on RS, so that each St.St. section is folded along its length at centre. Accentuate the lower edge curve into shape on each section as you go along. Once you have worked to the end, carefully lay the surfle RS up on a dry towel and open up the "accordion" pleats slightly so that the top edge of the surfles (the straight edge which will be attatched to the garment) is laying flat on the towel and the pleats are half open in an arching formation. Allow to dry completely in this position.

Thread a tapestry needle and embroider a shell, as illustrated on page 267, at the centre of each Chart B (between rows 19 & 22) on back, front and sleeves.

Sew back and front together at shoulder seams and press the seams lightly on the WS using the tip of a warm iron and damp cloth.

With extra circular 2.75mm needle and RS of neck surfle facing, knit up 132[136,140,144] sts along the straight edge of the surfle, working into the inside loop of the edge st and working 1st on each purl ridge and 3 sts evenly over each St.St. section. Break off yarn and set surfle aside.

With set of double-pointed or circular 2.75mm needles, beg at right shoulder seam and knit up 5 sts to back neck holder; pick up and k the 49[51,53,55] sts from holder; knit up 30[31,32,32] sts evenly along left side of neck to front neck holder; pick up and k the 23[23,23,25] sts from holder; knit up 25[26,27,27] sts evenly along right side of neck to shoulder seam. 132[136,140,144] Sts.

With RS facing, place the neck surfle in front of the neckline sts and with neckline needle, k together the sts from surfle and neckline all around. Place a marker at beg of rnd and p2 rnds. K 20 rnds. Cast off knitwise. Finish off end and allow collar to roll so that the purl side is outward. Sew surfle ends together on the WS and press seam lightly as before.

Pin straight edge of cuff surfles to WS of sleeves above the Pique row (row 5 of border) and catch stitch in postion. Press seam lightly on WS as before.

Sew up side and sleeve seams, sewing cuff surfle seams along with main sleeve seam and leaving cuff border ends free. Press seams on WS as before. Turn sleeves to RS and sew up cuff border seams.

Pin centre top of sleeves to shoulder seams and underarm seams together and then pin and sew sleeves into armholes. Press seams as before.

TECHNIQUES USED IN
# GLAMOURIE

The techniques used in *Glamourie* include felted knitting and appliqué as shown above in the floral arrangement on the front of the Lapwing design. The photograph at right shows the back of the Lapwing design's peplum overlaid with a triple feather pattern.

## CASTING ON

I have specified different types of cast-on methods in some designs as there are times when the cast-on has an important effect. When I have not specified the cast-on, I have used either the Long Tail or the Cable Edge as they are both excellent general purpose methods.

### The Knit Cast-on

This is the cast-on to use for making a light, elastic edge such as that required for the pointed feathers in the Raven designs. The finished effect gives exactly the right degree of openess and its inherent elasticity means that the feathers can be blocked out to give maximum stretch.

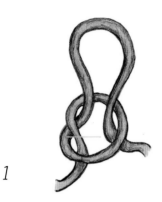

*1*

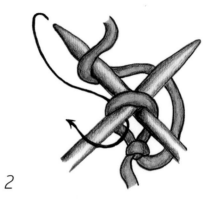

*2*

Make a starting loop as shown in step 1 and place the loop of the left-hand needle. Insert the right-hand needle, from front to back, through the starting loop.

Wrap the yarn around the right-hand needle and pull a loop through as shown in step 2.

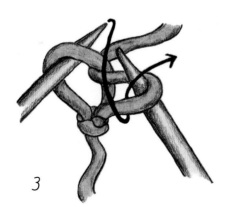

*3*

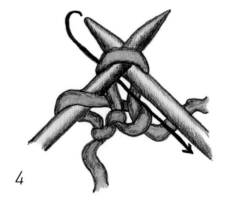

*4*

Place this loop on the left-hand needle, turning it (see arrow in step 3) so that it sits in the correct postion on the left-hand needle as shown in step 4.

There are now 2 stitches on the left-hand needle. Now insert the right-hand needle into loop of the stitch just made and repeat the process shown in steps 2 and 3 until you have the required number of stitches.

## The Cable Edge Cast-on

This is an attractive and practical cast-on for when a firm edge is required. The first 4 steps are exactly as shown for the Knit Cast-on when you will have 2 stitches on the left-hand needle.

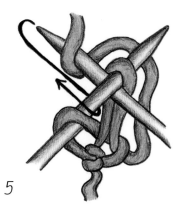

5

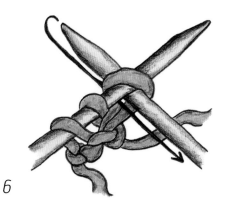

6

To make all following stitches, • insert the right-hand needle between the two stitches, wrap the yarn around the needle as shown in step 5.

Place the loop on the left-hand needle turning the loop as for the Knit Cast-on. Withdraw the right-hand needle as shown in step 6. Repeat from • until you have the required number of stitches.

## The Long Tail Cast-on

This is a good general purpose cast-on, sometimes referred to as "the thumb method". It is firm but has a good degree of flexibility.

To begin, measure out a length of yarn (the long tail) approximately three times as long as the edge to be cast-on, and make a starting loop at this point and place it on the needle. Err on the side of generosity with the long tail as there is nothing more irritating than to run out of length before you have finished.

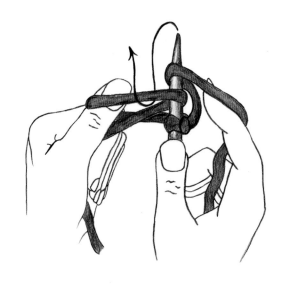

Holding the needle with the starting loop stitch in the right hand, wrap the long, measured out yarn around your left thumb in a loop as shown; make the next stitch by inserting the needle through the thumb loop; wrap the main yarn round the needle and draw through a loop for the next stitch as indicated by the arrow. Gently tighten the stitch by putting a little tension on both tail and main yarn, and then repeat the process until you have the required number of stitches.

## EMBROIDERY

Simple embroidery stitches can be applied to knitting for a wide variety of decorative effects. The free-form embroidery I applied to the Mountain Hare costume and the mermaid's purse works on knitting when the piece is felted beforehand, because the process closes up the fabric so that it becomes a solid surface. Applying embroidery to knitting that is not felted is more limited as there are tiny gaps in the knitted mesh. Therefore it is important to ensure that when you draw the needle through the knitting, you do so through the yarn and not through a clear gap between stitches. For example, a French Knot will disappear and become a knot in the embroidery yarn if you attempt to work it through a gap, whereas it will sit right on the surface if you ensure that you pass the needle through a strand of yarn

in the knitting. If you have not attempted to embroider on knitting before, I recommend that you experiment with a swatch before working on the garment. I do this in any event as I always experiment with size of stitches and colours on the swatch.

For all embroidery stitches worked on knitted fabric, begin by lightly working the threaded needle through the knitted fabric for a couple of centimetres on the wrong side, to secure the yarn end. This should be done close to the point where the embroidery is to be worked, and make sure that the fastened end does not show through on the right side. Then take the needle through to the right side, through a strand of yarn, at the point where the stitch is to begin.

### Stars

Stars are easy to work and versatile. Each star consists of three sets of cross stitches worked one on top of the other.

Work an upright cross of your chosen size as shown in diagram A.

Then work a diagonal cross directly over the upright cross as shown in diagram B.

Then finally work a small diagonal cross on top as shown in diagram C.

You can vary the overall size and also vary the lengths and widths of the individual crosses as I have done in the Mountain Hare Hat. I worked a number of the stars with a longer vertical stitch on the upright cross, then I worked a shorter horizontal, placing it above the centre line of the vertical so that the lower part of the vertical upright is longer.

I prefer to vary the stars so that they are not all exactly even and centred, as I think the effect is more organic.

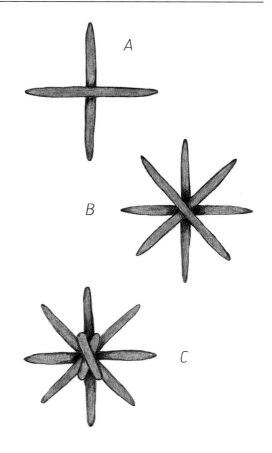

## Shell

This stitch is sometimes called Wheel or Spider Web but I have always called it Shell as it reminds me of a barnacle, both for its circular, ridged appearance and the fact that it sits highly raised on the fabric. It is simple to work but care needs to be taken to keep an even tension on the yarn as you stitch around the spokes of the circle.

First work an upright cross; then a diagonal cross on top so that each point marks the diameter of a circle as shown in diagram A.

Then bring the needle through to the right side at the centre of the circle but clear of the embroidered stitches. From now on, all of the embroidery takes place clear of the knitted fabric thus: * take the needle back over and then insert under one spoke, and then forward under the next spoke of the circle as shown in diagram B and gently pull the yarn through to make a stitch, being careful to keep an even tension; then repeat from * so that the thread is wound around every spoke of the circle.

Ensure that the spokes are not pulled out of position as you work. Keep stitching around the spokes in this manner until they are all covered. The more you stitch around the circle, the more raised the shell will become. For the Sea Anemone design, I stitched all around the spokes four times.

It is worth practising this stitch on a swatch until you are confident that you can keep the tension even. Having said that, if you do mess up a shell on the garment it is easy to remove it because other than the initial crosses, none of the stitches are attached to the knitting. This means that you can carefully snip the embroidery thread on the wrong side and lift off the whole piece.

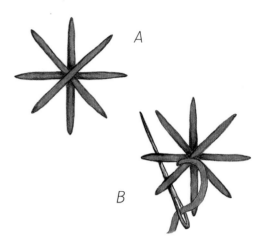

You can work the shells in a different shade to the knitted garment as I did on the Sea Anemone costume. You can also use different colours of yarn for making each circular "trip" around the spokes of one shell.

## French Knots

This is one of my favourite embroidery stitches as it is very simple and can be used to great effect either singly or massed to produce varying degrees of texture and colour.

To begin, bring the needle through the knitted yarn to the right side at the point where the knot will sit (A on the diagram). Twist the thread once round the needle as shown, and making sure it stays twisted, insert the needle back into the knitting through the knitted yarn immediately next to point A, thus forming a knot.

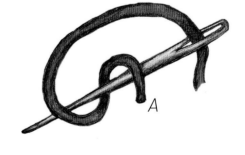

## Felting

To successfully felt knitted fabric it is essential to use the right type of wool yarn. My Hebridean yarn is ideal for this process as it is woollen-spun, has a high crimp and is of a very fine quality. Worsted (wool, which is made of long, combed fibres) and treated yarns such as superwash, will not give good results as they will resist the felting process. If you are not sure about the properties of the yarn you plan to use, then I recommend that you make a small swatch or object such as a button and try it out first.

Felting knitting goes against the grain of everything you have ever heard about washing garments made with pure wool. Very hot, soapy water and friction will cause your precious wool garment to shrink dramatically. Yet this is exactly what you need to do to to felt knitted wool fabric successfully. So if the idea of doing this brings you out in a cold sweat, then do try it out: it is great fun and opens up endless creative possibilities. Felting using a washing machine is an easy option, but other than putting the piece on the hottest programme you really have no control over the result. Hand felting is infinitely preferable as this gives total control: it means you can felt until the piece reaches exactly the finish you desire and you can mould and enhance the shapes during the process.

To felt the buttons and the appliquéd items in the designs you will need the following equipment:
 • A pair of household gloves. Those with textured palms work best.
 • A kitchen sink or basin for very hot water and a basin or other container for very cold water.
 • Pure soap. I use an olive soap bar and grate it into a fine powder as needed.
 • A comfortable absorbent shirt to wear because it is sweaty work.

Fill a container with very cold water. Then don the sweat shirt and run the hot tap until it is too hot for your bare hands, but bearable when wearing household gloves: in other words as hot as you can stand it. Pour in a generous amount of grated soap and swirl around quickly until you have plenty of suds. Work one piece at a time. For example, if you are felting a dozen buttons, throw them all in the hot sudsy water but then pick one. Cover it well with suds and proceed to roll it

vigorously between your palms until it feels like a little stone. This will happen very suddenly as the heat, friction and alkalinity of the soap causes the microscopic hooks in the fibres to lock tightly together. Once this happens, place the button in the cold water. This has the effect of shocking the fibres further to tighten them up more. You can leave it in the cold water whilst you go on to felt all the remaining buttons, one at a time. Once complete, rinse all in warm water, lay out on a towel and leave to dry thoroughly.

For other small pieces such as flower petals, roll or rub them in your hands, stopping every now and then to mould the shape. Just before placing in the cold water, make sure you mould again into the final shape. The fabric is very malleable at this stage and you can mould very easily. For the Lapwing design, I manipulated the shapes of the little leaves so that the tips turned upwards.

If you want to emphasise a shape further then you can use any suitable object as a mould to dry the piece on. The mermaid's purse is an example: I increased and then decreased stitches to form a "belly" on both sides of the purse – this is where the dogfish egg is encased in a real mermaid's purse. Once I felted the pieces, I found two suitable large pebbles and placed them under the shaping of each piece and left them to dry. For the Lapwing design, I manipulated the shapes of the little leaves by hand so that the tips turned upwards.

For larger pieces such as the swatches for the Cailleach's costume and book, the mermaid's purse and the Mountain Hare jacket, I felted the pieces by hand-rolling them repeatedly in a bamboo mat which I have for the purpose. As I mentioned in the embroidery section, felted knitting can be embellished with any amount of free-form embroidery.

Finally – though I am sure that all knitters will have figured it out immediately – I made the piece of "seaweed" attached to the mermaid's purse handle by knitting a swatch, then giving it a firm pressing with a hot steam iron. Then I cut it up one edge, ripped it out and bound one end of it to form a weedy tassel. A homage to all the ripping out I have done in my life.

Loose
Ends

# The Glamourie Photoshoots

A crucial element of *Glamourie* was to take our work back into the landscape that inspired it. Weather and terrain are always a risky issue but the rewards are immense if fortune smiles upon you. The venture involved finding intrepid models and crew, capable of climbing up mountains, down cliffs and across bogs. We planned three photoshoots, each to take place in the summers of 2015, 2016 and 2017 respectively.

As well as the photographer, Jade was also the stylist on all the different photoshoots we undertook. She created fabric printed with our photographic images of the landscape and life therein; using this fabric she then designed and made the garments worn with the knitted designs and costumes. Thus, our ideas and creations came full circle – back into the wild, where they all began.

This felt pleasingly symmetrical because when I was a child I became used to living intimately with nature in its most elemental and awe-inspiring form. In summer out on the Lewis moor, we lived in the society of wild creatures and so it was inevitable to become knowledgeable in the art of observation: to identify a bird flashing by at top speed; to see a mountain rock suddenly leap into the shape of a hare, or the whole side of a

273

silent hill shift into a herd of deer. Events often took dramatic turns; carnivorous plants quietly caught their prey; beasts turned into beauties through metamorphosis; the colours of moor and sky shifted and moods transformed within moments. That was the glamourie of nature and the sense of wonder it engendered is the source of everything you will see in this book.

The practical considerations of the *Glamourie* photoshoots were complex. The islands of Lewis & Harris are stunning – the landscape ancient and other-worldly. Capturing this landscape in a fashion photoshoot is another matter as the weather can be – to put it mildly – challenging. In addition to this, getting an entire crew up to the island and out to some of the locations had (literally) mountainous logistical difficulties.

The Mountain Hare needed to be photographed with an island vista spread out below her. This involved a crew of eight taking two hours to carry all the lighting, camera kit and clothing across rocks and heather to the top of a mountain in Harris. The hair and make-up then had to be done in the open air, with Suzi and Rachael having to shelter amongst the boulders in order to accomplish this without the wind making off with most of the powder eye shadows. The Sea Anemone was a scramble down a precipitous cliff to an incredibly beautiful shingle beach. Again, it took eight of us to get down with everything.

Each character in this book was photographed in a location that is special to our family in one way or another – places to which we have been hiking, scrambling or bog-hopping for many years. We wanted to share these places, from the moorland in the very centre of the island to the truly breathtaking beaches. That we were able to do so is down to an immense amount of preparation, and the hard work and willingness of everyone on the crew, plus – the luck of the weather on the day.

If we could have ordered weather for these shoots it would have been three weeks of a light diffused layer of cloud with a slight breeze and moderate temperature. We did not get even one single day of that kind of weather. Instead there was bright sunshine, threatening rain and an almost ever-present very brisk wind, but as it turned out, the drama of skirts and hair billowing, the diamond-bright colours brought out by the sun, and the particular quality of the light just before rain was what the individual characters needed.

The third shoot was by far the most stressful, purely because it was the last. There was always the possibility that it would rain for seven days straight, and with it being the end of the project there was no room for contingency. As it turned out, we got two days of glorious but windy sunshine which we used to the fullest extent, working from morning until sunset. As soon as we were finished the rain set in once more, almost as if our island home was saying – I will allow you this, but not a minute more. AS

*A note on the styling:*

One of the most exciting parts of this book was receiving emails full of snapshots of ever-more elaborate costumes photographed by my mother on a tailor's dummy outside the house. Much discussion would then ensue and I would start to design styling to work in harmony with the knitwear.

For the Mountain Hare costume, the White Raven, Damselfly, Otter and Sea Anemone designs, I created fabric from photographs of the island. So the Mountain Hare costume has a skirt with fabric printed with a design undershot with images of the lichen on the very hilltop rocks that she stands amongst. The human Damselfly has a skirt printed with reeds in water, and the human Sea Anemone has a skirt printed with images of a dark rock pool.

Other costumes and designs required the sourcing of different fabrics. The Eagle demanded a suede skirt and dress in russet brown, shot through with gold and fawn. The making of it contributed strongly to the demise of a very faithful sewing machine which has seen me through the styling of many a garment. The Cailleach costume had to be quietly opulent, so a simple wool fabric was chosen. I designed a dress with pleats from the shoulders that could be belted-in for the design but allowed to flow for the costume.

In consultation with Alice I designed and made all of the styling for this book, with the exception of the two pieces listed in the credits. JS

# Abbreviations

| | |
|---|---|
| alt | alternately |
| beg | beginning |
| cm | centimetre |
| cn | cable needle |
| DD | double decrease thus: slip 2 sts together knitwise; k1; pass the 2 slipped sts over the k st. |
| dec | decrease |
| foll | following |
| g | gram(s) |
| inc | increase |
| k | knit |
| kb | k into the back loop of the st thus twisting it. |
| LHN | left-hand needle |
| m1 | make a new st by knitting or purling, as required, into the loop of the st in the row below the next st to be worked. |
| mm | millimetre |
| p | purl |
| pb | purl into the back loop of the st thus twisting it. |
| patt | pattern |
| PDD | purl double decrease thus: insert the right-hand needle into the back loops of the next 2 sts purlwise (inserting into second st before first st) and slip them together in this position; p1; pass the 2 slipped sts over the p st. |
| psso | pass the slipped st(s) over. |
| pw | purlwise |
| rem | remaining |
| rep | repeat |
| rnd(s) | round(s) |
| RHN | right-hand needle |
| RS | right side |
| sl | slip |
| ssk | slip, slip, knit – slip the 2 sts separately knitwise, then insert the left-hand needle point through the fronts of the slipped sts from the left, and knit them together from this position. |
| St.St. | Stocking Stitch – k right side rows; p wrong side rows. |
| st(s) | stitch(es) |
| tbl | through back loops |
| tog | together |
| WS | wrong side |
| yb | with yarn at back |
| yf | with yarn at front |
| yo | yarn over needle from front to back, making a loop for a new st to be worked on the next row. |

# Credits & Yarns

**Alice Starmore**, from the Isle of Lewis in Scotland, created all the costumes and design variations in this book, with the exception of *The Otter*. She designed and knitted them over a three-year period, 2015 to 2017. *Glamourie* is the latest in a long list of her books, which are renowned and used worldwide. Her books on Fair Isle and Aran knitting are respected standard texts on these subjects.

**Jade Starmore** designed and knitted *The Otter* costume and its human variant. She organised the three *Glamourie* photoshoots and was the photographer and stylist for all of them. The styling involved her designing and making numerous fabric garments to partner the knitwear. Jade was also the technical artist for the *Techniques* chapter. She is a graduate of Glasgow School of Art with a BA in Visual Communication and an M.Des in Fashion Design.

**Graham Starmore** designed this book and produced all of the technical charts.

Together, Alice, Graham & Jade Starmore comprise the **Windfall Press**, which is a graphic design and publishing company based on the Isle of Lewis in Scotland. Windfall Press conceived the *Glamourie* project and saw it through to final fruition with the invaluable input from the following members of cast and crew –

**Jade Adamson** modelled for the Raven and Otter costumes and stories. Jade is a dancer, teacher, choreographer and a founding member of Glasgow-based contemporary dance company Barrowland Ballet.

**Suzanne Christie** did hair and make-up for the Mountain Hare, White Raven, Sea Anemone, Selkie, Lapwing, Eagle & Cailleach costumes, and for the entire design section of *Glamourie*. Suzanne is a professional make-up artist and hair stylist based in Edinburgh. In 2015, she won Professional Beauty North's *Warpaint* award of *Editorial Make-up Artist of the Year*. She is also an expert driver whose skill with the RV was a boon on narrow, twisting roads.

**Stephanie Davidson** designed and made the turquoise tufted skirt seen with the Raven Cardigan in the Mara colourway and Raven Poncho in Driftwood. Steph is a textile designer and maker based in Glasgow.

**Margaret Finlayson** knitted the Cailleach Cardigan in the design section of *Glamourie*. Margaret is an expert knitter, and by profession a midwife, from the Isle of Lewis.

**Rachael Forbes** modelled for the Mountain Hare, Sea Anemone, Cailleach costumes, and the design section of *Glamourie*. Rachael is a fashion and costume designer, artist and illustrator. She graduated from Edinburgh College of Art and has a fashion label: *The Imaginarium Apparel*. Rachael designed and made the skirt worn with the Lapwing costume: it works so well with the flow and shape of the knitted costume that the Lapwing appears to float across the machair flowers.

**Beth Hopkins** modelled for the White Raven, Selkie, Lapwing & Eagle costumes, and the design section of *Glamourie*. Beth is a professional photographer based in Leeds, and is as accomplished behind the camera as she is in front of it.

**Rachel Keenan** documented the process of our final shoot in a series of photographs which can be seen at **www.virtualyarns.com**. Rachel is a freelance photographer from Glasgow and the official photographer for Caledonian MacBrayne.

**June Long** did the hair and make-up for the Raven costume and the Otter and Damselfly story. Her skills can also be seen in our previous book *Tudor Roses*.

**Melanie Long** modelled for the heartbroken Damselfly and assisted with hair and make-up on the first *Glamourie* shoot. Melanie is a master diving instructor and free diver who is currently studying for a degree in Marine & Freshwater Biology.

**Sophie Morrison** modelled for the young Damselfly, both costume and design. Sophie, from the Isle of Lewis, is currently in secondary school where she excels at Mathematics. She is also training in various forms of dance.

**Pete Williamson** created the Eagle headcap and mask. He designed it to give an impression of the sharp force and speed of the bird itself, while toning beautifully with the colours of the landscape and garment. Pete is a designer, who makes unique and adventurous creations for a range of different clients and projects.

With extra additional thanks to –

**James Acheson** for his assistance with the photographic kit during shoots 2 & 3 and for his lively conversation throughout. James is an erudite Irishman ... *whose fair discourse hath been as sugar, making the hard way sweet and delectable* (*Richard II, Act II, Scene III*).

**Rachel McInally & Calum Green** for helping us down the cliff and up the mountain.

And to **Jock Russell & Senga Hodgson** for keeping the RV going and getting the cast and crew safely back home to Fife.

The yarns used in *Glamourie* are *Alice Starmore*® Hebridean 2 Ply & 3 Ply available exclusively from *Virtual Yarns*.

See the whole range at
**www.virtualyarns.com**

Virtual Yarns delivers worldwide and provides free air mail delivery on orders over £25

# L'envoi

*For six decades these twin wands I have plied,*
*The glamourie of knitting to pursue;*
*The spells I've cast spread magic far and wide,*
*Yet ever must I seek horizons new.*